I0690334

HEALING HANDS

THE WITCHES OF WHEELER PARK: BOOK 7

CHRISTINE POPE

This is a work of fiction. Names, characters, places, and incidents are either the product of the author's imagination or are used fictitiously. Any resemblance to actual events, places, organizations, or persons, whether living or dead, is entirely coincidental.

HEALING HANDS

Copyright © 2021 by Christine Pope

ISBN: 978-1-946435-42-2

Published by Dark Valentine Press

Cover design by Lou Harper

Ebook formatting by Indie Author Services

All rights reserved. No part of this book may be reproduced in any form or by any electronic or mechanical means, including information storage and retrieval systems—except in the case of brief quotations embodied in critical articles or reviews—without permission in writing from its publisher, Dark Valentine Press.

LAUREL WILCOX WAS JUST ABOUT TO STIFLE A yawn when her computer chimed. She blinked, then leaned forward in her seat to get a better look at the screen.

Hiker Claims Mysterious Healing Encounter With Stranger After Suffering Fall

The headline—from the Carson City *Courier*—had a time stamp of only thirty-six hours earlier.

Frowning now, all thoughts of yawning forgotten, Laurel quickly scanned the article. Not that there was much to it—just a couple of short paragraphs that had probably been buried on one of the back pages of the physical paper, although of course she was reading the online version.

MaryJo Gaffney, thirty-eight, had been hiking along the north shore of Lake Tahoe when she slipped and fell on the rocky terrain. The woman stated that she'd been lying there in pain, far from any help, when a man appeared out of nowhere and laid his hands on her leg, which she swore had suffered a compound break of the tibia, or shinbone.

"And the pain just disappeared," she claimed in her interview with the reporter. "The bone was healed, and the gashes on my leg were gone, too. It was like a miracle."

The description she gave was of a man in his late thirties or early forties, with brown hair and brown eyes, tall and slim. He hadn't told her anything about who he was or where he came from, although MaryJo Gaffney said he gave her a reassuring smile before he turned away from her and disappeared into the trees. With her wounds healed, she was able to hike back to the spot at the trailhead where she'd parked her car.

Although the reporter—someone named Cole Michelson—had clearly done his best to report the incident in a properly neutral journalistic way, Laurel could practically feel his skepticism slipping out in each phrase. However, he didn't offer any speculation as to what might have really happened to Ms. Gaffney.

But Laurel, her heart beginning to beat a little faster in excitement, could read between the lines, could see something promising in the woman's account.

"Jake!" she called out. "I think I've got something here."

Her cousin had been in the PC room, discussing a software upgrade with his brother Jeremy, Trident Enterprises' resident computer genius. No response to her call at first, but then a moment later, the two brothers came into the main computer lab. They were both tall and dark, like most of the Wilcoxes, Jeremy's features just a bit more rounded than Jake's chiseled magazine-cover looks.

Right then, they both appeared almost startled by her announcement, and Laurel really couldn't blame them. After all, it had been a *very* long time since they'd gotten even the slightest ping on the sophisticated witch-finding system Jeremy had set up. In fact, the last time had been in late September, more than eight months earlier. That blip had turned out to be Sloane Kennedy, an orphan witch with strong mind-reading abilities…a witch who was now Jeremy's girlfriend.

Ever since then, however, it had been complete radio silence, which was why Laurel had been fighting a yawn and wondering if she could come up with a plausible excuse for bailing early so she could go shopping with Autumn Garnett, her best friend and another Wilcox cousin.

"What is it?" Jake asked, stepping closer to Laurel's computer screen so he could take a look at the images there.

"Looks like maybe a healer," she replied, and obligingly slid her office chair a little out of the way to give him better access.

For a few moments, Jake was silent as he scanned the words on the screen. Jeremy also sidled closer, although he seemed content to hang back a little bit. Then again, it was entirely possible that he could read the article just fine from where he stood.

"This isn't much," Jake said at length, now sounding a bit disappointed. "Don't you think it's much more likely that this woman thought she was more badly injured than she really was, and in her panic just imagined the whole incident?"

Since Laurel had expected him to play devil's advocate, she refused to let his response get her down. "I don't think that's very likely," she replied. "If she actually hurt herself enough to start hallucinating from the pain, then she should have had some kind of cuts and scrapes after that kind of fall. The article says that her leg looked completely uninjured."

Jake scratched at the stubble on his chin. Most of the time, he tried to stay fairly clean-shaven, but with his wedding to Addie Grant now only a little more than a week away, he'd been busy enough that he'd allowed those sorts of minor details to fall by the wayside. At length, he said, "I still don't think it's much to go on."

"Let me run a search," Jeremy offered, speaking for the first time. "Sometimes the algorithms miss the really minor stuff, but now that I have a location and a particular talent to hone in on, maybe I can find more evidence of a healer working in the Lake Tahoe area."

"Okay, try that," Jake said, and Jeremy disappeared back into the PC room, which was where he did most of his intensive data hacking. In the next moment, Jake's phone pinged, and he pulled it out of his pocket and made a face that was almost but not quite a grimace. "I need to go," he went on. "Addie and I need to give the final sign-off on the menu for the reception."

"No worries," Laurel replied blithely. They'd all be waiting for Jeremy to come up with his own findings before they decided what to do next anyway, so Jake might as well go ahead and handle the wedding business. "I'll just hang here and wait to see what Jeremy has to say."

"Don't make any plans until I get back," Jake warned her, and she shot him a guileless smile.

"Why would you think I'd do something like that?"

"Because I know you," he returned, now

looking resigned. "I mean it. No going off half-cocked."

She shot him a thumbs-up, and he let out a sigh and headed toward the front door. A moment later, he was gone.

As soon as the door shut behind her cousin, Laurel's smile faded. She might have asked the universe how Jake could have possibly known she was already plotting and planning, but that sort of thing was to be expected when someone had known you for your entire life.

But really…how could she *not* already be scheming about how to go to Lake Tahoe to find this supposed healer?

I mean, Lake Tahoe, she thought. *Talk about your dream destination.*

Her life hadn't been quite as circumscribed as it had been for previous generations of Wilcox witches, thanks to the alliance that had formed between the Wilcoxes and the McAllisters about eight years earlier. She'd been able to visit the former mining town of Jerome—home base for the McAllister witch clan—and even travel as far south as Tucson, whereas before, she would have been confined to northern Arizona, to Wilcox country, which stretched across the northern third of the state, all the way from Kingman to the west to the New Mexico border to the east. Despite that newfound freedom, she'd still never left Arizona.

And Lake Tahoe sounded like such a cool place to visit. But would going there even be possible?

All of Nevada was Delmonico clan territory. Maybe once upon a time, it would have seemed unlikely that a Wilcox could even think about traveling there, but after Jeremy had managed to put the Walkers—the clan in South Dakota and part of Montana, with a particularly nasty *prima* at its head—in their place, the Delmonicos had reason to be grateful to the Wilcoxes. Before that, members of the Walker clan with the ability to hide their witch nature had been able to come and go in Nevada with impunity, but ever since their former *prima* had passed away, the Walkers had been lying low and staying out of trouble. In fact, it sounded as though they hadn't even made an attempt to leave their home territory.

Also, with Sloane and her mind-reading ability—an ability she'd used to consistently win at poker tables throughout the Southwest—now safely ensconced in Flagstaff, the Delmonicos also didn't have to worry about a freelance witch unfairly beating the odds and fleecing any clan-run casinos out of their earnings. True, the Delmonicos didn't own all the casinos in Nevada, but they ran a good number of them, and probably hadn't been too happy to learn that one particular witch had been utilizing her own special witchy talent to pad her wallet.

At any rate, the combination of those two happy shifts in fortune probably meant the Delmonicos had every reason to look favorably on the Wilcoxes…which also meant they might be a lot more open to having a Wilcox witch come and do a bit of investigating in their territory.

Or not. Laurel could freely admit that she knew very little about the Delmonico clan. Maybe they didn't have a healer, and therefore wouldn't want someone to come poking around and possibly steal a warlock who could be valuable to them.

She got up from her seat and headed into the PC lab. Jeremy was hunched over the keyboard in front of him, the two computer screens directly ahead filled with a mishmash of code. If she sat down and really studied what he was doing, she'd probably be able to make some sense of it, since she'd majored in computer science at Northern Pines University, but she didn't see the point. Her trying to hack Jeremy's magically enhanced algorithms was like a kid who'd studied science in high school trying to unravel the physics behind the discovery of the Higgs-Boson particle.

"Find anything?" she asked, trying not to sound too hopeful.

Although he was in profile to her, she could still see the way his brows drew together in annoyance. "I just started working on this five minutes ago," he said. "What do you think?"

Because she'd known Jeremy her whole life, Laurel wouldn't allow his gruff tone to irritate her. The guy was a total grump. Honestly, she didn't know how Sloane put up with him half the time. Okay, she'd allow herself to admit that he was cute —although since they were first cousins, she'd never let herself think of him at all romantically— and yet she thought there were plenty of other Wilcox warlocks who were almost as good-looking but didn't see the need to do an Oscar the Grouch impersonation every waking moment.

"Well, you're the whiz kid," she said, keeping her tone airy, unconcerned. "I figured it couldn't hurt to ask."

Jeremy's only reply was a slight hunching of his shoulders as his fingers continued to clatter across the keyboard. Still staring at the screen, he said, "Okay, there was an incident in January where someone crashed into a tree while skiing and woke up half an hour later, completely uninjured. They took the guy to the hospital to get checked out, since some other skiers found him passed out in the snow, but he was fine. No concussion, no bumps or bruises."

"Well, that sounds like something," Laurel

responded. "I mean, I assume if you skied at full speed right into a tree, you'd have some kind of injuries to show for your effort."

Another shrug. "You tell me. You're the healer."

Her shoulders tightened, but Laurel told herself not to rise to the bait. Technically, Jeremy was right—her gift was healing, but she'd never used it much. To be honest, she still found herself annoyed that she'd been blessed—or cursed—with a magical talent she didn't much want. It would have been far cooler to have Jake's power of telekinesis, or the weather control that his fiancée Addie Grant possessed. Or the ability to help things grow, or even to talk to ghosts, the way Angela, wife of the Wilcox clan's *primus* Connor, could.

But when you were a healer, you were pretty much at the clan's beck and call. You never knew when you'd get a phone call in the middle of the night to help deliver someone's baby, or to run to someone's house when their kid fell out of a tree and broke their arm. And all right, a lot of the Wilcoxes also relied on civilian doctors, so as not to put too much of a burden on Eleanor, the clan's other healer, but still, you couldn't exactly call your life your own.

That was the main reason why Laurel hadn't done much with her talent. Eleanor had been very understanding, and had only guided her through the basics so her gift wouldn't get out of control... and also so it could be of use in an emergency... but she'd assured Laurel that she didn't have any intention of retiring soon, and so there was no need for her to become the clan's second full-time healer.

Since Jeremy had paused in his typing and was now sending her a sideways, sardonic look, clearly expecting an answer, Laurel knew she had to respond to his comment. Trying to sound casual, she said, "I suppose it depends on how you hit the tree. If you were really slaloming and went full tilt into the thing, then you'd be lucky to get off with just a concussion and maybe a few broken bones. But even a small impact should have caused some cuts and bruises, especially since it sounds like this person hit hard enough to get knocked out."

Jeremy absorbed this information and went back to his typing. "The guy in the article doesn't recall seeing any strangers nearby."

"Well, how could he?" Laurel said reasonably. "The man got knocked out. If there really is an orphan warlock in the Lake Tahoe area, he probably just went up to the skier and healed his injuries while the guy was still unconscious. Obviously, he wouldn't be able to remember anything."

It seemed Jeremy found this explanation reasonable enough that he didn't bother to argue.

However, because it really wasn't in his nature to concede a point, he only said, "Oh…looks like there's another one."

"When?" Laurel asked, trying not to sound too eager.

"Last month," he said. "Here."

A blog post popped up on one of the screens, from a woman named Alison Crewe who called her blog *Tahoe Treasures.* As far as Laurel could tell, Ms. Crewe was a local who made a habit of hiking around the area, finding hidden spots or less frequented locales for those who wanted to go off the beaten path when they were visiting the area.

She leaned in closer, ignoring the annoyed glance Jeremy gave her as she made him shift his office chair a few inches in the other direction so she'd have better access to the screen. Apparently, Alison Crewe had been hiking in a spot outside Carnelian Bay when she lost her footing and slid down the hill, and crashed into a rocky outcropping. Luckily, she hadn't broken anything, but she was pretty banged up and in pain, and not sure whether she would be able to make it back to the place where she'd parked her SUV.

Out of nowhere, a tall man with brown hair appeared. He told her he'd seen her fall, and said he'd be happy to help her get back to her vehicle. There had been something so friendly and reassuring about the stranger that she found herself trusting him immediately, and she'd accepted his offer of help. With him to steady her, she made it back to her Nissan Pathfinder.

But after he helped her in and closed the door, he apparently vanished into thin air.

I wanted to think I'd imagined the whole thing, Alison Crewe wrote in her blog, *that maybe I'd conjured this "helper" because it was my mind's way of giving me the strength I needed to get back to my car. But the thing is, I discovered after I got home that all my scrapes and bruises were gone. I'd banged up my hands pretty badly as I tried to stop my fall, to the point where I was fairly sure I'd have to go to urgent care to have them looked at. All those cuts were gone as if they'd never existed in the first place.*

I don't know what happened, she concluded. *Maybe Lake Tahoe has its own guardian angel now, a man who's watching out for all of us.*

I'd like to think so, anyway.

Laurel finished reading and shot Jeremy a triumphant look. "That sure sounds like a healer to me," she said.

"One who can just vanish into thin air?" he replied, looking skeptical.

"Maybe he has multiple gifts," she said. That sort of thing wasn't unheard of, after all. It was fairly rare, but there were several people in the

Wilcox clan whose talents included several different magical skills, usually ones that didn't have any connection to each other.

"Those are two pretty strong gifts to have," Jeremy said. He still appeared dubious.

Laurel couldn't really blame him for being skeptical. The only people she knew of who could teleport were Connor and Angela, and they were a *primus* and a *prima*. Even so, they had to work together to bend time and space in such a crazy way. They couldn't do it on their own.

So if this brown-haired stranger really could heal and teleport at the same time, that meant he had to be an extremely strong warlock…and that also meant the Trident team needed to find him ASAP and discover what clan he was from. True, there was no need to worry about the government scooping him up, because Homeland Security's Project Daedalus had been disbanded a year earlier, but still, any warlock who was going around and flexing his magical muscles in such an obvious way ran the risk of discovery—a discovery that could be disastrous for the entire witching world, and not just the individual involved.

Of course, the most obvious question needed to be answered first. "Is he a Delmonico?"

Jeremy shook his head. "I don't think so. I've been working on cataloguing the members of the various witch clans, starting with the ones whose territories border ours. The Delmonico healer is a woman named Emilia. She lives in Reno and is in her sixties."

So, that was what Jeremy had been working on recently. Laurel knew he'd been feeling stymied by their lack of progress, but she hadn't realized he'd embarked on such an ambitious project. It made sense, though; the more they knew about the neighboring clans, the less chance they'd have of getting blindsided by someone with unusual gifts popping out of nowhere.

"Then our guy has to be an orphan," she said, hoping her firm tone would convince Jeremy that the anomaly he'd discovered was someone Trident Enterprises needed to seek out.

"Maybe," he allowed. "If he exists at all. We're only getting anecdotal evidence here—and these stories all involve people who were injured in some way, which means their judgment might have been somewhat impaired."

"You had less evidence to go on when you went after Sloane," Laurel argued, which was only the truth. Jeremy had been acting on the barest of hunches when he headed out to the Twin Arrows Casino to the east of Flagstaff in search of someone who might be gaming the system there, and yet that hunch had paid off in spades.

So to speak.

From the way his mouth curled at her

comment, she could tell she'd scored a point. Still, since it was Jeremy, he wasn't going to admit to such a thing.

"That was different," he said.

"How was it different?"

"Because I could tell she was a witch."

"You only found out she was a witch because you went to the casino. You definitely didn't know that when you drove out from Flagstaff to find her."

Faced with this obvious logic, Jeremy didn't reply right away. He settled against the back of his office chair and gave Laurel a direct look. "You know what Jake's going to say."

Unfortunately, she did. While she loved her cousin, sometimes he acted a little too much like an overprotective older brother. Maybe that was because she was an only child, and so he thought someone should step into that role. All the same, Laurel thought he needed to give it a rest. She was a grown woman of twenty-four, after all, and not some kid.

"Jake's busy," she said calmly. "It's not like he can go tearing off to Lake Tahoe, not with the wedding only a week away. And you know Trident is better off with you overseeing the surveillance stuff. I've been sitting here and twiddling my thumbs for months. Besides, my gift is healing. Doesn't it make the most sense to send someone with the same talent to track down this maybe-warlock?"

His mouth twisted, which meant he probably could see the logic in what she was saying, even if he didn't want to admit it. "Jake's not going to like this," Jeremy said.

"He'll get over it. I think we have enough to present our case to Connor, don't you?"

Because as much as Laurel would have liked to run home to her loft apartment, pack a bag, and get on the road immediately, she knew any inter-clan interactions like this had to be handled by Connor, at least at the beginning. He'd need to get in contact with the Delmonico *prima* and make sure they weren't stepping on any toes. If they were given the go-ahead, then Laurel could head off to Lake Tahoe with their blessing.

If not...well, she really didn't want to think about that. After all, it was about time for her to have her own adventure.

Voice steady, she said, "Let's call Connor."

2

Jason Ludlow stood in the office of the Ludlow *prima's*—his mother's—impressive house in San Francisco's Pacific Heights. The house had been built around the turn of the last century, and had survived the earthquake that leveled much of the town, thanks to the spells the *prima* of that time had used to bind the foundation, making it rock-solid and impervious to fire and quake and any other calamities it might have to weather.

Why Carolyn Ludlow had summoned him to the house, he wasn't sure. These days, he tried to have as little to do with his mother as possible. Ever since she'd made her power play four years earlier by trying to align their clan with Joaquin Escobar, the rogue warlock who'd taken over the Santiago clan in Southern California, Jason had done his best to distance himself from her and her machinations. At the time, he'd told her she was making a huge mistake, but she hadn't listened, had once again given in to the unreasonable demands of his little sister Brooklyn, the Ludlow clan's *prima*-in-waiting. Brooklyn's search for a consort hadn't been going well, and she'd decided that the otherworldly Levi McAllister would make the perfect consort for her.

Unfortunately for Brooklyn, Levi had other plans. As did the rest of the McAllisters, along with their allies, the Wilcoxes and the de la Paz clan in southern Arizona. When the Arizona clans had joined up with the Castillos from New Mexico, their combined might had been too much to withstand. Joaquin Escobar was defeated, and his death freed the Santiagos from his grip.

And the Ludlows had been forced to slink back to Northern California in defeat.

Brooklyn had ended up marrying the least objectionable of her eligible distant cousins, and their mother had done her best to carry on as if nothing had happened…not the easiest feat in the world, when a dozen of the Ludlow clan's witches and warlocks would have to live the rest of their lives without any magic, thanks to the way Connor Wilcox and Angela McAllister had stripped their powers from them in retaliation for attacking the McAllisters' home base in Jerome.

Luckily, Jason hadn't been sent on that particular foray. His talents were of a more subtle sort.

"What do you want, Mother?" he asked, not bothering with any sort of polite greeting.

Carolyn's brows drew together. She had been strikingly beautiful in her youth, and still managed to turn heads at a very well-preserved fifty-eight, slim and tall and with thick, dark gold hair like her son's. "Is that any way for a son to address his mother?"

He shrugged, hands jammed in the pockets of his trousers. While he rebelled against the family's strictures as much as he could, he still knew better than to appear at an audience with the Ludlow *prima* wearing jeans and a T-shirt. "I don't know," he replied. "Did you call me here as my mother, or as the *prima* of the Ludlow clan?"

Carolyn rose from her office chair of carved tiger maple and went to the window. A bright afternoon sun shone down on them, brilliantly illuminating the panoramic view of Russian Hill and the San Francisco Bay beyond, its waters glinting blue as the sapphire on her right hand, and gleaming in her carefully coiffed hair.

"As both," she said easily. "Unlike you, I can't separate the two. You are my son…but you also have gifts that can help with the problem at hand."

Those words made him stiffen. When he was

eleven and his talents started to manifest, he'd thought they had to be just about the coolest thing in the world. Later on, when he began to understand exactly how his mother wanted him to utilize those talents, he'd realized they really weren't that cool at all.

He didn't see the point in beating around the bush. "What do you want?"

She'd been wearing a faint smile, as if gazing down at her demesne pleased her, but it disappeared at once. "We've had word of a healer."

"Someone in the clan has finally developed that gift?"

Because as strong as the Ludlows were, what they lacked was a healer. Rose Ludlow, the clan's former healer, had died at the ripe old age of eighty-nine when Jason was only fifteen years old. In the eleven years that had passed since then, they'd had to struggle along with civilian doctors. He'd never viewed the lack as much of a hardship, since the clan's wealth meant they had access to some of the best medical care in the world, but Carolyn hadn't seen the situation that way. She disliked knowing that there might come a time when a member of the clan suffered an injury that would be difficult to explain to someone who wasn't a witch or warlock, and she viewed the clan as weakened because of the situation. In fact, she'd acted as though Rose's death had been a direct affront to her, although expecting the woman to cling to life indefinitely because they didn't have a replacement healer seemed a bit much to him.

"No," Carolyn said. "You misunderstand me. I've received word there's a good chance a healer unaffiliated with any clan has appeared in the Lake Tahoe area."

For a second, Jason could only stare at his mother. How was it possible that there could be a witch who was unconnected to a clan? He managed to find his voice and asked, "How do you know this person is a healer?"

"There are stories circulating," she said. "I need you to go to Lake Tahoe and find out if those stories are just civilian exaggerations, or whether this man they've described really is a healer."

Man. That was unusual; healers tended to be women. Already knowing what she planned to ask of him, Jason still made himself say carefully, "Lake Tahoe is in Delmonico territory."

"Only part of it," his mother replied at once. "Part of it is ours."

Which was true; the clan boundaries followed the same boundaries that separated Nevada from California. And even though the Ludlows controlled a much larger portion of Lake Tahoe than the Delmonicos did, that didn't mean this healer—whoever he was—might not be roaming around in the other clan's territory.

Since his mother knew that as well as Jason did, he didn't bother to answer, only crossed his arms and stared at her.

She made an impatient gesture with one hand. "You know it doesn't matter. You'll be able to go there and poke around, with the Delmonicos being none the wiser."

Again, only the truth. Because Jason's talent was illusions, the kind that could change his appearance so no one would ever be able to recognize him as himself. Even that handy magical gift wouldn't be enough, however, not when any witch or warlock he encountered would know right away that he wasn't a civilian.

No, his talent went far deeper than that. At the same time he could change his appearance, he could also shield his magical nature from others, making them believe he was no different from the vast majority of the population, those civilians who didn't even know magic was real, or that people with extraordinary powers lived among them.

Unlike any other witch or warlock he'd ever met, he'd be able to slip into Delmonico territory completely undetected.

And that was why his mother had summoned

him. Not because she wanted to see her son, but because she needed a spy.

Voice level, he said, "And what if I say no?"

Her expression didn't even flicker. They'd butted heads before, and so she knew what to expect…just as she also knew he would eventually capitulate to her demands. Same old dance, just a different day.

He was getting damn tired of it, though.

"You don't have any reason to *not* go," Carolyn said calmly. "If it turns out that there really is an unaffiliated healer in the area, why wouldn't he want to come back to San Francisco with you? We Ludlows could offer him a comfortable lifestyle, his every need met. It's not as though you'd be dragging him off to a gulag in Siberia."

No, but maybe this mysterious healer liked Lake Tahoe just fine and didn't feel like going anywhere else.

If he even existed.

"People don't always do what you want them to, Mother," Jason said, also keeping his tone even. Long ago, he'd learned that the only way he could ever manage to hold his ground with her was to not lose his temper. Getting angry only made her think she'd won.

Not even a blink. "I understand that, Jason," she replied. "But really, who would turn this down?" And she gestured toward the multimil-lion-dollar vista beyond the window.

Someone who doesn't want to sell their soul for a view, he thought, although he kept those words to himself. "You might be surprised," was all he said, but she merely smiled.

"Well, you bring this healer here, and then I can explain to him all the benefits of being a member of the Ludlow clan," she told him. "It's really not as though I'm asking anything terrible of you."

No, only to put on a false face, to hide his very nature...to walk into another clan's territory without permission. Jason didn't bother to point out any of that, however. His mother—and his little sister Brooklyn—had very flexible notions of right and wrong when it came to something they wanted.

He could protest further, but what would be the point? It wasn't as though he had a lot of options. When you were part of a witch clan, you did as the *prima* asked...even if she also happened to be your mother.

Or maybe especially if she was your mother.

"I'll leave tomorrow morning," was all he said, and her smile broadened.

"Thank you, Jason."

A nod, and he left her office. As he walked along the hallway to the staircase—a staircase whose bannister he'd once slid down, many years earlier—he wondered who he hated more…his mother for asking these things of him, or himself for giving in.

"You seriously get to go to Lake Tahoe?" Laurel's cousin Autumn Garnett asked.

"Well, I hope so," Laurel replied. "Jake hasn't given me the go-ahead yet. He has to talk to Connor first."

Because she knew that waiting to hear Connor's verdict on the Lake Tahoe plan was going to drive her crazy, Laurel had decided the best thing to do would be to meet Autumn for some coffee in the interim. And since Autumn was off from college for the summer and was only working about fifteen hours a week, she'd been available to drop by the coffee shop that was located directly under Laurel's loft apartment in downtown Flagstaff.

Autumn waved a hand. She had the same night-dark hair as most of the Wilcox witches, but her eyes were a startling dark blue. When they were little kids, Laurel had always imagined her cousin as Snow White any time she read the fairy tale.

Unlike Snow White, Autumn had a pretty take-charge attitude.

"Oh, you know Connor will say yes," she said, then lifted her iced coffee to take a sip. "He's not exactly what you could call a hard-ass."

That was true. Connor was pretty much the diametrical opposite of his late brother, who'd ruled the Wilcox clan with a heavy hand. "Unfortunately, it's not all up to him," Laurel replied. "He has to get permission from the Delmonicos before I can go anywhere near Tahoe."

Autumn considered that complication for a moment. However, it didn't seem to faze her much, because she said, "Connor's pretty good at sweet-talking people. I'm sure it will be fine."

Maybe "sweet-talking" wasn't exactly the phrase Laurel would have used, because their cousin wasn't the sort of smooth-tongued person who could get anyone to agree with them. However, she had to admit that most people generally liked Connor, and because he was so easygoing and unruffled, they found him easy to work with.

Would those qualities be enough to get the Delmonicos to agree to their plan? She knew absolutely nothing about the Nevada family, since, like most witch clans, they kept to themselves and minded their own business. Laurel supposed they probably were more used to working with civilians

—nonmagical people—than most, simply because there were so many tourists going in and out of Las Vegas all the time that they didn't have much choice but to deal with them.

Whether that would make them more open to allowing a Wilcox witch to come into their territory and start poking around, she wasn't sure.

"It's not like it would be the first time a Wilcox was in their territory, anyway," Autumn went on when Laurel didn't reply right away. "Jeremy went there when he was chasing after Sloane. And actually, didn't Jake and Addie head to Las Vegas when they were running away from Kanab?"

That was true. After Laurel's cousin Jake had rescued Addie Grant in the nick of time from being scooped up by Randall Lenz, the head of the Daedalus Project, Jake had thought it safer to detour to Vegas rather than head straight to Flagstaff, just in case anyone was pursuing them. A wise maneuver, since Lenz really had been hot on their trail—or at least, as hot as he could be, considering Jake had clocked the man in the head with a carefully aimed flower pot before beating feet out of Kanab.

The Delmonicos didn't seem to have had much of a problem with either of those forays, but then again, neither Jake nor Jeremy had hung around long. Laurel's mission would be something entirely different, an open-ended trip with no conclusion in sight.

Well, that wasn't exactly true. Even if she hadn't found the mysterious healer by next Friday, she'd have to head back to Flagstaff or miss Jake and Addie's wedding. Since she was the maid of honor, Laurel guessed that wouldn't go over too well. The bridal shower was over, and Addie had stated emphatically that she didn't want a bachelorette party, and so the only thing left to do was show up for hair and makeup on Saturday morning, but even so, she didn't have unlimited amounts of time to play with.

If she even got to go at all.

"They went there," she admitted, and reached for her own neglected cup of chai. The afternoon was warm enough that she probably should have gotten something iced, like Autumn had, but she'd compromised by letting it cool down to just lukewarm. "But they didn't stay long. I'm sure I'll need to be in Tahoe for at least a few days. It all depends on what I find."

Autumn gave a sympathetic nod. To Laurel's relief, she didn't ask about getting back in time for Jake and Addie's wedding, probably because she knew that her cousin had already done the necessary mental math and knew that the whole thing would be doable…if barely.

Just as Laurel was taking another sip of her

lukewarm chai, her phone let out a small bing. At once, she set down the mug and reached to dig the phone out of her purse so she could look down at the screen.

A text from Jake.

Connor says it's a go—the Delmonicos are on board. Come back for a meeting, and then you need to get packed.

She unlocked the phone and quickly typed back, *Awesome. I'll be right over.* After replacing the phone in her purse, she looked across the table at her cousin's expectant face.

"Well?" Autumn asked, blue eyes shining with curiosity.

"It's happening," Laurel said with a grin. "I'm going to Lake Tahoe."

She walked into the living room of the vacation condo the Delmonico clan had provided for her and let out a sigh of pure relief. Although they'd offered to let her break up the trip with a night in Las Vegas, she'd wanted to avoid wasting any precious time and press on toward Lake Tahoe, and so had done the entire eleven-hour drive in one *very* long day. By the end, she'd been drooping but also triumphant, since the farthest she'd ever driven before was the four-hour trip to Tucson.

It had been way too late to even think about going to a restaurant to get something to eat, but someone had thoughtfully put a few containers of yogurt in the fridge, along with several breakfast burritos in the freezer. Laurel grabbed one of those and nuked it in the microwave, knowing it was probably a stupid idea to eat when the hour was close to midnight, but also knowing that she needed to put something in her stomach. Her last meal had been a burger grabbed at an In 'N' Out in Vegas, and that was hours and hours ago.

She still couldn't quite believe she was here. Jake had made his objections—among them that Laurel was Addie's maid of honor, and therefore shouldn't be skipping off to Lake Tahoe with the wedding only a little more than a week away—but in the end, Connor had overruled him.

"You put her on the Trident team for a reason," the *primus* had pointed out. "Since there's no way you can go, and Laurel is a healer as well, it just makes the most sense for her to check things out. Besides, the Delmonicos will keep an eye on her."

Because that was the other crazy thing. Not only had Theresa, the *prima* of the Delmonicos, given Laurel permission to go poking around on the Nevada side of Lake Tahoe, she'd also said her own clan would give her any support they could. She told Connor that no one in the area had sensed a strange warlock anywhere around, and if there really was one on Delmonico land, then they wanted to know about him just as much as Laurel and the Wilcoxes did.

After that, the arrangements were made more quickly than she could have imagined. The very next morning, she was driving her Jeep Renegade westward on I-40 so she could cut through Kingman and go from there to Vegas before continuing north and west. It had been a grueling drive, but it had been worth it.

Or at least, she hoped it would be worth it.

She sat down on the couch with her burrito and a glass of water. A TV had been mounted above the stacked stone fireplace, but she was too tired to bother turning it on. No, she'd have her burrito and some water, and then go to bed. Luckily, the condo was a single story, and so she wouldn't have to worry about dragging herself and her luggage up the stairs.

As she'd driven, she'd made plans for her first day in the area. First, she'd drive over to Carson City so she could talk to Cole Michelson, the reporter at the Carson City *Courier* who'd covered the story of MaryJo Gaffney, the woman whose broken leg had miraculously healed itself. Yes, it was a Saturday, but Jeremy's hacking had discovered that apparently Mr. Michelson worked weekends and had his days off midweek. Jeremy had also dug up the address for Alison Crewe, the blogger, but Laurel thought it might be better to talk to the reporter first, if only because he wouldn't think it too odd that someone might track him down at his place of business. Alison Crewe, on the other hand, probably would be mildly freaked to learn that someone who'd read her blog had popped up on her doorstep.

Theresa Delmonico had given Laurel the contact info for several Delmonicos in Incline Village, so she knew she was covered in case any emergencies came up. But she doubted she'd need to reach out to anyone. From what she'd seen as she drove in, the little town seemed very quiet and very, very prosperous. If there was a low-rent neighborhood in the area, she sure hadn't seen any evidence of it yet.

And it would be nice to get some driving in during the daylight hours. It had been full dark when she got here, with a waxing moon giving some idea of the luxuriant pine forests on either side of the highway, along with a shimmer to her left that she guessed was the water of the lake, but she hadn't been able to see much more than that.

She really wanted to get out and explore. Being granted the freedom to go wherever she wanted in another clan's territory was a novel experience, to say the least, and Laurel intended to make the most of her current situation. And since her little Jeep had four-wheel drive, she knew she could go pretty much wherever the clues to the mysterious healer might lead her. Of course, once she found him, that would only be the start. They would still have to figure out which clan he belonged to.

But that was Jeremy's job. He'd done amazing work tracking down the various families of the people they'd liberated from the Special Enforcement Division's facility in Virginia where the Daedalus Project had been housed, so Laurel knew he'd be up to the task of locating this healer's clan. He would be one more person they could add to their database of orphan witches and warlocks who'd been restored to families they didn't even know they had.

Getting a little ahead of yourself, Laurel, she thought as she munched down the last of her breakfast burrito. *You still have to find the guy.*

But her spirits were high. Against all odds, she was here in Lake Tahoe, entrusted to handle this task on her own. And all right, she knew she could reach out to the Delmonicos in Incline Village if she ran into any problems, but even so, a lot of this was resting on her shoulders, and her shoulders alone.

She really hoped she wouldn't screw things up.

3

COLE MICHELSON, A NO-NONSENSE TYPE IN his late forties, with graying hair and piercing eyes nearly the same color, gave Laurel an assessing look. "Why are you so interested in MaryJo Gaffney?"

Time to find out if the cover story she'd cooked up sounded plausible. The reporter didn't seem hostile…but he also seemed like the sort of guy who could spot a fake at fifty paces.

Too bad her magical talent wasn't telling bulletproof lies.

"I have a friend who had a similar experience back home in Flagstaff," Laurel said. At least the part about living in Flagstaff was true. "She's been looking for the guy ever since so she could thank him. And then when I saw your article…."

She trailed off there, hoping Cole Michelson

would fill in the blanks. However, his eyes narrowed slightly, and he said, "How did someone living in Flagstaff even stumble across that story? It's not like the Carson City *Courier* gets a very wide distribution, even on the internet."

Laurel opened her eyes slightly. Did she look guileless and innocent, or just like an idiot? Since she couldn't see herself, she couldn't say one way or another. The only thing to do was press on, though.

"I was doing a search for unexplained incidents of people healing spontaneously," she said. "And your article popped up. I mean, it was a few pages back in my search, but it was the only one that sounded like my friend Autumn's experience."

Sorry, Autumn, Laurel thought. *Hope you don't mind me borrowing you for my little lie.*

For a moment, the reporter didn't say anything, only sat there and watched her closely. Then he released a breath that wasn't exactly a sigh and said, "I'm afraid you've come a long way for nothing. I don't have much of anything to tell that wasn't already included in my article."

"There has to be something," she replied immediately, since she'd already prepared herself for this kind of disclaimer. "I mean, it's been a while since my high school journalism days, but I still remember the editor making a lot of cuts for length."

He almost smiled. Almost. But his tone was a bit friendlier as he said, "I doubt it's been that long since your high school days, Ms. Wilcox. However, you're right. We did cut some of the more...fantastic...elements from the article."

"Fantastic how?" she asked, trying to ignore the way her heartbeat sped up slightly at those words.

The stern look was back in Cole Michelson's eyes, and he shook his head. "It's nothing. We were right to cut those bits. It sounded like something out of the *National Enquirer,* or maybe the *Weekly World News.*" A pause, and he added, "If your friend experienced something similar, then shouldn't you already know what we cut out?"

Damn it. Laurel narrowly avoided biting her lip, knowing if she did something like that, it would be a dead giveaway that he'd put her on the spot.

Then she remembered how Eleanor had told her once that some healers actually had hands that glowed as they worked, although her magic—or Laurel's own—wasn't nearly that flashy. Had MaryJo Gaffney witnessed something similar?

Fortune favors the bold, Laurel told herself, and she said, "Were the man's hands glowing as he healed MaryJo's wounds?"

A blink was the only response she got, but

that was enough. She'd surprised the reporter…
and caught him a little off guard.

Her suspicions were confirmed when he said,
"How did you know that?"

Voice steady, she replied, "Because my friend
saw the same thing."

Cole Michelson's fingers tapped on the desk-
top. Irrelevantly, she noticed that he was wearing
an Apple watch and a scratched white gold
wedding ring. A long pause, and then he said,
"Okay, yes, we cut out that part. Honestly, it just
confirmed that Ms. Gaffney had to have been
hallucinating during the entire episode."

That would be the easiest explanation, and the
sort of thing a civilian would immediately latch
onto. So many of them desperately wanted to
believe the world was entirely mundane, that there
was no such thing as magic.

And of course, the witch world did its best to
encourage those sorts of beliefs, since the last
thing any of them wanted was for their secrets to
be discovered.

"Maybe I could talk to her," Laurel suggested,
and Cole Michelson immediately shook his head.

"That's not a very good idea. For one thing,
I'm not allowed to give you her contact informa-
tion. Also, she's not a local—she lives in the Bay
Area."

Right in the heart of Ludlow territory. No way

in the world could Laurel go there to get MaryJo Gaffney's story, even if the reporter had been willing to break the rules and hand over her address or phone number.

It was looking more and more like Laurel would have to go speak to Alison Crewe, even if by doing so she'd inadvertently end up weirding out the woman. She'd have to figure out a way to approach her that wouldn't seem too stalker-ish.

Yeah, good luck with that, she thought.

"I do have one thing," Cole went on. He got up from his desk and went over to an old-fashioned metal file cabinet pushed up against one wall of his tiny office. A bit of rummaging around, and he drew out a small piece of paper. He came over to Laurel and handed it to her. "MaryJo sketched this for me. We ended up not including it with the article because my editor was worried about liability issues, but I can make a copy for you as long as you agree not to share it on the internet or on social media."

Laurel stared down at the piece of paper. On it was a surprisingly detailed sketch of a man's face done in pencil. He was handsome, with hair that waved back from a high forehead, and friendly, regular features. "This is the man MaryJo says healed her?"

"Supposedly. She made that sketch for me."

"It's very good."

"She's an artist. That's why she was hiking around—she was scouting places to set up her easel so she could come back and paint the landscape."

That made sense. The man in the sketch was a complete stranger, but MaryJo had filled in the details of his appearance well enough that Laurel was pretty sure she wouldn't have any trouble recognizing him if their paths should cross.

"I won't share it," she said. "But it would really help me to have a copy."

"Be right back," Cole responded.

He left his office and headed out into the main part of the *Courier's* slightly shabby head-quarters. Laurel sat in her chair, mind racing. It would help her so much to have an accurate rendering of the strange healer's appearance, rather than a vague description of a man with brown hair and brown eyes in his late thirties or early forties. True, she would still have to track him down, but at least now she would be able to rule out certain candidates almost immediately.

Assuming, of course, that MaryJo Gaffney's portrait was an accurate one and that she really hadn't hallucinated the whole episode.

Cole Michelson returned and handed Laurel a fresh copy of the portrait, the paper still slightly warm from being spat out of a photocopier. "I hope this helps. But you realize there's no guarantee that this man is still in the area—even if he actually exists at all."

"I know," she replied. "But it still gives me something to go on. Thank you very much, Mr. Michelson."

"Not a problem." He paused there, and gave her another of those keen, gray-eyed glances. "Do me a favor, though."

"Yes?" Laurel said, hoping he wouldn't ask for something she couldn't provide. He'd offered her more assistance than she'd expected, but still, this was witch business, and there was a whole lot she had to keep private, for obvious reasons.

"Let me know if you find him. This story has been nagging at me, for some reason, and I'd like to get a little closure."

"Um…sure," she replied. That wouldn't cause too much of a problem, would it? She could tell the reporter she'd found the stranger but not offer any particular details.

Then again….

But it was too late, because Cole Michelson actually cracked a bit of a smile and said, "Thanks."

After that, he politely saw her out, and wished her the best of luck in her search.

She had a feeling she was going to need it.

Jason had to prevent himself from startling as he watched Cole Michelson escort a very pretty girl probably a few years younger than his own twenty-six through the front doors of the Carson City *Courier's* offices. They were close enough that Jason experienced a low hum in his right ear as the girl walked by—a sure sign that she was also witch-kind.

Then Michelson said, "Best of luck, Ms. Wilcox," and offered her a somewhat rusty smile before he headed back inside the building.

Wilcox?

That gorgeous girl was a Wilcox witch?

It sure seemed that way.

A tingle of shock flashed down his spine, even as Jason told himself there was no way she could possibly know who he was. Since he could hold an illusion much longer if it wasn't too complicated, he hadn't done a lot to change his appearance. He still looked like a tall man in his middle twenties, only his hair was dark brown instead of dark blond, and his eyes were dark to match, his skin a deeper tan than normal.

Most of his energy had gone toward making sure that the spark of his witch nature was tamped down so fiercely, no one could possibly be able to detect that he wasn't a run-of-the-mill civilian. He'd gone to that effort since he knew he'd be deep in Delmonico territory and would have to do his best to avoid notice. Not once had he thought he'd have to be dodging the Wilcoxes as well.

What the hell was a Wilcox witch doing here?

Even as the question flashed through his mind, however, Jason thought he could guess. Although the Ludlows didn't have any direct contact with the Wilcoxes—for obvious reasons— rumors had begun to circulate through the various witch clans that apparently the Wilcox family had taken it into their heads to try looking for any witches or warlocks who were operating outside the normal clan structure, and then was reuniting the people they found with their families. What the Wilcoxes got out of the deal, Jason wasn't sure.

What he was pretty sure about was that this girl must have come to this part of the world in search of the same healer Jason was looking for. The real question was, had she come here alone, or did she have other Wilcoxes with her?

She was already a few yards down the side- walk, moving quickly, as if she had a destination already in mind. If he didn't follow soon, he'd lose her altogether.

And although he'd come to Carson City to do the exact same thing she'd obviously already done —namely, talk to the reporter who'd written the story about MaryJo Gaffney—Jason had a feeling there was no point in initiating such a discussion now. Reporters tended to be naturally suspicious people anyway, and this Cole Michelson would smell something fishy right away if someone else showed up and started asking questions about the mysterious healer.

No, much better to tail the Wilcox witch and see what she was up to.

It turned out her destination was a public parking lot a few blocks away. As luck would have it, Jason had parked in the exact same lot, only one row down from the spot where she climbed into an iron-blue Jeep Renegade and pulled out.

He hopped into his Range Rover and did his best to follow her without seeming too obvious. She made several turns, then headed south on Carson Street. Although he didn't know the area well, he'd taken basically the same route this morning as he headed into town.

Clearly, she was planning to drive back to Lake Tahoe. Since she obviously had to remain in Delmonico territory, he guessed she was probably staying in Incline Village…just as he'd taken over a vacation condo in South Tahoe so he could be safely inside Ludlow clan lands. His magical gift only protected him while he was awake; the illusion would fall away as soon as he was asleep, as would the blocking of his witchy nature. No way would it have been safe for him to stay anywhere on the Nevada side of the border, even if it might have put him closer to the mysterious healer he sought.

When they got closer to the turnoff for Highway 50, Jason lagged back a little ways so a car or two could get in between them. Although this was the first time he'd ever had to tail someone by car, he guessed that his black Range Rover was pretty conspicuous, and he didn't want to rouse the Wilcox witch's suspicions. Besides, her little blue-gray Renegade was also a vehicle that tended to stand out from the others, so he didn't think it would be too difficult to keep an eye on her from a few car lengths back.

The countryside around him was some of the most beautiful in the world, but Jason couldn't allow himself to be distracted. No, he hung back as a big Dodge pickup truck blocked his view of the Wilcox witch's SUV for a time, all the while praying that she wouldn't make a sudden turnoff at someplace like Glenbrook or Sand Harbor. He could maybe course correct and circle back, but that kind of maneuver would be incredibly obvious.

To his relief, though, she continued to head north on Highway 50 all the way to Incline Village, then turned off onto Country Club Way before making another right onto a road whose name he didn't catch, but which led to a street with several hotels and a condo complex.

The condos seemed to be her destination; she pulled in there, while Jason slowed and weighed his options. If he turned into the complex as well, she'd probably notice him right away, since the other cars who'd been providing cover during the drive had dropped off one by one.

Instead, he pulled into the parking lot of a place called the Tahoe Prosperity Center, then brooded over what to do next. Yes, he could tell she was staying in one of the condos, but the complex had around twenty of the low, single-story units, and since he hadn't dared risk tailing her into the parking lot, he had no idea which one was hers.

It seemed the best thing to do was wait until she came back out. It was a little past noon, so maybe she'd leave soon enough to get something to eat.

And then what? he asked himself. *You're just going to follow her all over the greater Lake Tahoe area until she leads you to the healer?*

Considering he didn't really have any other concrete plans, that sounded like a good idea to him.

Especially since she was probably the prettiest girl he'd seen in a long time, with that fall of wavy, warm brown hair and the fresh, bright smile she'd worn as she thanked Cole Michelson and headed off to her car. Jason had only been able to catch the briefest glimpse of her eyes before she settled a pair of tortoiseshell Ray-Bans on her nose, but he thought they were a light amber-brown, striking against her dark hair and tanned skin. He was fairly sure he'd never seen a woman with eyes that color before.

You're here to look for a healer, not chase girls, he chastised himself.

Then again, if he could do both things at the same time….

His phone pinged, and he pulled it out of the cupholder where he'd set it and looked at the home screen. Irritation flickered through him.

Any luck?

How typical that his mother would expect him to come up with a lead when he hadn't been in Lake Tahoe for even half a day yet. Never in a million years would he inform her that a Wilcox witch was apparently pursuing the same healer, so he only replied with a terse, *Not yet,* and then set the phone back in the cupholder.

Just as he was looking up, the witch's smoky blue Jeep Renegade pulled out of the condo parking lot and headed over to Village Boulevard, moving north.

Luckily, Jason had left the Range Rover's engine running, so he didn't waste any time in pulling out after her, although once again he did his best to hang back so he wouldn't be right on her tail. She drove a couple of blocks, and then pulled into a parking lot that seemed to be shared by several different restaurants, along with a 7-Eleven.

The girl got out of her Jeep and locked it, then headed toward someplace called Inclined Burgers and Brews. Her hair swung as she walked, and he was able to get a better look at her long, slim legs in their skinny jeans, her graceful tanned arms providing a contrast to the bright pink peasant-style blouse she wore. A couple of guys in hiking gear were just getting out of their own Jeep as she approached, and Jason noted at once how their gazes seemed to be inexorably drawn toward her.

For some reason, he felt a stir of irritation at the way they were looking at the Wilcox witch. Logically, he knew that kind of reaction was stupid—he certainly didn't have any claim on her —but at the same time, he didn't like the idea of them trying to glom onto her as she was sitting down to eat a quiet lunch.

If that was even her intention. For all he knew, she'd come here just to get some takeout that she could bring back to her condo.

He didn't make any kind of conscious decision, but in the next moment, he shut off the engine and then hurried toward the entrance of the restaurant, cutting in front of the two hikers.

One of them grumbled, "Hey, man," but that was the limit of their response.

And then he was inside. The restaurant was obviously a casual one, the kind of place where you put in your order at the counter and then had your food brought to you. Jason was able to slide into line behind the Wilcox witch, who approached the man at the cash register and ordered a burger and some fries, along with an iced tea. She had a light, pretty voice that matched her appearance perfectly.

He wanted to hear more of it.

Once she was done, she took the little number in its metal stand that the guy handed her, then headed outside to one of the tables on the patio. The guy at the cash register looked at Jason and said, "What would you like?"

"Um…cheeseburger and fries," he mumbled, since he'd been so busy looking at the witch, he hadn't glanced up at the menu board mounted to the wall behind the counter.

"To drink?" the guy asked in bored tones.

A beer sounded great, but Jason knew he was already off kilter enough without throwing alcohol into the mix. "A Coke," he said, mostly because he hadn't had one in months…and also because he knew that if his mother had been there, she would have highly disapproved of his choice. Carolyn Ludlow thought soft drinks were the devil.

He paid the bill in cash, then took the number the guy gave him as he was informed that his order should be out in about ten minutes.

Now for crunch time.

Did he have the guts to approach the Wilcox witch out of the blue like this? Even though he knew there was no way in the world she could possibly guess who he was, there was still the very distinct chance that she'd tell him she wanted to eat alone. After all, a witch traveling by herself by necessity had to be somewhat circumspect.

Still, he figured he'd better try. He'd liked her face, liked the openness he'd seen there, an attribute that was quite separate from the prettiness of her features. It wasn't a quality he would have expected of a Wilcox, since that clan didn't exactly have the best reputation in the world.

Or at least, they didn't used to have a very good reputation. Once upon a time, the Wilcoxes had been the bad guys of the witching world. Now, though…now the Ludlows had taken up that mantle, thanks to throwing in their lot with Joaquin Escobar. Almost four years had passed since the dark warlock's death, but Jason had a feeling it was going to take many more years to wash off that particular stink.

He pulled in a bracing breath, one that had a

savor of frying burgers and fries to it, and made himself head outside into the bright sunlight. The air was just on the pleasant side of cool, but the sun warmed things up enough that it should be pretty comfortable to sit outdoors as long as they weren't in the shade.

The Wilcox witch had taken a seat at a small round table near the edge of the cramped patio, which didn't have room for more than a half dozen tables and one sofa-style bench placed against the wall of the building. The sunlight picked out shimmers of warm brown and deep umber in the long waves of her hair, and she was staring off toward the parking lot, expression distant, as though she was focused on something very far away.

Had he ever approached a woman like this? He didn't think so; the whole time he was getting his degree at Stanford, he'd done his best to hold himself aloof from his female classmates, since he'd always known his mother would never allow her only son to marry a civilian. And the Ludlow cousins who were distant enough relations to be considered acceptable had known him their entire lives, so it wasn't as though he'd had to do what he was doing now, which was walk up to a complete stranger and ask to share a table with her.

He cleared his throat. "Excuse me."

The Wilcox witch startled, then sent a wild

glance around her, as if she was sure he must be addressing someone other than herself. When she realized there wasn't anyone else around—the other occupied tables were on the opposite side of the patio—she tilted her head up at him and said, "Um…yes?"

"Do you mind if I sit with you? There aren't a lot of tables out here, and it feels weird to take one up all by myself."

She lowered her sunglasses slightly, as if to get a better look at him. As he'd thought, her eyes were a shimmering amber-brown, like cognac when backlit by firelight. They were probably the most beautiful eyes he'd ever seen.

For one horrible moment, Jason was sure she was going to shoot him down, and he'd have to figure out another way to get close to her and spy on what she was doing. But then she flashed him a smile, one that showed the faintest hint of a little dimple on the left side of her mouth.

"Sure," she said. "I guess it was kind of rude of me to be hogging this whole table to myself."

He thought her voice matched her looks almost perfectly. Once again, he realized that he wanted to hear her talk some more. And since she hadn't said no….

He sat down across the small table from her, and set the number for his order next to the place where hers was already waiting, facing toward the restaurant so the waitress would have a clear view of both numbers as she walked toward the table.

"I'm Jason," he said, figuring using his actual first name was safe enough. It was a pretty common one, after all. "Jason Nichols."

"Laurel Wilcox," she replied with a smile.

He wasn't as surprised to hear her real name as he would have been if he hadn't heard the reporter at the *Courier* refer to her as "Ms. Wilcox." It seemed pretty obvious that she wasn't doing much to hide her identity. Then again, why should she? The Delmonicos had to have given their blessing for her to be here, and the Wilcox surname wouldn't hold any particular significance for a civilian, which she obviously believed him to be, thanks to his handy talent.

"Do you live here in the Lake Tahoe area?" she inquired next.

A natural enough question. Luckily, Jason had an answer ready for her.

"No," he replied. "I live in San Francisco. I'm just here for a few days of R&R. You?"

"I'm from Arizona. Flagstaff," she added, as if she wanted to distinguish herself from the millions of people who lived in the greater Phoenix area.

"I've heard it's nice up there."

"It is," Laurel said, then sipped from her iced

tea. "I wish we had a lake like this, though. It's gorgeous here."

Since that observation was nothing more than the simple truth, about all Jason could do was nod in agreement before he swallowed some Coke.

Should he ask any probing questions, or try to be casual for now and see what else she let slip?

Probably better to play it safe. He didn't want to scare her off. Besides, it was nice to sit here in the warm sun and listen to her pretty voice and watch the sunlight awaken all those warm glints in her dark hair. He could almost pretend he wasn't anything more than what he professed to be, just a regular guy getting a few days away in one of the world's most beautiful spots.

"You drove all this way by yourself?" he asked next.

Something flickered in her eyes, although he couldn't quite say what. Wariness?

"Yes," she said lightly, although he got the impression it had been a big deal for her to come to Tahoe all by herself, so far away from her own clan. "But I have family friends in the area, so I'm not really on my own."

So, she wasn't quite as careless as he'd first thought. Jason guessed she was probably referring to any Delmonicos who lived in Incline Village or its surroundings, which cemented his hunch that she was here with their blessing.

"That's good," he said, and was saved from having to add something clever to his comment by the arrival of the waitress with their burgers.

They spent the next couple of minutes eating quietly, but their silence didn't seem as awkward as he'd feared it might. Actually, it felt good to sit here with her across the table, as if they'd done this sort of thing many times before and didn't see any need to fill the time with idle chatter.

However, after he'd eaten about half his burger, Jason reminded himself that he was in Lake Tahoe for a reason…and that reason wasn't having lunch with a Wilcox witch, no matter how pretty she might be. He drank some Coke, then asked, "So…are you here for the same reason I am? Just wanted to get away for a few days?"

Silence for a few seconds. Laurel had just taken a bite of a French fry, so maybe that was the reason why she didn't answer right away. But then she sipped her iced tea and said, "It's going to sound kind of crazy."

Although Jason knew he needed to look calm, he couldn't quite hold back the little ripple of excitement that passed over him. She wasn't going to tell him the *truth,* was she?

"I'm okay with crazy," he replied, allowing himself to send her an encouraging smile.

She trailed the end of one French fry through the ketchup she'd squeezed into her burger basket, although she didn't look as though she planned to eat the fry any time soon. "I'm looking for someone," she said. "There's supposedly some guy hanging around the area who can heal people." She paused there and looked up at him, shimmering amber eyes framed by thick, dark lashes only lightly touched by mascara. "I need to find him."

4

UNTIL THE WORDS LEFT HER MOUTH, LAUREL honestly hadn't intended to blurt them out. But Jason had been sitting there, watching her with sympathetic dark eyes, and she'd figured, *What's the harm? He's a civilian, after all.*

She found herself wishing he wasn't, though. The second he'd walked through the door of the restaurant, she'd thought he was probably the best-looking guy she'd ever seen. His features were so perfectly sculpted, he looked like he should be in a museum. Dark hair and eyes, but not as dark as most Wilcoxes. A nice tan. And arms that bulged with some decent-looking muscle under the sleeves of the plain dark blue T-shirt he wore.

Luckily, the guy at the counter had asked for her order in the next moment, or she probably would have embarrassed herself by continuing to stare at the newcomer. The very last thing she'd expected was for this Adonis to approach her at the outside table where she'd sat down and ask if she wouldn't mind sharing it with him.

Anyway, she wished the guy had turned out to be a warlock. She'd dated civilians in college because she figured that was easier, but in her heart, she'd always known she'd settle down with someone who was also witch-kind. None of her distant Wilcox relations had done it for her, though, and neither had any of the unattached McAllister warlocks she'd met.

But Jason Nichols *definitely* did it for her.

More than once, she'd admonished herself to keep her cards closer to her vest, but she'd never been very good at that sort of thing. And really, what was the harm in telling Jason why she was here in Tahoe? She could leave out all the witchy stuff and merely say she was looking for the healer because someone in her family needed his help. That would be all right, wouldn't it?

"'Heal people'?" Jason repeated. One eyebrow lifted, but it didn't seem as though he was mocking her. No, he looked genuinely interested. "Like, a faith healer or something?"

"Not exactly," she replied, quickly cooking up a plausible-sounding story. "I'm trying to find him because of my grandmother. She has cancer, and the doctors want to move her into hospice care. If I can't get her help soon…."

Laurel let the words trail off there and hoped Jason would get the message. It was probably awful to lie about having a sick grandmother— both of her real grandmothers were in the peak of health and basically the exact opposite of the story she'd just told.

Immediately, his expression shifted to one of concern, and she experienced another pang of guilt. She really wished she didn't have to lie to him, even though she knew she could never tell him the truth…at least, not the *whole* truth.

"I'm so sorry," he said.

She acknowledged the words of comfort with a nod and hurried to go on. "I saw some stuff online about a guy here in Lake Tahoe who's been going around and healing injured hikers and skiers. No one knows who he is, because it sounds as though he disappears from the scene as soon as he's done his work. But I thought it was worth a shot to come and see if I could find him."

"How does he heal people?" Jason asked. "Like, laying on hands or something?"

Again, he sounded more curious than anything else, head tilted to one side as he watched her. A faint heat touched her cheeks that had nothing to do with the warm sun shining down on their table. "Sort of," she said. "At least, that's what the stories I read made it sound like. One of the people he helped actually lives in the area, so I thought I'd try to talk to her, since the others were tourists and are long gone."

"Need any help?" Jason asked, and she stared at him in surprise.

"Oh, I couldn't ask you to do that—"

"No, really," he said, cutting off her protests. "Tracking down a healer with mysterious powers sounds like a lot more fun than hiking around by myself, or trying my luck at the poker tables down in Stateline."

Laurel hesitated. While she also had to admit to herself that her errand would be made much more interesting by having Jason Nichols at her side and playing amateur sleuth, she could only imagine what Jake or Jeremy might have to say on the subject. This was supposed to be clan business, and she shouldn't be dragging a civilian into it.

Then again, she'd already sort of brought Jason into her business by mentioning the healer at all. If some part of her hadn't wanted his help, she would have kept their conversation on light topics like the weather or things to do in Lake Tahoe, rather than blurting out the real reason for her being here…or at any rate, the partial reason.

Apparently guessing the reason behind her reticence, he said next, "But if you want to do this on your own, I get it. I probably shouldn't have tried to butt in like that."

"You're not butting in," she said quickly. "It's just…I have no idea how long this is going to take, and I don't want to drag you into my mess when you're supposed to be here on vacation."

He smiled and picked up his Coke. Good lord, what a great smile he had—a flash of even white teeth, friendly crinkles showing at the outer corners of his warm brown eyes. "I already told you that it sounded like more fun than anything I had planned."

Well, that much was true; he had just said that. Laurel pulled in a breath and tried to come up with a list of reasons why having Jason Nichols help her on her quest was a really, really bad idea. After all, what if he was a serial killer or a sex fiend or something? She knew absolutely nothing about him.

However, none of those objections had a chance of lasting for very long under the glow of that megawatt smile. In general, she had pretty good instincts about people, and nothing about Jason had tripped any of her internal alarms.

Sometimes you just had to take a chance.

Besides, Jake and Jeremy were hundreds and hundreds of miles away. There was no reason they'd ever need to find out that she'd enlisted a civilian's help in tracking down their mysterious healer, especially since Jake was preoccupied with wedding preparations. Jeremy might be more of a problem—Laurel wouldn't put it past him to surveil her phone or her laptop, although once when she'd asked him if he would ever do such a thing, he'd claimed that of course he wouldn't... not without her permission anyway.

Since she hadn't given that permission, she figured she was probably safe.

She hoped.

"Okay," she said after a long pause. "If you're sure."

"I'm sure," Jason responded without hesitation.

Now that she seemed to be committed to this plan of action, Laurel actually found herself relaxing a bit. She hadn't looked forward to visiting Alison Crewe on her own—cold calling people had never been her idea of a fun time—but now she'd have Jason at her side, which could make the situation a little less weird. If nothing else, he was awfully easy on the eyes, and might get them entree to the woman's home when Laurel wouldn't have been able to accomplish such a feat on her own.

"Then I was thinking that after lunch we could go talk to someone named Alison Crewe," she said. "She lives right here in Incline Village, so we won't have to go chasing all over the place."

"Sounds like a plan," Jason responded, brown eyes shining with what looked like anticipation.

That matter settled, they finished the remainder of their meals and then took their burger wrappings and other discards and put them in the trash can placed by the door to the restaurant.

"I'll drive," Laurel said, and although she got another eyebrow lift in response, Jason didn't argue with her.

"Sure," he said easily. "You're the one who knows where she's going."

In theory, anyway. Jeremy had gotten Alison Crewe's address for her, and Laurel had it already stored in the Jeep's navigation system. Theoretically, there shouldn't be much work involved, although even with the nav guiding her along, she'd still have to keep on her toes, since she knew next to nothing about the area.

Jason followed Laurel out to the parking lot and got in the passenger seat while she was buckling her seat belt. Once he'd secured his as well, she went to the saved destinations in the nav system, selected the one for Alison Crewe's house, and backed out of her parking space.

The house was only about five minutes away; Incline Village wasn't a big place. It also seemed to be filled with one luxury home after another, and Alison Crewe's place appeared to be yet another multimillion-dollar mansion. Because it was located up among the trees and not on the water, it might not have been as expensive as some of the other houses they'd passed, but Laurel still found herself wondering where the blogger's money had come from to afford the big two-story house with its sharply peaked roof and banks of huge windows that overlooked Lake Tahoe.

She pulled into the driveway and turned off the engine, doing her best to ignore the nervous butterflies fluttering around in her stomach.

"Nice house," Jason commented, staring up at Alison Crewe's home.

"I guess Incline Village doesn't have any low-rent districts," Laurel joked, and he shook his head.

"Guess not."

They got out of the Jeep Renegade and followed a curved flagstone path to the double front doors. Artsy-looking wreaths of grapevine and subtly toned silk flowers adorned those doors, and a rose bloomed in a pot to one side of the entry. All in all, the impression should have been welcoming enough, but the only thing Laurel could think of was how nervous she felt.

She really didn't want to blow this.

"I can ring the doorbell, if you want," Jason offered, and she shot him a grateful smile.

"Sure."

He pressed the button, and a simple *ding-dong* sounded somewhere within the depths of the house. A few minutes later, the door opened, and a woman who appeared to be in her late fifties or early sixties looked out at them. She had artfully gray-streaked dark hair pulled back into a sleek ponytail, and wore a simple chambray shirt and jeans. But probably the biggest pair of diamond studs Laurel had ever seen winked from the woman's ears, and the band she wore on her left hand was encrusted with equally impressive stones.

"Hello?" she said, in an understandably puzzled tone.

"Hi," Laurel responded, knowing she needed to jump in feet first before she lost her nerve. "My name's Laurel Wilcox, and this is my friend Jason Nichols."

Okay, maybe calling him her "friend" was pushing things a bit, since they'd only just met, but she knew it wouldn't sound very good to proclaim that they hadn't known each other at all before a half hour earlier.

"We were hoping we could talk to you about your blog post about the mysterious man who healed you after you took a fall at Carnelian Bay," Laurel continued, and Alison Crewe's eyes flared with surprise before she gave a nod of understanding.

"You saw that?" she asked, and Laurel nodded.

"It would really help us if you could give us a little more information about what happened."

A long pause, during which Laurel was sure the older woman would tell them to go away, that she wasn't in the habit of allowing perfect strangers in her house. But then Alison surprised her by saying, "Of course. Come in."

She stepped out of the way so Laurel and Jason could enter. Because she didn't want to gawk, all she got was an impression of a foyer with enormously high ceilings and a slate floor before Alison led them from the entryway and into the living room, a gorgeous space with glossy oak underfoot and what appeared to be a wall of windows allowing a breathtaking view of Incline Village and the gleaming dark blue waters of Lake Tahoe beyond.

"Please, sit down," Alison said, gesturing toward the set of cream-colored leather couches that occupied the center of the space.

Laurel went ahead and sat, and Jason settled himself on the couch next to her. It was somehow awkward and yet reassuring at the same time to have him so close, although she thought it would have been even more awkward to be doing this on her own.

"Would you like some water or iced tea?" Alison asked.

"Water would be fine," Laurel managed, and Jason also murmured his request for water.

Their hostess told them she'd be right back and headed off toward the hallway, presumably going to the kitchen.

"So far, so good," Jason said in a low tone.

"I know," Laurel replied. "I'm still surprised she let us in."

"Maybe she's been wanting to talk to someone about the healer, too," he said. "I mean, it's probably not the sort of thing her country club friends would want to discuss."

Laurel wanted to ask him how he knew for sure Alison Crewe was a member of a country club, but she figured that was a pretty safe assumption to make, considering the house where they now sat. People who owned houses like this had to belong to country clubs, didn't they? It was just part of what you did when you were in a certain income bracket. Lord knows all of her cousin Lucas's civilian golf buddies from the country club in Flagstaff were pretty much rolling in cash.

However, she kept silent until Alison returned with two glasses of water. She handed each of them to her guests, then sat down on the sofa opposite theirs.

Before either of them could say anything, she spoke. "I suppose I could ask you how you tracked me down, but I know it's not that hard to find that sort of thing on the internet these days."

"A friend of mine," Laurel admitted, figuring it was probably better if she didn't mention it was her cousin who was the real computer hacker. Otherwise, Jason might have wondered why Jeremy hadn't come on this trip to help their ailing grandmother. "He's really good at digging up information. I know this must be seem like a real imposition, but I really did need to speak with you. So…thank you for giving us a chance to talk."

"It's fine," Alison replied. She had dark blue eyes almost the same color as the waters of the lake outside that bank of windows, and her gaze sharpened slightly as she regarded her two guests. "I don't think you would have come here looking for information about this man if it weren't important."

She really hated to have to lie to this woman, but Laurel knew she could never tell her the truth. "It's about my grandmother," she said. "She has cancer and is about to go into hospice. I thought —well, I thought if I could find this man, he might be able to help her."

At once, Alison made a murmured sound of pity. "I'm so sorry," she replied. "I know what he did for me seemed miraculous, so maybe it's possible he could help your grandmother…if you can find him. He seemed to vanish into thin air after he was done helping me."

Next to her on the sofa, Jason shot a sideways glance at Laurel. She hadn't mentioned that little detail to him, mostly because she didn't want the story to sound any more fantastic than it already was.

"You mean, you saw him vanish?" she asked, and Alison Crewe shook her head.

"Not exactly. He helped me to my car and waited to see that it started and I was able to pull away safely. I saw him standing by the side of the road, but when I looked back in my rearview mirror, he was gone."

That did sound a little strange, although Laurel supposed the healer could have simply walked far enough to go around a bend in the road and so have it look as though he'd vanished. "Did you see his car?"

Alison shook her head. "No, my SUV was the only vehicle parked anywhere near there. It's not very accessible unless you have four-wheel drive."

Laurel reflected that Alison Crewe didn't look like the sort of person who did a lot of four-wheeling, but appearances weren't everything. The winters could be rough in this part of the world, and having a rugged vehicle could make all the difference if a particularly bad storm blocked the roads for hours or even days.

"But he could have hiked away from where you were parked," Jason said, and Alison shrugged very slightly.

"I suppose so. I wasn't watching him the whole time. Honestly, I don't know how he got there or how he knew where to look for me. When I fell, it was so sudden that I don't think I made any kind of sound or anything like that." She paused there, expression oddly calm. "I know it must sound strange for me to say this, but I really do think he was a guardian angel of some kind. How else could he have known to be in exactly the right place at the right time?"

Laurel didn't have an answer to that question, because she honestly didn't know, either. Some sort of sixth sense for knowing where and when someone would be in need of his healing powers? That explanation seemed to make the most sense, because even though she obviously believed in magical powers, she couldn't quite stretch that belief to allow herself to accept the reality of angels. The Wilcox clan was nominally Christian, but none of them were what you could call devout churchgoers.

She smiled and said, "Maybe it was just luck."

"I'm not sure I believe in luck," Alison said. "Or at least, not that kind of luck. Especially not when this same man has helped other people in the area besides me."

"You know about that?" Laurel asked, surprised, and the older woman tilted an amused eyebrow at her.

"I may be retired, but I still pay attention to what's going on around me. Yes, I've heard about the skier and the artist from the Bay Area. Their experiences sound very similar to mine."

Yes, they did. And if Alison Crewe wasn't ready to believe in luck, then she most likely wasn't going to be a big fan of coincidence, either.

Jason sipped some of his water, then paused, glass held in both hands as he asked, "Do you know of any other instances of this healer showing up besides you three?"

"No," Alison replied. "And I've asked around. But that doesn't mean they haven't occurred. We get so many tourists around here—it's very likely that if any of them had this sort of experience, they just didn't stick around to tell anyone about it. Some people don't want to admit that they've overreached by hiking on trails that are too advanced for them or attempting a black diamond ski run when they've barely had a few lessons."

Those words made a lot of sense. Laurel could recall a few times when she'd gotten a little too ambitious when hiking the trails around the San Francisco Peaks back in Flagstaff. No, she'd never done much more than slip on a patch of scree and fall on her rear, but she knew she could have been in serious trouble if she hadn't managed to catch herself in time. She'd never told anyone about those falls because she was embarrassed by her carelessness...and so she could see other people doing pretty much the same thing to cover up their reckless behavior.

She reached in her purse and pulled out the photocopy of the sketch MaryJo Gaffney had drawn. "Is this the man?"

Alison looked down at the sketch and nodded. "Yes, it's a very good likeness. The artist—Ms. Gaffney—did this?"

"Yes. I got a copy from the reporter at the *Courier* who covered her story."

A brief silence as Alison studied the sketch for a bit longer, and then she said, "I think his hair wasn't quite this dark, and I think his mouth was just a little wider, but otherwise, this is definitely the man who came and helped me."

"What did his voice sound like?" Jason asked then. "Did he have any kind of an accent?"

"No accent," she replied at once. "Or at least, he had a neutral American accent. He didn't sound like he was from the South or the East Coast or anything like that. It wasn't a particularly deep voice, but it was...." A pause as she seemed to stop and replay the scene in her mind, and then she said, "It was warm. Soothing, almost. Any doctor with a voice like that would have a very good bedside manner."

All of which was interesting, Laurel supposed, but it didn't help them much when it came to figuring out who—or what—this healer actually was. Then again, she told herself she needed to be realistic in her expectations. Alison Crewe had just provided a few more data points; it wasn't as though they could expect her to have all the answers, or she would have put them in her blog.

"Thanks so much, Ms. Crewe," Laurel said. She gave the teeniest sideways glance at Jason, and he offered a very small hitch of his shoulders, seeming to indicate that he didn't have any other questions to ask, either. "This has helped a lot."

Whether that was strictly true, Laurel didn't know for sure, but she wasn't going to tell the other woman that she'd just wasted fifteen minutes of her life. Besides, you never knew when some random bit of data was the one thing that might solve a mystery.

Alison seemed to have picked up on something of what Laurel was thinking, because she said, "I wish I had more to tell you. There wasn't anything about what the man was wearing that seemed at all distinctive—he had on faded jeans and a T-shirt from the local Hard Rock casino, and he was wearing hiking boots."

That particular detail seemed to catch Jason's

attention, because he sat up a little straighter and said, "The Hard Rock?"

"Yes." Alison smiled then and added, "I suppose you could ask around there to find out if anyone had seen him, but hundreds of tourists go in and out of that place every day."

"True," Jason replied. "Still, it's a clue."

A clue that just happened to be a little closer to Ludlow territory than Laurel preferred. Still, it was a casino, and therefore on the Nevada side of the border. It should be safe enough…and she knew Jake and Jeremy would never let her live it down if she avoided investigating such an obvious piece of evidence.

"Yes, I think we should definitely check it out," Laurel said firmly, hoping that the resolve in her tone would translate to a bit more inner confidence on the subject. "And thank you again, Ms. Crewe—we really appreciate your help."

"Alison," the other woman replied. "I don't like to stand on ceremony. Why don't you give me your phone number? If I think of anything else, I'll send you a text."

That sounded like a good idea. She waited while Alison extracted her phone from her jeans pocket, then rattled off the digits to her number so the other woman could enter them in her phone. Jason appeared to listen intently during this exchange.

You know, if you want my phone number, you can just ask for it, Laurel thought, barely smothering a grin.

After Alison had the number safely stored in her phone, they made their goodbyes, and Laurel and Jason walked back out to her car. As soon as she'd backed out of the driveway, he said, "I guess we'd better caravan down to Stateline, since I'm staying in South Tahoe anyway."

While she experienced a little pang at not being able to make the drive with Jason there in the passenger seat, she had to admit to herself that it made more sense for them to each take their own vehicle. "Okay," she replied. "Your car's still parked back at the restaurant, right?"

He nodded. "It's a black Range Rover. It's over by the 7-Eleven."

Armed with that information, Laurel drove over to the little complex that included Incline Burgers and spotted the SUV in question. It was very shiny and new-looking, and she found herself wondering exactly what Jason Nichols did for a living. In a witch clan, it wasn't quite as odd for a guy in his mid-twenties to be driving a vehicle that cost upward of $80K, but in general, most people their age didn't have the cash for that kind of car.

Maybe she should have asked. They hadn't exchanged a lot of chitchat about their personal lives, which at the time had suited her just fine. The less he knew about her, the better.

Well, it didn't seem as though he was ready to give up the search for their healer any time soon, so she just had to hope that the opportunity to ask some more questions about his background would present itself at some point.

"It's super-easy," Jason told her after he'd gotten out of her Renegade and paused over by the driver-side window. "I mean, let's try to stick together, but if we get separated, all you have to do is head south on Highway 50 until you get to Stateline. The Hard Rock will be on your right— you'll turn on Lake Parkway and follow the signs."

That did sound pretty simple. "Got it," Laurel said, and flashed him a thumbs-up.

He sent her another of those scintillating smiles and climbed into his Range Rover. She pulled enough forward so he could back out of his parking space, and then she followed him to the highway.

As she drove, she couldn't quite keep a silly little grin off her lips. She didn't know what was going to happen next…but it looked like Jason Nichols planned to stay by her side.

And that had to be a good thing.

5

His phone buzzed as Jason was driving down to the Hard Rock Casino in Stateline. A quick glance told him the call was from his mother, and so he ignored it. In a way, there was something liberating about being able to blow her off like that. The hundreds of miles that currently separated them might have been a flimsy barrier at best, but he'd take it. Since he was currently carrying out an errand at her behest, he didn't think she would push him too hard about being incommunicado.

At least, he hoped she wouldn't.

Well, he'd worry about that later. For the moment, it was enough to have Laurel's little blue Jeep in his rearview mirror and to know that they'd get to spend a few more hours together. Meeting her had been an unexpected and utterly wonderful gift, and he wasn't going to question the universe's intentions in having their paths cross.

Still, he also couldn't quite ignore the guilt he was experiencing at the way he'd deceived her about his identity…the way he would have to go on deceiving her. Some might have argued that she was doing pretty much the same thing, since she was obviously pretending to be a regular civilian, and was probably lying about the sick grandmother as well. Deep down, though, Jason knew their lies weren't exactly on a par. By hiding her witch nature, Laurel was only doing what any other member of witch-kind would have done under similar circumstances. It just wasn't allowed to tell civilians about the witch world, about the people with magical powers who lived side by side with ordinary human beings.

While he, on the other hand….

Since he'd had a lot of practice over the years shoving unwelcome thoughts aside, he did the same with that one as well. For the time being, he only wanted to enjoy knowing that he would get to spend some more time with Laurel Wilcox. Any more clues they might be able to unearth about the mysterious Lake Tahoe healer would just be the icing on the cake.

After about a half hour of driving, he pulled into the parking lot of the Hard Rock Casino.

He'd never been there before—he was staying at a vacation condo owned by the Ludlow clan—so he had to guess at the best place to park. Luckily, there were two spots next to each other in the row almost directly in line with the casino's front entrance, and he pulled in there. A few seconds later, Laurel maneuvered her Jeep into the adjacent space and shut off the engine.

As she came around to meet him, the fresh breeze off the lake played with the ends of her hair, sending shimmers of sunlight along its length. Jason was struck by an almost overwhelming impulse to reach out and touch that hair, to push it away from her face…to cup his hands around her cheeks so he could bring her in close for a kiss.

Slow your roll, buddy, he admonished himself. *You're here on business.*

Technically, that was true. He knew, however, that finding the healer was definitely secondary in his mind at the moment. All he really wanted was to be with Laurel.

She smiled at him, clearly unaware of the chaotic thoughts flashing through his brain. Whatever her talent might be, he knew it couldn't be mind reading. Otherwise, she would have already known he was deceiving her.

"What's the plan?" he asked, trying to sound casual.

Her shoulders lifted. He loved the bright pink blouse she wore, which set off her light tan and the unusual amber tones in her eyes. "I have no idea," she confessed. "I guess if the healer guy was wearing a Hard Rock T-shirt, he probably got it at one of the gift shops in the casino. I suppose we should start there."

If it was even an authentic T-shirt. It could have been purchased at one of the many souvenir shops in town that catered to the tourist trade, the kind of shop that sold knockoffs rather than the real thing. But, as Laurel had already pointed out, they had to start somewhere.

"Sounds good," he said. "Let's go."

They passed the enormous guitar at the entrance to the building and headed inside. Almost at once, a cacophony descended—something that sounded like an old Bruce Springsteen song blared through the speakers, blending with the sound of voices talking and laughing, the clink of the slot machines and the clatter from roulette wheels and craps tables. Next to him, Laurel winced visibly, and he wished they knew each other well enough so he could reach over and take her by the hand.

However, since he realized their relationship wasn't quite at that stage—if it would ever be—so he settled for saying, "Don't hang out in casinos much, do you?"

She sent him a rueful grin. "Nope. There's a pretty big Navajo casino outside Flagstaff, but it's not quite like this. Also, I never went there to gamble, just to hang with friends and go dancing at one of the clubs."

A sudden vision of Laurel flashed in Jason's mind, of her wearing a close-fitting dress and heels while she danced and laughed with her friends. Even in jeans, her legs were long and slim, and he had a feeling she probably looked spectacular in club clothes.

Heat pooled in his belly, and he pushed the desire away. It had been a long time since he'd reacted to a woman like this—well, to be perfectly honest, he wasn't sure if he'd ever had this strong a reaction to an attractive female—but he needed to keep it together. Laurel had been friendly and open and fun so far, but he hadn't seen any signs that she reciprocated the sort of desire he was currently experiencing.

"There's a merch stand over there," he said after performing a brief scan of their surroundings...even as he hoped his voice didn't sound too strangled.

"Oh, I see it," she responded, sounding relieved. Did she want to get this over with as quickly as possible, or was she just happy that they wouldn't have to ask someone where the T-shirts were sold?

Either way, she set off at a brisk pace, Jason trailing for a step or two before he caught up. Enough people crowded the casino floor that they had to zigzag a few times to avoid bumping into someone, but eventually, they reached the merchandise stand, which was set up not too far away from the front desk.

No one appeared to be manning the thing, which seemed strange. Jason didn't think it was very wise to leave a bunch of expensive merchandise unattended like that. As soon as Laurel began to reach for one of the T-shirts, however, a woman who looked only a few years older than either of them popped out from a door that was nearly hidden by the kiosk.

"Can I help you with something?" she asked.

Jason noted that the name on her badge was Brandi. "Hi, Brandi," he said. "We wanted to know if you remember selling a T-shirt to a particular person."

Almost at once, the salesgirl's expression turned wary. "We sell a lot of T-shirts," she said, her tone dubious.

Laurel flashed her a reassuring smile. "We have a picture, if that will help." She reached in her purse and pulled out the photocopy of MaryJo Gaffney's drawing, then handed it to Brandi.

The woman took the piece of paper, stared down at it for a few seconds, and shook her head.

"Nope, I don't remember anyone who looked like that."

"You're sure?" Laurel asked, voice a little too tight.

Brandi shrugged. "Pretty sure. He's cute, so I think I would probably remember him. But I only work twenty hours a week here, which means it's totally possible someone else might have sold him a shirt."

"Are any of the other salesclerks on shift right now?" Jason asked.

"No, we're on a rotation unless there's a big event going on and we need extra people to help out." She paused there and glanced down at the sporty watch she wore on her left wrist. "Mel will come on shift in about an hour. You can hang until then and ask her."

Judging by the way Laurel's mouth drooped at that suggestion, it didn't look as though she was too keen on the idea of loitering around the casino until this Mel person appeared. However, Jason figured that was probably the best thing to do. There was no point in driving back to Incline Village when they had only an hour to wait—and as much as he would have liked to take Laurel to his condo, which was only about five minutes away, he doubted that would be a very good idea.

"Sure," he said smoothly. "Thanks for the tip."

He began to move away from the kiosk, and

Laurel trailed after him, still looking less than thrilled with life. "We just ate a little while ago," she said once they were a safe distance away. "What are we supposed to do for the next hour?"

"Well," he replied, "we're in a casino. Why not try some gambling for a bit?"

From the way her brows lifted, you'd have thought he'd suggested that they spend the next hour playing strip poker. "I'm not really big on that kind of thing," she said, her tone dubious… and maybe just a little bit judgmental.

Jason chuckled. "I'm not saying you should jump right into playing baccarat or something. Let's play the quarter slots. It's kind of hard to get into too much trouble doing that."

"I don't have any quarters," she pointed out, and he couldn't help grinning.

"I'll go get us some change," he said. "My treat."

"You don't have to do that—"

"My treat," he repeated firmly. "It was my suggestion, so I'll pay. Really, it's not a big deal."

And it wasn't. As the son of the Ludlow *prima,* he wasn't exactly hurting for cash, to put it mildly. He could blow a thousand bucks in the next hour and not even notice.

Not that he planned to do anything nearly so extravagant. No, he'd get a hundred bucks in quarters, and that should be enough to keep them amused until this Mel person showed up for her shift and they could ask her whether she'd seen Laurel's mysterious healer.

Laurel looked as though she was going to protest further, but then her shoulders lifted and she said, "Okay. If you're sure."

"I'm sure," he told her.

They found two quarter slots next to each other toward the back of the room where it wasn't quite so noisy. Jason hurried off to get his change, then came back and set the cup of quarters down on the little table between them.

"There," he said. "That should be enough to play with."

Laurel peered inside the cup, amber eyes widening slightly at the amount of quarters it held. "How much change did you get?"

"Enough," he replied evasively.

Her lips pursed, but she didn't say anything, only reached in and extracted a quarter, then put it in the slot machine and pulled the lever. One bar…two bars…and then a lemon.

Cue the sad trombone sound, Jason thought, trying not to smile at Laurel's immediately crestfallen expression. "Try again," he said. "No one usually wins first thing."

She shook her head. "You'd think they'd have these things programmed to have people win right away. Then they'd be hooked from the start and would be more inclined to keep pumping money into their slot machines."

"You have a point," he responded, thinking how much he liked her quick, lively mind. "Maybe you should pass that idea on to the management."

His suggestion made her smile, but she didn't answer him, only reached into the cup and got out another quarter, then pulled down on the slot machine's handle. Nothing that time, either, but she didn't seem too worried about it.

Jason went ahead and put a quarter in his slot machine as well. Almost as if by magic, a waitress came by and asked if they'd like some drinks.

Oh, the hell with it.

"Anchor Steam, please," he said, and Laurel's eyebrows lifted slightly.

However, she only told the waitress, "Margarita on the rocks, please."

"Back in a few," the woman replied. She was attractive, with platinum blonde hair pulled up into a French twist, although Jason could tell she was probably at least ten years older than he, if not more.

She headed off toward the bar, and Laurel said, "So, we're drinking now?"

"One drink," he assured her. "That's all."

"Well, I'm paying for the drinks," she told him. "Fair's fair."

Oh, you innocent child, he thought, even though he'd already guessed that he had two or three years on her at the very most. "You really don't hang out in casinos, do you? Drinks are free if you're gambling."

Laurel's eyes widened. "Seriously?"

"Seriously."

"Then I think I'll have to make a field trip to Twin Arrows when I get back to Flagstaff."

He couldn't help chuckling, and Laurel laughed as well, as if she was okay with being the subject of a joke, if only a little one. The waitress returned with their drinks, and Jason tipped her generously with some of the cash he had on hand.

Laurel obviously noticed this whole exchange, but she didn't say anything, only sipped some of her margarita and then slid another quarter into the slot machine. For a few minutes, they played in silence, both of them interspersing pulls on the machines' arms with sips from their drinks.

And then her machine began ringing, and quarters started to pour into the metal basin in front of her.

"Holy shit!" she exclaimed, almost knocking over her half-drunk margarita. "I won!"

That she had. And not the five or ten dollars' worth of quarters that were often used to entice people to keep playing, but one of the big payouts, probably something like a thousand dollars clinking its way into the slot machine's tray. There was so much of it, in fact, that it began to spill out onto the floor.

Jason leaped up from his stool and grabbed a couple of the extra paper cups that the casino had thoughtfully placed nearby for situations just like this. He gave one to Laurel and then dropped to his knees so he could scoop up all the quarters that had scattered their way across the busily patterned carpet.

Eventually, the flow of quarters ceased, but they ended up having to use four cups to contain all of Laurel's winnings. He set the last one down on the little table where their drinks still rested and remarked, "How do you feel about casinos now?"

"Much better," she replied with a grin. "But seriously, I never win *anything*. I'm not like my cousin Lucas, who—"

She broke off abruptly there as Jason sent her a curious look. What had she been about to say? That her cousin won all the time, was maybe luckier than the average person?

Whatever it was, she didn't seem inclined to continue. She grabbed her margarita and drank most of what remained in the plastic cup, then said, "Well, I'm just not generally a lucky person. But this is really cool."

Since he could tell she wasn't going to say

anything else about her cousin Lucas, Jason didn't bother to press the issue. He only said, "We should get all these quarters exchanged for something a little more manageable."

That obviously sounded like a good idea to her, because she got up from her stool and grabbed two of the cups full of quarters. Jason gathered up the rest, and together, they headed over to the cashier's cage.

Altogether, Laurel had won almost twelve hundred dollars. Her eyes grew gradually wider as the cashier counted out all the bills from her winnings. As they were walking away, however, she thrust a wad of twenties at him.

"Here," she said. "You should have some of this. I wouldn't have won anything at all if you hadn't given me the quarters to play with in the first place."

Even though he didn't need the money, he couldn't help being struck by her generosity. And sure, one could argue that as a member of the Wilcox clan, she wasn't exactly hurting for cash, either. Still, Jason knew quite a few people with pretty impressive net worths whose first impulse wouldn't have been to pay back the money he'd contributed to their little gambling adventure.

"It's fine," he said. His hands closed on hers, preventing her from letting go of the bills. "I told you, I don't need it."

Her amber eyes, somehow even more intense in the casino's wild lighting, stared up at him. "But I don't feel right keeping all of it."

"You should, though," he reassured her. "They're your winnings. Do something fun with them."

And then he realized he was holding her hands still, could feel the smooth, warm flesh under his fingertips. He wanted to tighten his grip, pull her toward him so he could kiss her over and over again, but somehow he managed to hang onto his admittedly shaky self-control long enough to let go and take a step back.

Something flashed over her face then. Regret? Had she wanted him to keep holding her hands?

Stop flattering yourself, Ludlow, he thought.

And yet....

Laurel looked away from him so she could stuff the bills into her wallet, and the moment was lost. Probably better that way.

"Well," she said, now sounding falsely cheery. "Has it been an hour yet?"

He pulled his phone out of his pocket and took a quick glance at the time stamp on the home screen. "A little more than an hour, actually. Mel should definitely be on duty by now."

"Unless she's late, or called in sick," Laurel responded, her expression now almost worried.

"No, I don't think so," Jason told her, and

grinned. "Let's go find her—after all, this seems to be your lucky day."

As they headed back to the kiosk, he couldn't help reflecting that this day had been pretty damn lucky for him, too.

6

LUCKY DAY, LAUREL THOUGHT, WALKING NEXT to Jason as they headed back to the merchandise stand. Most of the time, she didn't think of herself as an especially lucky person—that was Lucas's thing, not hers—but she had to admit that the stars did seem to be smiling down on her today. Not only had she gotten an unexpected windfall in the form of some gambling winnings, but she'd met Jason Nichols...and that was definitely the luckiest thing that had happened to her in a *very* long time.

He probably hadn't meant anything by the way he'd taken her hands, except as a means of preventing her from giving him some of the money she'd just won. Even so, she could still feel the pressure of his fingers on hers, could sense how strong his hands were, how warm and friendly.

It was hard not to imagine those hands touching her face…gliding along her throat….

Heat flashed in her cheeks, and she thrust those thoughts away as best she could. Yes, the guy was unbelievably hot—and nice on top of it, which was more important than looks—but she couldn't really tell whether he was attracted to her or not. There might have been just the briefest flicker of something in his eyes once or twice this afternoon, although she could also be flattering herself into imagining something that wasn't really there.

And there shouldn't *be something,* she told herself fiercely. *He's just helping you out. And he's a civilian.*

Not that there was anything intrinsically wrong with getting involved with a civilian. However, when people in witch clans found themselves in relationships with nonmagical folks, it was almost always with someone who lived in their same territory. The expectation was always that the civilian would join the clan, and having someone pick up stakes and move into a clan's area wasn't always feasible.

Jason lived in San Francisco, which was a very long way away from Flagstaff…and in the middle of Ludlow territory, to boot. It wasn't as if they'd bumped into each other at the produce section at Sprouts. Laurel didn't think there was much chance of things working out between them.

Long-distance relationships were sometimes manageable…but not when the people involved were a witch and a civilian man.

Luckily, they were approaching the T-shirt stand by that point, and Laurel could push aside those unwelcome thoughts and unlikely speculations in order to focus on the matter at hand. The woman now working the booth looked to be in her middle thirties, with blonde-streaked brown hair she had pulled back in an elaborate French braid.

Having learned from her last encounter at the merchandise stand—and because those unexpected winnings were burning a hole in her pocket—Laurel picked up a maroon T-shirt with the Hard Rock logo emblazoned on it and said, "How much for one of these?"

"Twenty-eight dollars," Mel replied immediately.

Laurel dug out two twenty-dollar bills and handed them over. A couple of feet away, Jason watched this exchange with a faint smile on his lips, as if he'd guessed exactly why she'd decided to open the dialogue with a purchase rather than immediately ask the salesclerk about the healer they were looking for.

Transaction handled, Laurel took the change and put it in her wallet, then awkwardly draped her new acquisition over her purse. Belatedly, she realized the photo of the healer was still inside there somewhere, and she stuck her hand in the purse and began scrabbling around for the piece of paper she needed.

"I was wondering…." she said, and trailed off. Damn it, where *was* that thing?

Jason came to her rescue, saying, "We were hoping you could help us with something."

"Like what?" Mel responded, a hint of suspicion entering her dark eyes. Although she was only in her early or middle thirties at the most, she already had the beginnings of lines showing in the skin around her mouth, and she looked as though life had handed her plenty of reasons to be wary.

"We're looking for this guy," Laurel said as she finally managed to yank the elusive piece of paper out of her purse and hand it over to the salesclerk. "Do you remember if you sold him a T-shirt?"

Mel took it from her and studied it for a moment before giving a faint nod. "Yeah. He was here about a week ago."

Although Laurel wanted to shoot Jason a glance of triumph, she managed to restrain herself and instead asked calmly, "Can you tell us anything about him?"

In response to that question, Mel put a challenging hand on her hip and sent them a narrow look. "Like what? Are you two cops or something?"

Laurel couldn't help letting out a laugh at that remark, although she sobered quickly as she realized that the salesclerk didn't look as though she thought there was anything funny in what she'd said. "No, we're not cops. It's just that he's someone I wanted to interview for a story."

Honestly, she hadn't even intended to make up that particular fib. But there was something in the way Mel kept shooting her those suspicious looks that made Laurel realize saying anything about the mystery man's true abilities would have been a big mistake.

"You're a reporter?" the salesclerk asked, and now she looked almost amused, as if she somehow knew that was even less of a possibility than Laurel and Jason being with the police.

"We're in journalism school at the University of Nevada, Reno," Jason put in, and Laurel shot him a grateful look for that bit of quick thinking.

"My condolences," Mel remarked.

Ouch. Then again, the journalism field had taken kind of a beating over the past decade, according to what Laurel had heard her parents say on the topic. It wasn't the sort of thing she paid much attention to, since she'd never wanted to be a reporter.

"Anyway," she went on, trying to keep the discussion from getting completely derailed, "this guy has been doing kind of a Banksy thing, you know? Going around and creating art in public spaces. Super stealth. No one even knows his name."

Who knew she would be so good at lying on her feet? True, they were harmless enough lies, but still....

Mel let out a breath, looking as if she would have preferred to be exhaling cigarette smoke. "If you know what he looks like, then he's not that much like Banksy, is he?"

"Close enough," Jason replied. "Anyway, we were hoping that if you sold him a T-shirt, he might have mentioned his name."

"Or there might have been a credit card receipt with his name on it," Laurel put in, although she had a feeling that particular scenario was probably a long shot. Someone who was so good at coming and going without a trace probably wasn't roaming around town leaving a trail of credit card transactions.

"Nope," Mel said. "He paid cash. I remember that because he paid with a hundred-dollar bill, and you don't see as many of those anymore."

Damn. Laurel had guessed a cash transaction

would be the most likely scenario, and yet she'd really been hoping for something more. "Did he say his name?"

"No. But," she went on, "he did mention something about camping in the Mt. Rose Wilderness."

"Mt. Rose?" Laurel said eagerly. "Where's that?"

"North shore of the lake, up past Incline Village," Mel replied.

In other words, pretty much right back where they'd started. Laurel would have allowed herself a sigh of annoyance, except that they wouldn't have gotten even this small piece of information if they hadn't made the drive down to Stateline.

"Are there campgrounds up there?" Jason asked.

Mel gave him a skeptical look, as if wondering how a couple of students attending school in Reno could be so ignorant about local attractions. Then her shoulders lifted slightly, and she said, "A couple. But most of it is just dispersed camping on U.S. Forest Service land. People like to stay out there because it's free."

If that was what their healer was currently doing, then good luck finding him. Laurel had never even heard of the wilderness area until a moment earlier, but if it was anything like the camping areas around Flagstaff, they were talking about hundreds of square miles of wildland. It would be like looking for the proverbial needle in the haystack.

Still, it was the only real clue they currently had, and maybe they could figure something out that would help narrow down their search.

"Thanks," Laurel said, and Mel only shrugged again.

"No problem. Hope you packed some hiking boots."

As a matter of fact, Laurel had, just because she hadn't known what she might encounter during her search for the healer. She thanked the salesclerk again, and Jason took that as the clear signal it was. They both walked away from the merchandise stand and paused in the lee of a bank of slot machines.

"So, we're going to have to tromp through the wilderness to find this guy?" Jason asked.

"Sounds that way," Laurel replied. "Unless you have a better idea."

"Not really." He paused there for a few seconds, as if pondering the situation. Then his lips lifted slightly, and he said, "It's too late in the day to be starting that kind of search. We'll need to start fresh in the morning. Which means…."

"Which means what?" Laurel asked, hoping she didn't sound too suspicious.

"Which means I should take you out to

dinner in Incline Village. I've heard the food at the Lone Eagle Grille is great."

Even though she thought that prospect sounded amazing, Laurel still found herself protesting, "Oh, you shouldn't be buying me dinner. Not after I used your money to win at the slot machines."

A grin lit up his face. "Okay. Then what if you use your ill-gotten gains to buy dinner for both of us? Maybe you won't feel so guilty about it then."

How could she resist a smile like that? He looked like he should be in a toothpaste commercial…although she wondered if anyone in a toothpaste ad had ever had quite that kind of devilish glint in their eyes.

"Deal," she said before she could change her mind and talk herself into something much more practical, like spending the evening alone in her borrowed condo. "Is the restaurant fancy? I didn't bring any dress-up clothes along on this trip."

"Not super fancy," he replied. "I mean, no one's going to expect you to wear a cocktail dress or something. But probably not jeans."

"That's all I brought," Laurel told him, heart sinking. She really wanted to go out to dinner with Jason, but it didn't sound as though her travel wardrobe would be up to the task.

However, he didn't look fazed at all. "There's

got to be someplace around here where you can get something. Let's check."

He pulled out his phone and opened the Yelp app, then did a quick search. Laurel watched, feeling slightly off-kilter but also excited. She loved shopping, especially when she got a rare opportunity—like this one—to do it in a place she didn't know very well and had the chance to go exploring and discover fun new stores.

"There's a place inside Harrah's that sounds good," he said. "Let's go check it out."

"You're really okay with hanging around while I look at clothes?" she asked, not bothering to keep the skepticism out of her voice.

"Well, I won't say it's my favorite pastime, but this is in a good cause, right?" A pause, and he added, "And being dragged shopping with my mother and little sister has given me plenty of experience."

That comment made her chuckle, as he'd probably hoped it would. "All right," she said. "Lead on."

They left the casino, and Jason pointed to the east, toward Highway 50. "Harrah's is right over there. We don't even have to move our cars if you don't want to."

"Might as well, though," Laurel said. "I mean, we're going to be leaving from there, right?"

He agreed that made sense, and they both got

in their vehicles and drove the short hop from casino to casino. The description on Yelp said the boutique was near the front desk, so they parked as close to the front entrance as they could and headed inside.

"I'll hang out here while you browse," Jason said as Laurel hesitated near the front of the boutique.

Letting out a sigh of relief would have been way too obvious, but she couldn't deny that his offer made her feel a lot better about the situation. She liked him a lot, and yet she still had to acknowledge that it would be pretty awkward to have him hanging around while she tried on dresses.

"Great," she replied, knowing she probably sounded a little too perky. "I'll try not to take too much time."

Whether she'd be able to keep that promise was hard to say. Once she was inside the boutique —and glad that the woman working there said she'd be happy to help if her customer needed anything, but otherwise seemed content to stay out of the way—Laurel realized there was an awful lot of fun-looking stuff packed into a fairly small space.

However, the store was organized well enough that she knew she could ignore big chunks of it. Obviously, she wasn't looking for jeans or T-shirts or swimsuit cover-ups. No, she either wanted a top and a skirt or a dress, and a dress seemed easier just because she'd only need to try on one item instead of a bunch of skirts and tops.

Well, and she needed to find some shoes to match. She had a feeling her hiking boots or flip-flops probably wouldn't work with whatever she ended up choosing.

Still, by the time she was done shuffling through the racks, she had four likely candidates. She took them all into the dressing room and tried them on one after the other, rejecting the first because it turned out to be way shorter on her than it had looked on the hanger, and deciding the second one wouldn't work because it pulled weirdly across her chest.

But the third dress—a simple wrap style in a dark teal shade—fit her perfectly, and the contrast with her eyes made them seem to glow.

We have a winner, she thought happily, knowing she wouldn't need to even try on the fourth dress, and draped the winning item over one arm as she headed out to look at shoes. A pair of sleek strappy sandals in a warm, deep brown seemed to go just right, and she headed over to the cash register with her selections in hand, glad that she'd managed the task so efficiently.

The total for just those two items seemed a bit steep, but she reminded herself that she was in a resort town and the prices probably reflected the kind of clientele they usually got in Lake Tahoe. Anyway, since she was paying for the dress and sandals with her slot machine winnings, it wasn't as though she had to worry about dipping into her travel money to cover the cost.

Laurel emerged from the shop to see Jason sitting on a bench not too far away, forehead puckered in a distracted frown as he stared down at his phone. However, he looked up almost immediately as she approached and stood, shoving the phone in his pocket.

"Everything okay?" she asked, and he nodded.

"Sure," he said easily. "I tend to frown when I'm reading. It makes everyone think I've just gotten bad news."

"Oh," she replied. That made sense. She knew she often bit her lip if she was concentrating really hard on untangling some computer code. "Well, I found what I needed. So…."

"So," Jason said, and paused. "I was thinking —since I'm staying here in South Tahoe and need to get changed, I thought I'd just head back to my condo and then come by and pick you up a little before seven-thirty. That's when I was able to get us reservations."

Clearly, he'd been using his time well as he waited for her while she shopped. Laurel wasn't sure if she liked the idea of splitting up, but his suggestion was a logical one. It would probably be weird for her to go with him to his condo and hang around while he got changed, and this way she'd have plenty of time to primp in preparation for their date.

If it even was a date.

It's dinner at a fancy restaurant with a guy, she told herself. *It's a date.*

And a happy little flush went through her at that thought.

"Sure," she said. "Let me give you the address of the place where I'm staying."

She got out her phone and looked it up in her notes, since she knew the street name but didn't have the condo's exact address memorized. They also exchanged phone numbers, something they probably should have done earlier but had overlooked.

Well, she had a feeling he'd been paying attention to her number when she gave it to Alison Crewe earlier, but this made it all official.

Afterward, they walked out to the parking lot and made their goodbyes, with Jason promising he'd be at her condo around seven-fifteen or seven-twenty. Then they both headed out to the highway, although Laurel pointed her vehicle north toward Incline Village, while he drove in the opposite direction, to South Lake Tahoe.

And as she sailed along Highway 50 back to

her temporary home base, all she could think of was her upcoming dinner with Jason...even though she knew that wasn't the reason why she'd come to Tahoe.

Still, she wasn't going to let her official mission distract her from the obvious fact that Jason Nichols was probably the best thing that had happened to her in a very long time.

Since he was now back in his condo, Jason figured it was safe enough to finally answer his phone. "Hi, Mom."

"Don't you 'hi, Mom' me," Carolyn Ludlow snapped. "What have you been doing all day? Why haven't you been answering your phone?"

"Because I was busy," he said calmly. Several decades of dealing with his mother had allowed him to achieve that apparently unflappable exterior...although underneath, he still bristled with annoyance. It would be nice if she treated him as a son just once, instead of as a sometimes useful adjunct to her office as *prima*. "You did send me here to do a job, not go sightseeing, right?"

"Busy doing what?" she asked, ignoring his comment. Which was also like her; Carolyn Ludlow only acknowledged what she wanted to acknowledge. Everything else might as well not even exist.

"Gathering clues," Jason said. "I've got a couple of leads. No name, but I have a better description of the guy, and maybe some information on where he's been staying in the area. I'm going to check it out tomorrow."

"Why not today?"

"Because he may be camping in some pretty rough country, and I didn't see the point in heading out there when the afternoon was already half over," he replied, even though he had a feeling that explanation wouldn't sit well with his mother. "I'm not really in the mood to slide down a ravine in the dark."

"If you did, maybe this healer would come and find you, and help you out," she returned.

"So, you want me to be bait?"

A pause, during which Carolyn probably realized even she had gone a little too far. "Of course not," she said. "I'm only saying that maybe that's what would happen if you did run into trouble."

Jason rolled his eyes. Since his mother couldn't see him, he figured doing so was safe enough. "I'm going to head out tomorrow morning," he told her, knowing it was probably better not to address her comment directly. "I'll get an early start and see what I can find. Like I said, though, it's out in the middle of nowhere, so I doubt I'll have any kind of a cell signal. I'll just have to call you when I'm done."

Once again, she didn't say anything right away. He could tell she wasn't too happy about him being out of contact for a large chunk of the day, but even his mother had to acknowledge that she had no control over modern cell phone technology. She would just have to sit and wait to hear back from him like a normal person.

And Jason had to admit to himself that he was probably more elated than he should be at the prospect of spending a whole day in Laurel Wilcox's company without having to worry about whether his mother would interrupt him once again with another of her annoying phone calls. She rarely texted, seeing it as an activity beneath the dignity of a *prima.*

"Well, at least you have a lead," Carolyn said at length. "That's something. And no one suspects anything?"

"Of course they don't," Jason replied. "I went into Stateline today and asked around a bit, and no one noticed a thing, even though I know I passed a Delmonico at Harrah's."

This was another total fabrication; he honestly hadn't encountered a single member of the Delmonico clan so far. But since Laurel hadn't been able to tell he was a warlock, Jason knew that his talent was holding just fine.

"Good. Here's hoping you find this man tomorrow and can get back to the Bay Area quickly. It's not good to push your luck, even if everything seems to be going well so far."

How nice of you, Mom, to worry about someone discovering me now, after you sent me on this stupid mission.

But he wouldn't utter those thoughts out loud. He'd learned long ago that standing up for himself wouldn't change a damn thing.

And really, the mission wasn't completely stupid. If he hadn't been sent up to Lake Tahoe to find the healer, he would never have met Laurel Wilcox. While Jason had absolutely no idea how all this was going to turn out, he had to admit he was enjoying the ride so far. It was actually a little frightening to realize just how much he was looking forward to their dinner together.

If the thought of their date had just a little extra spice because of the way he'd managed to avoid any mention of Laurel to his mother, well, so be it.

She didn't deserve to know.

"I have to go," his mother said then. "But keep me posted if anything changes—and do try to keep a low profile."

"Sure thing, Mom," he replied.

A noise that sounded suspiciously like a "hmph," and the call ended. Jason stared down at his iPhone for a moment, then shook his head. He needed to put Carolyn Ludlow and her machinations out of his mind.

It was time to get ready for his date with Laurel Wilcox.

7

SHE DIDN'T KNOW WHY SHE'D BOTHERED TO pack her curling iron for a trip like this, but now Laurel was really glad she'd thrown the thing in her luggage. Although her hair waved naturally on its own, she wanted to make sure it looked perfect for her date.

Actually, she wanted *everything* to be perfect.

Because she had so much time, she'd showered and washed her hair again, then spent almost an hour on her makeup, although she decided against false eyelashes just because she worried that Jason might find them a little over the top. She hadn't packed any fancy jewelry, either, but it was pretty hard to go wrong with silver hoop earrings and a chunky silver bracelet.

Her efforts were rewarded, because when she opened the door to her rented condo in answer to

Jason's knock, he stood there for a few seconds, practically goggling at her.

When he recovered himself enough to speak, he said, "You look amazing."

"Thanks," she replied, knowing her cheeks had flushed a bit at the compliment. "Come on in."

He entered the condo and took a brief glance around. Right then, she was awfully glad that the Delmonicos had given her such a nice place to crash. Somehow, Jason Nichols didn't seem like the type of guy who hung around cheap motels.

Because although Laurel didn't know much about men's clothing—she didn't have any brothers, and the Wilcoxes tended to be a casual lot— she could somehow tell that the dress trousers and button-up shirt Jason wore had to have been pretty expensive, as was the slim silver watch he had fastened to his left wrist. Dressed like that, with his dark hair combed away from his face, he looked like James Bond…or at least, a twenty-something James Bond.

"I'd offer you a drink," she said, speaking quickly to fill up the awkward silence that had fallen while they gazed at each other. "But I don't have anything except water."

Jason shook his head. "That's fine. We should probably head over to the restaurant anyway."

That sounded like a great idea. She hadn't thought to buy a wrap to go over her dress, and she didn't think her jean jacket exactly fit the bill, so Laurel hoped it wouldn't get too cold while they were out.

After she locked up the condo, they walked over to the guest parking where Jason had left his Range Rover. They both buckled their seat belts, and he began to back out of his parking space.

The scent of expensive leather seemed to fill the air inside the SUV, and Laurel blurted, "So, what exactly do you do for a living?"

He waited until they were moving forward before he answered, although the side of his mouth had lifted slightly as soon as she asked the question. "I don't do anything," he said.

"But…." The word trailed off as she looked at the Range Rover's gleaming dashboard.

Appearing to take pity on her, Jason said, "Trust fund baby. One of those guys people love to hate."

"Seriously?" Laurel supposed one could argue that most members of witch clans were trust fund babies in a way, since all of them received a monthly stipend paid out of the family's investments. Still, almost everyone she knew also had a real job as well.

Besides, Jason was a civilian. It wasn't as though his money had come from generations of witchy wealth.

"Seriously," he echoed. "It's old California oil

and gas money, with some land speculation thrown in there somewhere. I came up to Lake Tahoe because I was bored and I wanted a change of scenery." A pause, and then he added, "Do you hate me?"

"Of course not," Laurel replied immediately. "I could never hate you."

He didn't answer right away. Something about the lines of his throat seemed to tighten, although the sun was setting behind the pine-topped ridges to the west and the light wasn't all that great. "Well, that's good to know."

They drove in silence the rest of the way. Jason handed his SUV over to the valet at the Hyatt without blinking, leading Laurel to believe that he'd done that sort of thing many times before. Personally, she'd always been kind of wary of valet parking, although that particular institution was in short supply in Flagstaff.

After that, they headed inside the resort and over to the restaurant. It occupied a spot that afforded an absolutely amazing view of the lake, and when the hostess guided them to a table by the window, in a lovely octagonal room that jutted out from the rest of the building, Laurel couldn't quite stop herself from wondering if Jason had offered some kind of bribe to get them such a great table on such short notice.

She pushed the thought aside as the waitress

handed her a menu. A quick peek inside told her the place was pretty pricey, something she supposed she should have expected. But even sixty-dollar filet mignon wouldn't put a huge dent in what remained of their winnings.

Now, if Jason suggested a five-hundred-dollar bottle of wine, then she might be in some trouble.

They perused the menu, and both decided on some form of steak. Because of that, it was easy enough to find a cabernet they both could agree on. Or rather, Laurel let Jason choose, mostly because she didn't know much about wine, especially when it came to California cabernets.

The wine was expensive—$149 a bottle—although a quick glance at the wine list had told her that was on the low end of the restaurant's offerings. Once the waiter had taken their order and departed, Jason quirked an eyebrow.

"You look like you're suffering from sticker shock."

"Maybe," she allowed as she lifted her glass of ice water and took a sip. "I'm just not used to seeing prices with four figures on a wine list."

"They weren't *all* that much."

"Thank God."

He chuckled, then reached for his own glass of water and swallowed some. "You don't have fancy restaurants in Flagstaff?"

"Not like this." And she was fine with that.

She'd had some wonderful meals in her hometown, but the mountain city didn't have a lot of pretense. Curious, she asked, "Have you ever had a three-thousand-dollar bottle of wine?"

"A couple of times," he admitted. Then he leaned toward her and said in a mock-whisper, "I honestly couldn't tell the difference…but don't let anyone else find out."

Laurel couldn't help grinning at the conspiratorial wink he gave her after making that pronouncement. "So, it's all a scam?"

"I didn't say that." He sipped some more water. "I just guess my palate isn't as refined as some people's. Which is fine. Wine that expensive makes me nervous. I mean, think how you'd feel if you accidentally knocked over the bottle."

That mental image made her wince, but she didn't have a chance to reply, since the waiter returned with their much more modest $150 bottle, and proceeded to expertly uncork it and offer a sample taste.

Laurel sent Jason a helpless glance, and he came to her rescue by offering to take that first swallow. He did so, and said, "It's excellent. Thank you."

With a nod, the waiter poured for both of them, then said their salads would be out in a few moments. After he was gone, Jason lifted his glass.

"We should have a toast."

"To finding what we're looking for," Laurel said at once, and he gave an approving nod.

"Yes—to finding what we're looking for."

They clinked their wine goblets together with a musical little clash of fine crystal, and she sipped from her glass. Yes, that was very good—rich and dark, with enough fruit to let her know what was going on without being too jammy.

As if you know whether or not having jammy cabernet is a good thing, she mocked herself, which was only true. She'd overheard her cousin Connor, who co-owned a vineyard, get into technical discussions about wine with Lucas and a few other Wilcoxes who fancied themselves aficionados, but she'd never paid too much attention. Most of the time, as long as a wine wasn't too expensive, tasted halfway decent, and wouldn't give her a hangover, it was a winner in her book.

"Like it?" Jason asked. His dark eyes had an amused glint in them, as if he'd guessed that what she didn't know about wine could fill a book.

"It's really good," she said. "I'm sure it'll go great with our steaks."

"That's why I chose it."

By that point, the sun had sunk behind the western hills, but a warm golden light lingered over the water, with shimmers of wispy clouds to the west adding echoes of pale orange and copper. Along the edges of the sky, purple tones had begun to steal in, making the world seem as though it had fallen into a hush, as if it hid a special secret waiting only for her. The conversations of the other diners and the little clinks and clanks of cutlery and dinnerware suddenly seemed very far away.

"This is so beautiful," she said as she stared out over the water.

"It is," Jason agreed.

But his gaze wasn't fixed on the view, but rather on her face.

Once again, a flush touched her cheeks, although Laurel tried to reassure herself that her summer tan probably hid most of it.

"So," she said. "What time do you want to get started tomorrow?"

His lips curled slightly, as if he'd recognized the way she'd tried to steer the conversation away from anything intimate and was amused by it. However, he sounded neutral enough as he said, "I don't know. I suppose it depends on how late we're up tonight."

Was he saying…?

No, he couldn't be.

But….

The waiter appeared with their salads, and she gratefully accepted the interruption. Once he'd set down their plates and left again, however, Laurel knew she needed to make some sort of a response to Jason's comment.

"Well, it shouldn't be too late," she said, trying to sound as casual as possible. "Unless they serve three-hour meals around here."

He grinned outright at her comment. "If we throw in dessert, who knows? But since it takes me about a half hour to get up here, and I'm not exactly an early riser, I'm thinking maybe I'll come knocking around nine, if that's okay with you."

"Nine sounds great," she replied. Should she be this relieved? After all, she knew she was attracted to him. What if dinner turned into something else…something much more?

It won't, because you don't go jumping into bed with guys you've just met, Laurel told herself sternly. *No matter how good-looking they might be.*

And that was the truth. Maybe it was old-fashioned, but she'd never gotten intimate with anyone until they'd gone out four or five times. She wanted to know how well she got along with a guy before she took that next step. Hormones were great and all, but she'd never believed that you should allow them to rule your life…even if there was something about Jason Nichols that made her seriously want to reexamine that rule.

For a few minutes, they were quiet as they ate

their salads. Her burger at lunch seemed as though it had been consumed years earlier. Well, almost eight hours had passed since then, so she supposed she could forgive herself for being ravenous. Clearly, roaming around the greater Lake Tahoe area and looking for a man who might or might not possess healing powers used up a lot of energy.

After a bit, though, she slowed down enough to ask with some curiosity, "So, you really just sit around being a trust fund baby all day? You don't have a job?"

He grinned at her, the unself-conscious flash of it telling her that he hadn't been offended by the question. "Technically, I work for the family business. But it's not the sort of thing I have to do full-time."

"What's the family business?"

Belatedly, she realized that maybe she shouldn't be giving him the third degree like this, but to her relief, he said, "We own a lot of property in the Bay Area. I help manage our portfolio and work with several different companies who deal directly with our residential and commercial clients."

On the surface, that didn't sound so different from how the Wilcox clan made their money. Most of the people in the family didn't have much to do with the day-to-day management of all the properties the family owned, but Laurel knew there was a small but dedicated group of Wilcoxes who oversaw the operation and made sure the cash kept flowing.

"Your family's been in the Bay Area a long time?"

Jason nodded before spearing the last chunk of iceberg wedge salad on his plate. "A little over a hundred years, I guess. We've been there since before the turn of the last century."

That was a pretty decent chunk of time for a family to be in one place, especially in California. True, the Wilcoxes had been in Flagstaff for even longer than that, but generally speaking, once a witch clan put down roots, it tended to stay put.

"I've never seen San Francisco," she said next, her tone sounding wistful even to herself.

"It's a gorgeous city," Jason replied. Maybe the faintest pause before he added, "I'd love to show you around sometime."

Oh, no—had he thought she was fishing for an invitation? As much as she would have loved to visit the Bay Area and get a tour from a local, Laurel knew that was never going to happen. No way in the world would she ever dare to set foot in Ludlow territory.

"That sounds like fun," she said, hoping her lackluster response would be signal enough that she didn't really plan to take him up on his offer.

Luckily, the awkwardness of the moment was

broken by the waiter returning to take away their salad plates. Laurel murmured a thank-you to him and tried not to fidget with the napkin in her lap.

Either Jason didn't notice anything was off, or he'd also decided it was probably better to slide past that moment as if it hadn't occurred. "I had a chance to look up some info about the Mt. Rose wilderness area. It's got almost thirty trails and covers a lot of square miles, so don't be surprised if it takes us a couple of days to really cover a decent amount of ground."

"That's okay," Laurel replied. "I can take as much time as I need."

Well, that wasn't exactly accurate. She had to be back in Flagstaff by Saturday for Jake and Addie's wedding. But that blessed event was still five days off, so she figured she had plenty of time.

Jason sat back in his chair, eyebrow lifted at the skeptical angle she'd come to recognize already. "I guess this is the part where I ask you what you do for a living. Most places don't let people take open-ended vacations like that."

Damn it. What she'd told him was basically the truth—for once—but she realized that most people couldn't take off from work for an indeterminate amount of time without risking getting fired. She reached for her wine glass and took a fortifying sip, then said, "Oh, luckily, my boss is super understanding. He knows what's going on with my grandmother and told me to take as much time as I need."

"That was nice of him." Jason also drank some wine before adding, "What kind of place do you work?"

"Oh, I...." Laurel stopped there and tried to figure out a way to describe Trident Enterprises in a way that wouldn't start sending up all sorts of red flags. Since she failed after the first second or two, she said hastily, "I work at the computer lab at Northern Pines University. I got hired after I graduated, but because my boss already knew me from when I was a student there, he's a lot cooler about stuff."

That sounded like the worst explanation ever, but Jason seemed to buy it. He gave a nod and had another sip of wine, and then the waiter came by with their entrées, once again rescuing her from an awkward situation.

She'd have to make sure he got a very good tip.

To her relief, Jason didn't ask any more probing questions. Maybe—since he obviously came from a very wealthy family—he just didn't know all that much about what it was like to be a regular working person. Laurel honestly didn't, either, since the job at Trident was the only real one she'd ever had. And because Jake was pretty relaxed about how he ran things, she couldn't really compare that experience to having an actual job with a boss who wasn't your cousin and who tended to make allowances for you.

She cut some steak and took a bite. It really was amazingly good, with a black pepper wine sauce that made the whole thing want to melt in her mouth. And, just as Jason had promised, the cabernet paired with it perfectly.

"How far can we drive into the wilderness area?" she asked.

Jason's head tilted slightly as he seemed to consider her question. "It sounds like it depends on the trail you're taking. Why?"

"Just because it might be a better idea to take my Jeep," she said. "I know your Range Rover has four-wheel drive, too, but my Renegade might be better at getting through tight spots."

"Maybe," he said. "I don't know how much off-roading we'll really be able to do. But I'll also admit that I've never once taken the Rover off the pavement."

"Seriously?" she blurted before she stopped to consider whether that was the best way to respond. "Why'd you buy it, then?"

A sheepish sort of smile, one that made him seem even better-looking…if that was possible. "I just like it, I guess," he replied. "Unfortunately, there aren't a lot of opportunities to go four-wheeling in the Bay Area."

No, probably not. She didn't know the region at all, but the pictures she'd seen made it look as though pretty much the entire area was completely built up.

"You've gone off-roading in your Jeep?" he asked next.

Laurel nodded. "Not a lot, but I've done the drive around the San Francisco Peaks, starting on the back side near Lockett Meadow and then coming out near Aspen Corner and the Snowbowl." She stopped there, since Jason was watching her with a puzzled expression in his brown eyes. "The San Francisco Peaks are the mountains next to Flagstaff. They're gorgeous pretty much year-'round, but it's an especially nice drive in the fall when all the aspens are turning. The road is rough in spots, though, which is why it's good to have four-wheel drive. People have done the circuit in passenger cars, but I wouldn't try it. Too much chance of leaving your transmission on the ground after hitting a nasty rut at the wrong angle."

"That definitely doesn't sound like fun," he agreed. Another sip of wine, and he said, "But it also sounds gorgeous. We don't have any aspens in my area."

"No, you need the altitude," she agreed.

"'Altitude,'" he repeated, and blew out a breath. "That's the one thing I'm a little worried about. I can feel it even here near the lake, but some of the hikes I was reading about can take you up to eight or nine thousand feet."

Since Flagstaff sat at a hair below seven thousand feet, Laurel didn't think an elevation of a thousand feet more would probably make much of a difference to her. Jason, on the other hand, had spent most of his life right around sea level. No wonder he was concerned about the altitude.

"I think most hiking shops carry canned oxygen," she told him. "It might not be a bad idea to pick up some before we go."

"Oh, right," he replied. "I think I saw some of that at the place where I bought my hiking boots a couple of days ago."

"Perfect," Laurel said. "And if they're not open by the time you want to get on the road, then we can hit one of the shops here in Incline Village before we head out."

He replied that her suggestion sounded like a good idea, and they settled into eating the rest of their meals. The steak was so big that she didn't think she'd have room for dessert, but Jason talked her into sharing a slice of flourless chocolate cake, which was much more luscious and decadent than she'd expected.

Full dark had settled by the time they left the restaurant. Since Jason had also convinced Laurel to have a small glass of port with her cake, she was definitely feeling a bit elevated as they waited for the valet to bring around the Range Rover. Not drunk at all, and maybe not even tipsy, either, but just slightly floaty, as if the entire evening had taken on a dreamlike quality.

They were both quiet as he drove the short distance to her borrowed condo. There weren't a lot of other cars on the road; it seemed like the residents of Incline Village weren't much into late nights. Idly, Laurel wondered what Alison Crewe was doing that evening. The band of diamonds on her left hand had looked like a wedding or anniversary ring, but she'd never mentioned a husband. Did she live in that big house all by herself?

Those speculations came to an abrupt end, however, as Jason pulled into one of the guest parking spaces at the condo complex and turned off the engine. As he began to unbuckle his seatbelt, Laurel wondered if maybe it would be better for her to tell him that he didn't need to walk her to her front door. She shot that idea down almost immediately, since she knew he wasn't the kind of guy who would allow her to wander off into the darkness by herself.

True, the walkways in the complex were illuminated by low-slung landscape lighting, but still, many dark patches remained. To tell the truth, she didn't think she was too keen on making the trek by herself.

He came around to meet her on the passenger side of the Range Rover, and together they headed down the path that wound toward the building where her particular unit was located. The only discernible sound was the rustle of leaves overhead and a faint, mournful sigh as the night wind soughed through the pines that bordered the property.

It didn't seem as if anyone else was out and about.

They paused at her front door, and Laurel had to scrabble in her purse for the key. If she'd been alone, she would have simply touched the doorknob and her witchy powers would have done the rest, but obviously she couldn't pull that kind of trick with Jason standing there and watching her.

"I had a really nice time," she said, pausing awkwardly with the key in one hand.

"I did, too," Jason responded. The light next to the door wasn't bright enough for her to get a very good read on his expression, but it seemed the faint smile he often wore had disappeared, and now he looked very serious. "Is it okay if I kiss you goodnight?"

The question seemed both ridiculously old-fashioned and yet utterly charming at the same time. She nodded. "Definitely okay."

He bent and touched his mouth to hers. Because she'd dated several civilians before, she thought she knew what to expect. It would be a good kiss, something that should send a happy little thrill down her spine, but it wouldn't be mind-blowing, not like the sorts of first kisses witches and warlocks shared when they finally found the *one*.

Except....

The moment their lips met, a wave of warmth moved through her, heat flooding along her limbs. All the haze from the wine she'd drunk at dinner seemed to disappear, and instead she was left with an amazing alertness, as if every nerve ending in her body had been shocked awake from a deep sleep. She found herself clinging to him as he held her, wondering with one part of her mind if she would have been able to support her weight at all if it weren't for Jason Nichols' embrace.

This seemed to go on forever, although she realized the kiss had probably lasted for only a few moments. Even so, she somehow knew instinctually that nothing in her life would ever be the same after this.

Her heart was still thumping almost painfully when he finally pulled away.

"You're amazing," he murmured, and she managed to make her tingling lips curve into a smile.

"So are you," she said.

He reached out and took her hand, his fingers tightening on hers. For a long moment, he stared down into her face, dark eyes hot with desire. Laurel understood that need all too well, since her entire body ached with wanting him. She didn't want this evening to end with a kiss at her door.

And yet....

When Jason spoke, his words were both a disappointment and a relief. "I was going to ask you if I could come inside," he said, his voice huskier than usual. "But that would be pushing things, wouldn't it?"

"I—" She paused there, doing her best to gather her racing thoughts. "Probably. I mean...I want you to. But it's probably not the best idea."

A very faint smile tugged at his lips. "It's fine. You're worth waiting for."

He bent and kissed her again, but only on the cheek this time. Even so, that extremely chaste caress was still enough to send her blood singing all over again.

"I'll see you in the morning," he told her, then gave her hand a squeeze before he turned and headed back toward the parking lot.

Laurel watched him go, forcing herself to stay silent. Oh, she wanted to call out to him and tell him she didn't care if it was too soon, that she wanted him to come inside.

Some small speck of self-control remained in her, however, and so she stood near the doorway quietly for a moment more before she touched the door handle and let herself into the condo. Once there, she leaned her head against the door after she closed it behind her.

Maybe it was crazy for her to be feeling this way about someone she'd only just met…but she also knew she wouldn't change this bubbly, tingling sensation for anything in the world.

She couldn't wait for tomorrow to come.

8

THE REFLECTION THAT MET JASON'S EYES WAS his own—gray eyes, dark blond hair. He wouldn't use his gift to change his appearance until it was time to leave, partly because there wasn't any point in expending the energy until he absolutely had to, and partly because he wanted to be looking at his real face as he said the words.

"You're an idiot."

What the hell had he been thinking? All right, he knew he was attracted to Laurel Wilcox, and maybe it had been stupid to suggest such an overtly romantic venue for their dinner together. Despite all that, he should have been able to maintain some kind of self-control at the end of the evening.

But no, he had to go ahead and kiss her…and realize as soon as his lips touched hers that this was different, that this wasn't some kind of casual flirtation. He'd wanted her, yes, but that need had gone far beyond the physical. He'd wanted to kiss her and hold her…take her inside and fall into bed with her…but he'd also wanted to sit with her on the couch and watch their favorite movies together, wanted to know her favorite color and the name of her childhood pet. He'd wanted her to take him to Flagstaff to meet her parents.

All of which was entirely crazy. He couldn't go to Flagstaff. Laurel had absolutely no idea he was a warlock…a Ludlow warlock, at that…and he needed to keep it that way.

And now he was going to spend another day with her. Hiking around in the wilderness, true, but they'd be alone together for hours and hours. Absolutely anything could happen.

Nothing is going to happen, he told himself as he picked up his razor. *You're going to work on finding this healer, and nothing more. No playing kissy-face, no deep meaningful talks about your future. You don't have a future with Laurel Wilcox. Period.*

He scowled as he scrunched his face to get at the tricky spot under his jaw. That all sounded very logical. Too bad he had a feeling he'd throw all those resolutions out the window the second he was alone with her again.

Just what the hell was going on with him? He

didn't have a lot of experience with women, mostly because there had been no point in pursuing a serious relationship with a civilian, and he wasn't yet ready to meekly go along with his mother's choices of who would be "suitable" within the Ludlow clan. He'd dated some girls in college, had a couple of extremely casual flings because he didn't want to be the only guy to graduate from Stanford while still a virgin, but none of that had counted for much.

Not one of those women had affected him even a tenth of the way Laurel had. Even now, twelve hours later, his body thrummed with need for her. It was as though he could still feel her soft lips against his, could still breathe in the soft coconut scent of the shampoo she used. She might have been miles and miles away, but she was still with him.

He finished shaving, set down the razor, and then ran his hands under the water so he could slick his hair back from his face. Now that he was pretty much ready, it was time to darken his hair and his eyes, make his skin more tanned.

Turn himself into Jason Nichols.

Only…he really didn't want to do that.

A wild notion entered his head. What if he went to her and confessed? Told her exactly who he was and what he was doing here in Lake Tahoe?

This idea appealed for a second or two, until he realized that her most likely reaction would be to tell him to get the hell away from her. And who could blame her? The Ludlows were basically pariahs in the witching world, thanks to his mother's singularly ill-advised decision to throw in her lot with the rogue warlock Joaquin Escobar.

Not that she would ever admit how badly she'd screwed up with that one.

Still frowning, Jason left the bathroom and picked up his phone from the spot where he'd left it on the table in the condo's dining area. No voicemails from his mother, which was a relief. Then again, he'd already texted her to let her know he was heading out on his search very soon, and so in her mind, she was probably satisfied for now, relieved that he was being a good little drone and acceding to her demands.

He supposed that was true enough…for the moment, anyway…although he knew she'd go ballistic if she ever found out he was working with a Wilcox, not to mention had indulged in an after-hours liplock with that same Wilcox witch.

It just figured that the one girl who'd finally gotten his motor racing was the one he couldn't possibly have.

With an almost physical effort, he shoved that thought aside. It was almost eight-thirty, and he still needed to hit a hiking store to pick up some of that canned oxygen Laurel had told him about.

A blink, and his appearance shifted, hair and eyes and skin all darkening to the shades he'd determined would work best for his false persona of "Jason Nichols." Good thing that his gift allowed him to make those changes and then forget about them for the rest of the day. This would have been even harder if he had to continually stay focused on keeping the illusion intact.

He headed out the door and drove to the hiking shop he'd looked up on Yelp earlier that morning. The place was busier than he'd expected, probably because the people there were like him, and trying to pick up whatever various odds and ends they needed before it got much later in the morning.

But that little side trip only delayed him by ten minutes, and he thought he'd still be able to make it to Laurel's vacation condo just a little after nine. The closer he got to Incline Village, the more his body seemed to tense. How should he play this? Casual? Should he try to act as if the kiss they'd shared the night before was no big deal?

He didn't think he was that good an actor.

Maybe it would be better to take his cues from Laurel. If she was being nonchalant, then he'd try to behave the same way. If she ran over and threw her arms around him and gave him a good-morning kiss, he'd kiss her back...and try his damnedest not to drag her into the bedroom so they could take the logical next step.

Except there wasn't anything logical about going to bed with her. Getting any more intimate than they already had would be a huge mistake. It was entirely possible they'd already gone too far, but Jason knew he needed to do his best to walk away at the end of this without hurting her too badly.

If he himself ended up hurt, well...that was his own damn fault for letting things progress even this far.

He parked in the same spot he'd used the night before. As he headed toward the walkway, he scanned the signs in the guest parking lot, making sure that there wasn't a time limit for how long he could leave his vehicle there. It seemed the only prohibition was parking a car in the guest spots overnight, and he knew that wasn't going to happen. Even if they spent all day wandering around the Mt. Rose wilderness, they'd still be back before dark.

Laurel opened the door almost as soon as he knocked, and again his breath caught at just how gorgeous she was. Not like the night before, when that dress she'd bought at the boutique in State-line had hugged all her curves and shown off her fabulous legs, but the down-to-earth prettiness of a T-shirt and cargo pants and hiking boots, her long brown hair pulled up into a messy bun on top of her head.

"Hey," she said, sounding breathless.

"Hey," he replied. "Sorry I'm a little late. I had to stop to pick this up."

And he hefted the canned oxygen he held.

"Oh, that's fine," she said at once. "I overslept a little. Come on in."

She shifted so he could move past her into the condo. At once he saw it was airy and beautifully decorated, with a high-ceilinged living area that had clerestory windows letting in the fresh morning light, everything done in soothing shades of cream and gray, with a pop of teal and turquoise and plum here and there to keep the decor from being too monochromatic.

A backpack sat on the sleek, glass-topped dining table, and Laurel hurried over to pick it up. "I don't know what kind of supplies you brought with you," she said. "But I've got water and some protein bars, and a tube of sunscreen and a compass."

It sounded as though she was a lot more prepared than he was. He'd thought enough ahead to fill up a travel mug with some water and toss that in his pack along with the canned oxygen, but he hadn't even stopped to think that he should have brought some food along, too.

No point in giving himself grief now, though. "The protein bars are a good idea," he said. "I guess I was thinking we could just grab some sandwiches to bring with us."

That little dimple showed in her cheek as she grinned at him. "I'd *much* rather have sandwiches," she replied. "We can use the protein bars as backup."

He agreed that this sounded like a good idea, and they paused to consult Yelp as to the best place to get sandwiches to go. The Hillside Deli seemed to fit the bill, so after agreeing on the restaurant as their next stop, they gathered up their things and headed out to the covered carport where Laurel's Jeep was parked.

As he walked along next to her, Jason allowed himself an inner sense of relief. Their reunion this morning hadn't been awkward at all, showing that all his fears had been for nothing. Laurel seemed focused on the task ahead…or at least, she'd done a good job of acting as though searching for the healer was the only thing currently occupying her mind. Their gazes had met once or twice, though, and if the little flush he'd glimpsed in her cheeks meant anything, it seemed she wasn't quite as casual about the situation as she wanted him to believe.

That realization warmed him, even as he told himself he shouldn't be quite so happy that she was glad to be around him. The more their connection grew, the harder it would be to walk away when this was all over.

Even if he knew that was what needed to happen.

He climbed into the passenger seat, and buckled his seatbelt as she backed her little Jeep Renegade out of its assigned spot. The deli they'd chosen as their destination turned out to be only a few blocks away, so they'd barely gotten up to speed before she was pulling into the parking lot. Inside, they loaded up on amazing-looking submarine sandwiches, pasta salad, and several large iced teas in go-cups.

"Nothing like a little carb loading on a hike," he remarked as they settled themselves back in Laurel's car.

She chuckled, although he noted the way her gaze flickered toward the navigation system's screen on the console, as if reminding herself of where she needed to go. "We might have gone a little overboard," she agreed. "But I figure we can always wrap up any leftovers and use them for snacks later on."

This sounded like a good plan, so he nodded, and she drove them out of Incline Village and up into the mountains, following the road as it narrowed and eventually came to a dirt lot designated as parking for the Tahoe Meadows Rim trailhead. A number of other vehicles filled it almost to capacity, but Laurel was able to squeeze her Renegade into a spot at the far end.

"Doesn't look very secluded," she commented as she turned off the engine. "Maybe we should look for a different trail."

Privately, Jason was inclined to agree. But they might as well give it a try. "We're here already," he replied. "I know it seems like a lot of people are in the area, but once we're out on the trails, we might not bump into anyone. Besides, this healer guy obviously has to be around other people in order to find injured hikers and help them out, so it's not as if he's going to be hiding up in a cave somewhere, playing hermit."

Those words must have been the right thing to say, because Laurel's expression brightened immediately. "True. I hadn't thought of that."

They were silent for a few moments as they went around back to get their packs out of the cargo area, spending a little extra time to stow the food they'd just bought in the backpacks. Soon enough, however, they were both ready to go.

"I stored a .pdf of the trails on my phone so we can access it even if we don't have any cell service," she told him. "And I've got a compass."

She unbuttoned one of the cargo pockets on

her pants and pulled out her compass to show the device to Jason. It was small but rugged, with a rubberized casing, ensuring that it wouldn't break even if she fumbled and dropped it.

Once again, he was struck by how prepared she seemed to be. Yes, she'd told him that she hiked a good bit in the mountains near her home in Flagstaff, but all the precautionary measures she'd taken only served to remind Jason of what a city dweller he really was. The mountains looming all around them were a silent signal that Mother Nature didn't play games.

"Then it looks as if we're good to go," he said, trying to sound more confident than he felt. "Which way?"

Laurel pointed to a sign next to the trailhead. "Well, we need to start there. After about a mile, the trail forks, and we'll have to decide then whether we want to continue north or head west."

The casual way she used the cardinal directions told him she really did know which way was north. Jason couldn't help thinking of his little sister Brooklyn, who wouldn't be able to navigate her way out of a paper bag if she had to use actual directions. No, it was all "turn left at the Starbucks, and keep going past Bloomie's" for her.

"Lead on," he said.

For a second, Laurel looked at him sideways, as if surprised that he wanted her to take the lead.

But then her shoulders hitched slightly, and she replied, "Sure. This way."

She set off toward the trailhead with an easy, loping gait that told him she knew exactly how to pace herself to cover the most ground without using up too much energy. Jason followed, hoping that his regular workouts in the home gym at his house in San Francisco would be enough to let him keep up. He'd always thought he was in reasonably good shape, but even so, he had no idea how he'd fare on a multi-mile hike.

Well, it looked as though he was about to find out.

For the first stretch, they walked in silence. Maybe Laurel was doing the same thing he was—taking in deep breaths of the clean mountain air, enjoying the cool breeze as it glided past them, refreshing enough that Jason thought he wouldn't have to worry too much about getting overheated. That was a good thing, since, as a resident of the Bay Area, he didn't have a lot of experience with hot temperatures.

Every once in a while, he had a faint sensation of dizziness, but those moments came and went so quickly that he thought he should be okay without taking a whiff of the canned oxygen he'd brought along. All the same, he was glad he had it in his pack…just in case.

After about twenty minutes or so of walking,

they came to the first fork in the trail. Laurel brought out her phone and studied the map on it for moment, brow creasing slightly as she squinted at the screen from behind her sunglasses.

"The east fork is a steeper climb," she said after a moment. "But eventually, it'll bring us to a small mountain lake. There's a camping area nearby, so maybe that's where we should try looking. The other part of the trail leads into a wilderness area that's too rough for camping, so there's less chance our healer would be hanging out there."

"How steep a climb?" Jason asked, hoping he didn't sound like a total wimp for even bringing up the question.

"Um…." The word trailed off as she appeared to do some mental math. "We'll climb about two thousand feet over the space of three miles. You might feel the altitude change a bit, but there shouldn't be any rock climbing involved."

Two thousand feet? She sounded so casual about the whole thing. Jason reached for the bottled water hanging from his belt, took a sip, and then said, "What altitude are we at now?"

"A little over six thousand feet."

Jesus. Was he up to hiking around at eight thousand feet?

Jason supposed there was only one way to find out.

"Let's take the east fork," he said calmly.

~

Laurel tried not to look as though she was hover-ing, but she couldn't help sending quick little glances in Jason's direction to make sure the hike wasn't getting to him. Some sweat stood out on his brow, and he was breathing more heavily than she, but so far she hadn't seen any obvious signs of altitude sickness. She reassured herself that he had the oxygen with him, and if he started to seem as if he was flagging, she'd make him sit down on a handy boulder and breathe some before going any farther.

And also, if he really looked as though he was having trouble, she could always take him by the hand and send some subtle healing energy to him, although she would prefer not to do that. There was no reason for him to suspect that anything like magic would be involved, but even so, she didn't want to take the risk of revealing her talent.

So far, that didn't seem as if it would be a problem. They kept going at a decent pace, not talking much, which was fine with her. Laurel didn't know if she trusted herself to keep things casual if they spent much time in conversation. There was so much she wanted to know about him, and yet she knew the risk in letting herself to get too close.

It was just like the universe to allow her to

finally find the one guy she thought might be perfect for her, only to have him be a civilian who lived in the heart of enemy territory.

She wouldn't allow herself to sigh, mostly because she needed to save that breath for her own exertions. This hike wasn't the most strenuous one she'd ever been on, but it still required enough of her energy that she couldn't be wasting it on frivolities. As they slowed down to negotiate their way over a rocky patch, she paused and looked back at Jason, who was gamely struggling along a few paces behind her.

"Doing okay back there?" she asked, and he nodded and gave her a thumbs-up.

"Piece of cake."

Laurel wasn't so sure about that—his breathing sounded a bit more labored than she would have liked—but again, she told herself she didn't need to hover and that she definitely would stop if he fell any farther behind.

Besides, she knew they only had about a quarter-mile more to go before they got to a clearing. It would probably be a good idea to stop there and take a break, maybe have an early lunch, although she knew it wasn't even noon yet.

The clearing arrived on schedule, a quiet secluded spot with deep blue lupines and pure white wildflowers she didn't recognize waving amongst the fresh green grass, tall pines standing sentinel around the meadow. Laurel stopped at its border and waited for Jason to catch up.

"I thought we could have lunch here," she said when he paused next to her, hands pressed against his thighs as he bent slightly and pulled in some breaths. "You ready to take a break?"

He shot her a rueful smile. "What do you think?"

She grinned back at him, glad he still had enough energy to make a weak joke. "I see some tree stumps over there," she told him, pointing toward the stumps in question. "We can use those as chairs."

"Sounds good."

They headed over to their designated lunch spot. As they walked, Laurel paid close attention to the way Jason breathed and moved, but he seemed to be doing a bit better now that he was traversing more or less level ground rather than making a steady climb.

The tree stumps appeared to be quite smooth, except for some graffiti scratched into them, seeming to prove they'd been used as a resting place for a number of people over the years. Laurel hadn't wanted to use up any of the valuable space in her pack for something as superfluous as a tablecloth or a tarp, so they didn't have anything to protect themselves when they sat down.

We're wearing hiking clothes, she reminded herself. *They're meant to get dirty.*

At least the stumps were worn and weathered enough that they'd ceased oozing sap long ago. Once she and Jason had sat down, they got out their sandwiches and the little tub of pasta salad, along with fresh bottles of water.

"We're just going to have to share the pasta salad," she said as she set it down between them. "I hope that's okay."

"It's fine," Jason replied, and for a moment, his gaze lingered on her lips, as though he was recalling that they'd shared an open-mouthed kiss the night before and didn't have a problem with it.

This time she knew he wouldn't be able to see how she blushed, not with the flush of their hike up here already warming her cheeks. She picked up her submarine sandwich and took a bite. It was laden with three different kinds of meat and two different types of cheese, garnished with olives and peppers and oil and vinegar, and was quite possibly the best thing she'd ever tasted.

"These sandwiches are amazing," Jason said after swallowing his own mouthful of sandwich. "God bless Yelp."

"Seriously," Laurel responded. Sure, the app had steered her wrong a time or two, but most of the time, she'd had nothing but good experiences when using it to guide her to a new restaurant.

Wearing a slight smile, she added, "I'm sure the next part of the hike will be even easier with this kind of fuel helping us along."

He nodded, but he didn't say anything. True, he'd just eaten another bite of his sandwich, and probably didn't want to talk with his mouth full.

Or was he worrying that even with all that meat and cheese and bread to give him energy, he wasn't sure whether he'd be able to manage the second, steeper part of their journey?

It's going to be fine, Laurel reassured herself. *We've already covered several miles and climbed almost a thousand feet. If he could handle that much, then he can manage the rest, too.*

She paused in eating her sandwich to try some of the pasta salad. It was also delicious, with thick chunks of buffalo mozzarella and red peppers and olives.

"Want some?" she asked, extending the plastic fork toward Jason, and he nodded.

"Definitely."

He helped himself to a mouthful, clearly not worried about sharing the same fork. Laurel swallowed some water, then returned to her sandwich. She could tell there was no way in the world she'd be able to finish the massive thing, so once she got to a point where she felt sated, she stopped and carefully wrapped up the sub's remaining third.

Jason got a bit farther with his own sandwich,

but he also had enough left over that he could probably use it as a snack on the hike back down, should he be so inclined. Once they'd stowed their partially eaten subs in their packs, they drank water in silence for a moment or two.

It was hard not to stare at him, to avoid drinking in the way the sunlight warmed his brown hair and found little glints of dark gold and even russet in its thick strands. Those same Ray-Bans—the black version of her own pair—he'd been wearing when she first saw him covered his eyes, but the sunglasses couldn't conceal the fine lines of his jaw and chin, the strength in his throat as he swallowed some water.

He seriously was the most stare-able man she'd ever seen.

As he took the bottle of water away from his mouth, he said, "What's next?"

Laurel pointed at the far side of the meadow, glad for the distraction of his question. "The trail continues from there," she replied. "It winds through the woods and gains more altitude until it reaches the lake. The camping area is on the far side."

"And that'll bring us up another thousand feet?"

"Around there," she said. Jason's tone had been faintly curious and nothing more, and yet she got the impression that he was steeling himself for the next leg of their hike. The sweat on his brow appeared to have mostly dried, and he didn't look pale or sound out of breath, and so she reassured herself that he seemed to be adapting pretty well to the altitude, at least when he was at rest. She'd have to do her best to make sure that she didn't move too quickly for him to keep up. After all, this wasn't a race. They wanted to find the healer, but they definitely didn't have to kill themselves in the process.

He brushed his hands on the thighs of his pants and then stood up. "Well, I'm ready when you are."

"Okay—then let's go."

She set off toward the northeast edge of the clearing, where the continuation of the trail was just barely visible through stands of pine and aspen. As they got closer, the rustling of the leaves seemed to fill her ears, a sound Laurel found somehow comforting. Aspens had always been her favorite trees.

Once they were past that pretty little grove, though, the trail moved out into more open land, with sun-warmed grass to either side of the trail, as well as rocky outcroppings that served as reminders of the ancient stone that made up these majestic hills. The breeze felt brisker here, although the sun seemed warmer as well.

Laurel allowed herself a quick glance at Jason.

The sweat had returned to the tanned skin of his forehead, but his breathing didn't seem too labored and he appeared to be chugging along just fine. So far, they hadn't encountered any other hikers, which was both good and bad. Although she was glad of the chance to be alone with him, she wondered why no one else had come along this part of the trail. Was the west fork that much more interesting? She'd have thought the mountain lake at the end of this particular trail would make it a more enticing destination, but maybe she was missing something.

They passed a clump of boulders that she'd read was a natural marker indicating they were only a quarter-mile or so from their destination. And even though Laurel was used to high altitudes—and had once hiked all the way up to the summit of Mt. Humphreys, an ascent that brought you more than twelve thousand feet above sea level—even she could feel it a bit now. Not too bad, just the slightest bit of lightheadedness, and the sensation that the breaths she was taking weren't making it quite to the bottom of her lungs the way they might have at a lower elevation.

"Almost there," she said, and her voice sounded a bit breathless as well.

"Good," Jason replied. That was all he said, but there was a roughness to the edges of his tone that told her he was working hard to get out even that much.

They came around a curve in the trail, one where low-hanging branches concealed part of their route, and Laurel saw at once why no one else had come this way. Large boulders lay scattered across the trail, blocking the path. Obviously, they had fallen here earlier in the spring as the snow on the peaks melted, and no one had yet come to clear the way.

"Well, damn it," she said, more annoyed than anything else. You'd think with all the research she'd done on the trails in the area, one of the websites might have mentioned that the north fork of this trail was basically impassable. Then again, she knew she was only assuming that the boulders had fallen earlier in the spring. She had enough experience hiking around Flagstaff that she knew sometimes a rock could decide to fall long after the last time it had snowed or rained in an area. "I guess we'll have to go back."

For a moment, Jason didn't reply. His eyes narrowed as he took in the tumble of boulders blocking the trail. "I don't know," he said after a moment. "It looks to me as if there's a way to get through. See?"

He pointed toward the spot that apparently had caught his focus. Laurel stepped closer so she could see what he was talking about. Yes, there did seem to be a narrow passage through the boulders, although some sections were so tight that it would be a very tough squeeze.

"Maybe," she replied, knowing how dubious she sounded. "I don't know if we could get through there with our backpacks, though. And honestly, I'm not sure it's worth the risk. It's not as if we know for sure whether the healer is even hanging out up here. I honestly think it's better if we just go back and try the west fork of the trail instead."

Jason ran a hand through his hair. The movement distracted her, making her wonder what it would be like to do the same thing, to feel those heavy locks run over her fingertips. Then she wanted to shake her head at herself. What a time to let herself get distracted by something so trivial.

"I think we should try," he said. "I mean, if this healer is doing his best to stay away from people except for the times when he actually wants to go out and help someone, camping up beyond this rock fall would be kind of a perfect setup, wouldn't it?"

She had to admit that he had a point. Irresolute, she stood and stared at the boulders, her desire to find the mysterious man warring with her common sense, which told her in no uncertain terms that it just wouldn't be smart to try to squeeze through that maze.

"It's no big deal," Jason said, his tone now coaxing. "Here, I'll show you."

Before she could utter a word of protest, he'd slung off his backpack and had begun to move through the rock fall. A muttered curse escaped her lips, and she also removed her pack so she could follow him.

"I really don't think—" she began.

She wasn't able to complete the sentence, however, because in the next instant, Jason made a muffled grunt of pain, then dropped his pack.

"What's the matter?" she asked, worry surging through her.

"I put my foot down wrong," he said. "Slipped on some rocks and twisted my ankle."

Oh, no. A burst of anxiety-fueled adrenaline surged through her, making her hands tingle. What if he'd hurt himself badly enough that he couldn't get back down the mountain?

Even as that terrible thought darted through her head, she knew she had the power to fix whatever was wrong with him. Problem was…did she dare?

"Can you get out?" she asked. Yes, she possessed healing powers, but if Jason had really wedged himself in good, she couldn't exactly teleport him out the way Connor or Angela might have.

"Think so," he replied, voice tight with pain. "I'll need you to take my pack, though."

Without replying, she stepped forward so she could get the backpack as he handed it to her. She backed out of the rock maze, biting her lip with worry. What if he really couldn't un-wedge himself?

That particular fear disappeared as he emerged from the boulders. However, she couldn't allow herself to be too relieved, not when she saw how badly he was limping. At once, she dropped both packs and went to support him, easing him over to a large fallen log off to one side of the trail.

"Thanks," he said. The sweat was back on his brow, but now he appeared pale rather than being flushed with exertion.

"Can I take a look?" she asked.

Jason shot her a dubious glance that also managed to be tinged with amusement. "You a nurse or something?"

"No," Laurel said calmly. "But I have first aid certification."

There. It might have been a lie, but it also sounded plausible enough for someone who spent a lot of time hiking in the mountains. Also, if he'd only sprained his ankle, she could wrap it up—she always carried an Ace bandage in her kit, just in case—and use a little bit of magic on his ankle, just enough that he shouldn't suspect anything out of the ordinary was going on.

An eyebrow lifted, but he looked more impressed than skeptical. But then his brows drew together, as if a sudden thought had just occurred to him. "Maybe we should wait a while and see if the healer shows up. I mean, that's what he does, right?"

Such a notion hadn't even crossed her mind. In a way, it made sense, but....

"I don't know," she said, knowing how dubious she sounded. "I mean, there's no guarantee that he would even come. It doesn't exactly sound as though he's fixed every single sprained ankle and scrape that's happened in the greater Lake Tahoe area, after all."

For a second or two, Jason didn't say anything. Clearly, he was mulling her words and doing some quick mental math on how long he was willing to sit here in pain on the off chance that their healer would actually make an appearance...especially since MaryJo Gaffney's account in the paper and Alison Crewe's write-up on her blog made it sound as though in both cases, he'd showed up pretty soon after the original incident had occurred. If he'd really been lurking in the area, waiting to flex his healing muscles, wouldn't he have found them by now?

Jason seemed to have reached much the same

conclusion, because he blew out a gust of breath and said, "You're right, of course."

He bent over and unlaced his hiking boot, then pulled off his sock. The ankle was already swelling, showing livid red and purple. Laurel swallowed, even as she told herself that a bad sprain could look much worse than it actually was.

However, when she touched Jason's tanned skin, her powers alerted her at once to the thin fracture running through the bone beneath. There was no way in the world he'd be able to hike out of here with a broken ankle, even with her supporting him.

Which meant....

Oh, hell.

She knew what she had to do.

9

"Well?" Jason asked. He was actually pretty proud of himself for sounding so calm, even though his ankle felt like a ball of flaming agony.

How could he have been so stupid?

Because he'd wanted to go charging up the last leg of their journey and find the healer—and at the same time, show Laurel that he wasn't a useless city boy. But since he was out of his element on this mountain, he'd underestimated the risk of what he was doing.

Well, the universe had just reminded him of who was really in charge.

For a long moment, Laurel didn't reply to his question. Since her eyes were concealed by her sunglasses, he couldn't get a good read on her expression. However, from the way her mouth tightened a fraction, Jason had a feeling the news wasn't good.

But then she looked up at him and smiled. Something in that smile seemed a little too taut, although he supposed it was natural for her to be worried about whether he was in any kind of shape to get back down the mountain.

"I think it's just a sprain," she said. "I'm going to wrap it up real well, and then you can see how it feels when you walk on it."

"You're sure?" he asked. There had been a moment as he lost his balance and he felt his ankle give way beneath him that he was almost sure he'd heard something snap—that something being one of the fragile bones in his ankle. But maybe he'd only imagined the sound. After all, the rocks sliding and slipping beneath his feet had made a good bit of noise.

"I'm sure," Laurel responded. She got to her feet and went over to her pack, which she'd laid down next to the fallen log where he sat, and fished out an Ace bandage and removed the little clasp that had been keeping it coiled in a tight roll. "This might hurt, though. Do you think you could drink some water?"

He nodded. Actually, he wasn't sure how much water would help with the throbbing ache in his ankle, but he figured drinking it might help to distract him a bit, if nothing else. Luckily, his water bottle still hung from the sling at his belt, so he was able to release the clip holding it in place and lift it to his lips.

It did feel better to get some water going down his throat. Thankfully, his mouth seemed a little less dry—although he had a feeling it was about to get very dry in the near future.

Laurel wrapped her hands around his ankle. Almost at once, a warm, somehow soothing sensation ran through his flesh, centering on the searing ache in his bone. And the longer she held on, the more the pain subsided, becoming lesser and lesser until all he could feel was just the barest twinge.

A pause, and then she let go of his ankle. Jason was able to get only the briefest glimpse before she began briskly wrapping the Ace bandage around the wounded area, but he could have sworn the flesh that had been livid purple and red only a moment earlier now looked almost normal.

What the hell?

Almost at once, a suspicion began to grow in his mind. Naturally, Laurel had said nothing about her magical gift to him, since she thought he was a civilian, and witches didn't go blabbing that sort of information to just anyone.

However, if his eyes—and his very flesh and

bone—weren't deceiving him, then he guessed she must be a healer…just like the man they were seeking.

He remained silent as she continued wrapping his ankle. There was no way in the world he could confess his suspicions to her. At the same time, the very fact of her being a healer seemed to shoot down his theory that the Wilcoxes were seeking the man with the healing powers because they had no one like that in their own clan.

Why, then, was she so intent on finding him?

A few more passes with the bandage, and then she was securing it in place with its little silver clip. "There," she said. "Does that feel better?"

"Much," he replied. "You definitely have the touch."

Her brows drew together briefly at that remark, but then she gave a very small shrug and got to her feet. "See if you can stand," she told him. "I'll help steady you."

She held out a hand, and he took it gratefully. Yes, she'd healed his ankle, but it still hurt a little, and he could tell that the shock of the injury, combined with the challenge of moving around at this altitude, had made him sort of unsteady.

Even so, he was able to get to his feet without too much trouble. He took an experimental step, then let go of Laurel's hand and took another. "I think I'm okay," he said. "I won't be running any marathons, but I think I should be able to get down the mountain just fine."

Her head tilted slightly to one side. "You're sure?"

"Pretty sure," he replied. "I might have to take a break here and there, though."

Although her expression had been a bit clouded earlier, now she actually smiled…a smile that seemed much more genuine than the one she'd worn a few minutes ago. "I can handle that. It's not as if we have any place we need to be."

No, he thought as they began to make their way back down the trail, *although we did have someone to find.*

Only….

The notion struck him with such force, he almost stumbled. At once, Laurel shot him a concerned look, but he gave her a reassuring smile. "Just getting my sea legs," he explained, and she seemed to relax.

They picked their way along the trail, Jason's thoughts racing furiously. His mother had sent him to Lake Tahoe to find a healer…but did it really matter *which* healer?

Not that he had any intention of taking Laurel back to San Francisco by force. Of course not. No, he just needed to find the best way to break it to her that he wasn't exactly who he pretended to be. From there, he could talk about their obvious chemistry, how he'd never felt about any woman the way he felt about her. If those feelings were reciprocated, then it shouldn't be that hard to convince her to stay with him, to come to the Bay Area and become the Ludlow clan's healer.

Right, he thought sourly as he limped along, *and after that, you'll both ride off into the sunset on a unicorn that's shooting rainbows out its ass.* That scenario seemed a lot more plausible than the belief that Laurel would be just fine with all his deceptions and wouldn't have any problem at all with joining the hated Ludlow clan.

But even though he mocked himself, he couldn't quite let go of the thought. When they reached the meadow where they'd had lunch, he sank down onto one of the tree stumps and released a breath.

"How're you doing?" Laurel asked, her worried gaze focused on his ankle.

"Fine," he replied. "I just need a couple of minutes to catch my breath."

"Take as long as you need," she said. A pause, and she added, "I should probably look at your ankle again."

"It's doing okay," he told her. "It just aches a little."

"That's good, but I should still check."

Since it didn't seem worth arguing the point with her—and because Jason knew he wouldn't mind at all feeling her hands pressed against his skin—he only nodded and let her go to work. She undid the bandage and removed his sock and hiking boot, then ran her fingers over the site of the injury. Once again, that strange warmth moved through his body, sinking through skin and flesh to the injured bones beneath. The ache he'd been experiencing dwindled to almost nothing, just the smallest, nagging reminder that he'd done something spectacularly stupid an hour earlier.

"Looks okay," she said, although Jason noted how she wouldn't meet his gaze directly. Was she scolding herself for taking such a risk in healing a civilian? Very likely. Witches and warlocks weren't supposed to use their powers around nonmagical people if there was even the smallest risk of detection. That she'd done so in this instance seemed to tell him she cared enough to take the chance.

She cares because she thinks you're someone else, he reminded himself. *You know she'll freak out if she discovers you're a Ludlow.*

Or maybe not. Laurel seemed light and easygoing, but there was also a steadiness to her that he appreciated. There were witches in his own clan who probably would have lost it if they'd been caught in a similar situation, stuck up in the mountains with an injured hiking companion. Or had Laurel managed to remain calm because she knew she could handle the situation?

That explanation seemed likely enough, although he also thought there was more to her than that…a whole lot more.

They made another stop at one of the way points on the lower section of the trail and drank some more water. His ankle had begun to throb again by that time, although since Jason knew they were in the home stretch, he demurred when Laurel asked to look at his ankle again.

"It's really okay," he told her. "I'd rather keep going and get back to your car."

She frowned slightly but only said, "All right. Luckily, it's not too much farther."

The remaining distance was only about half a mile, but by the time they got to Laurel's Jeep, Jason was damn glad to know all he'd have to do for the next while was just sit in the passenger seat and hope that the ache in his ankle would begin to subside soon. That was the problem with healing magic—it could work literal miracles, but the human body still needed time to recover from the trauma it had suffered. It wasn't like a healer could snap her fingers and instantly restore you to exactly the way you'd been before the injury.

Which was fine. From what he'd heard about how healing worked, he should wake up the next day feeling about ninety percent of the way there, and the day after, it would be like he'd never broken his ankle at all. Or rather, all his coordination and function would be returned. The healed break would always be there and would show up on an X-ray, but it wouldn't prevent him from doing whatever he needed to, up to and including running a marathon.

Not that he had any plans to do such a thing. No, he had more important matters to deal with at the moment.

Once they were back on the road, Laurel stole a quick glance over at him before returning her attention to the narrow forest lane in front of them. "Still doing okay over there?"

"Much better now that I'm sitting down."

Even in profile, her smile was luminous. "I'll bet. Well, we'll get you back to the condo, and then you can put your feet up for a while."

That sounded like a good idea. Jason knew he'd have to drive back to his own borrowed place in South Tahoe, but a few hours spent relaxing at Laurel's condo in between would be just what the doctor ordered…so to speak.

"And have a beer or something?" he asked.

She chuckled. "I don't have anything in the

fridge, but if you want, I can stop at a liquor store on the way back."

"That would be great. If you don't mind, of course."

"No, I don't mind. After that little adventure, I could use a beer."

Her tone was light, and she didn't sound overly worried. Then again, why should she be? She'd healed the break and knew he would be fine. If she were truly the civilian she was pretending to be, then she probably would have insisted that they stop at the urgent care in Incline Village to have his ankle looked at by a professional, but there was no real need for him to do that, not when her magic had fixed him up just fine.

"Sorry I screwed up everything," he remarked, and she gave a little shrug, although her hands remained fixed on the steering wheel.

"It's okay," she replied. "I can totally understand wanting to plow ahead. And who knows? Maybe our guy will do another rescue soon, and we'll have another data point to work with."

That would be convenient, although Jason wasn't going to hold his breath. "Sure."

Laurel seemed to understand that he wasn't too sanguine about the possibility of another rescue happening while they were waiting around for his ankle to get better, because she didn't say anything right away. In fact, it wasn't until they were on the main road that snaked down into Incline Village that she spoke again.

"You'll probably need to stay off that ankle for a day or so. In the meantime, I was thinking about reaching out to MaryJo Gaffney, the artist who had the first encounter with our healer. And maybe there's someone in Incline Village who remembers the incident with the injured skier and might be able to point us in the right direction to find him, if only to give us a name."

Clearly, she wasn't about to let Jason's injury sideline the two of them. And unfortunately, there wasn't much he could say to dissuade her. It wasn't as though he could tell her that he'd been tasked with finding a healer, and since she herself was one, there didn't seem to be any reason to continue their search.

No, that sort of comment would go over like a ton of bricks.

"That sounds like a good idea," he said, since he could tell Laurel was waiting for him to make some sort of response. "I don't know how much additional information they'll be able to give you, but I suppose every little bit helps."

"Well, it'll give me something to do, anyway." She shot him an apologetic glance and quickly added, "I didn't mean it to sound that way. It's just—"

"No, I get it," Jason cut in. "I screwed up. I'm

glad you're thinking of other angles to make this work."

She shook her head. For the first time—probably because she had her hair pulled up and they were sitting in close proximity—he realized that she had multiple little diamond studs in her ears. They caught the light coming in through the car windows and twinkled like stars. "You really need to stop beating yourself up. It could be me who went charging through those boulders. My mother always used to give me grief for going off half-cocked."

Jason would admit that sometimes Laurel seemed a little impulsive, but she wasn't the one who'd thought she could negotiate that treacherous ground. Not this time, anyway.

"Well, I promise to be more careful in the future," he said.

"Fair enough."

She seemed willing to let it go there, so he remained silent. A few minutes later, they were back within the town limits of Incline Village. They headed down the main drag, and then she pulled into the parking lot of Incline Spirits.

"Be back in a few," she told him as she undid her seatbelt. "What's your preference?"

"I like Anchor Steam," he replied. "Or since it's a warm day, a decent hefeweizen if they've got it."

"I'll see what I can do."

Laurel flashed him a dazzling smile and hopped out of the Jeep, then headed in through the liquor store's entrance. Some might have said that a combo of cargo pants, hiking boots, and a slouchy T-shirt wasn't exactly the most visually appealing sight in the world, but right then, he thought she was probably the most beautiful woman he'd ever seen.

As soon as she disappeared from sight, however, he let his head slump against the back-rest. He really had it bad, didn't he? And all this was going to be for nothing just as soon as she found out he was a Ludlow.

Well, he'd have to do what he could to put off that evil day for as long as possible. It might have been amusing to entertain the notion of telling her the truth and letting the chips fall where they may, but he knew better. The minute she realized who he really was, she'd be right out of his life.

He waited, and smiled a little at the delay his injury had caused. His mother wasn't going to be too thrilled to learn he'd hurt himself and wouldn't be able to get out into the field, so to speak, for a day or so. If someone other than Carolyn Ludlow had been involved, she might have shown some concern for her son's condition, but because he was only a little banged up and nothing more, Jason knew she wouldn't have much patience for the situation.

Which was fine. She could brood about it as much as she wanted, but she wouldn't be able to change anything. No, she'd sit in her big house on Lombardy Street and fume and stew, and that was about it.

Laurel emerged from the liquor store, a six-pack of beer in one hand and a brown paper bag in the other. She handed them off to Jason as she said, "They didn't have any hefeweizen, but there was Anchor Steam, so I got you some of that."

He peeked into the bag she'd handed him. "And a couple of bottles of wine?"

"Well," she said, her tone blithe, "I didn't have any at the condo, and I thought it might come in handy, depending on how long you planned to stay around. Not that I'm trying to kick you out or anything," she added quickly.

He shot her a grin. "I wasn't thinking that. And I will agree that wine is generally a good thing to have around the house."

A dimple flashed in her cheek, and she maneuvered the Jeep out of the parking lot and back onto the road, heading toward her condo complex. "I guess it's just the shopper in me. It's hard for me to leave a store with only one thing in my hand."

That admission made him laugh outright. "You sound like my sister."

"She's a shopaholic?"

"Big time. Her master bedroom closet is bigger than my dorm room was at Stanford."

"Sounds nice."

Was that a note of envy he detected in her tone? "What, are you closet-deprived or something?"

"Kind of. My apartment is a loft in downtown Flagstaff. It's very cool, but let's just say they weren't big on walk-in closets in the 1920s when it was built."

Probably not. The traditional Ludlow *prima's* house, where his mother still lived and where Jason had grown up, had been built in the early 1900s, but it had been updated and remodeled so many times since then, he really had no idea what it must have been like in its first incarnation. "It must be a pretty nice loft, then, if you're willing to put up with not much closet space," he said.

"It is," Laurel replied as she guided her Jeep into the condo's parking lot. Really, if it hadn't been for his bum ankle and the fact that they were driving anyway, the place was so close, they might as well have walked. "Sooner or later, I'll probably look for something bigger, but for now, it works. I like that it's right in downtown Flagstaff so I can walk to a lot of places."

That did sound like a pretty good setup. His own house was over in the Marina District, a fun neighborhood with a lot of restaurants and bars—not to mention the Palace of Fine Arts and the gorgeous park that surrounded it—and he also liked being able to leave his car in the garage and go most places on foot. That sounded like yet another thing he and Laurel had in common.

But he probably shouldn't be thinking about that. Otherwise, he'd let himself get lost in how much he liked her, and that wouldn't help his situation at all. He was here to do a job. Maybe he was messing it up royally, but he still needed to soldier on as best he could.

"Hang on a sec," Laurel told him after she'd parked the Jeep and turned off the engine. "I want to come around and help you out."

"I'm fine," Jason protested. "You don't need to treat me like an invalid."

"I know that," she responded calmly. "But there's not much point in you getting out and twisting your ankle the wrong way and undoing all my work, is there?"

Because he couldn't very well point out that her "work" had mostly involved using her innate healing talents, he gave a fatalistic shrug. "If it makes you feel better."

"It does."

She climbed out and came around to the

passenger side, where he'd already opened the door. Trying not to feel like a complete idiot, he allowed her to take his hand and assist him out of the vehicle. He didn't stumble, although he couldn't quite stop himself from tightening his grip on her fingers when he went off balance for a second.

That could have been a flush of pink in her cheeks from his touch…or maybe she'd forgotten to put sunscreen on her face.

"There," she said, trying a little too hard to sound casual. "Was that so tough?"

"No," he replied.

"Good. Let me just get the packs out of the back. You can carry the booze."

Since he'd set the bag from the liquor store and the six-pack of beer in the footwell before maneuvering himself out of the Jeep, it wasn't too much work to bend down and pick up those items. While he was doing that, Laurel went around to the rear hatch and opened it, then got out both their packs.

After slinging them over her shoulders, she paused and asked, "Ready?"

"Sure."

He followed her down the path to the condo, wishing he could have carried one of the backpacks so her slender form wouldn't look quite so heavily burdened. However, he knew if he tried to take his pack from her, he'd get an earful about how he shouldn't be exerting himself like that, so he wisely maintained his silence.

It wasn't too long a walk to her condo, but by the time they'd gotten there, his ankle had begun to ache again. Not too badly…just enough that he knew it was a good thing he didn't have any plans to go running any time soon.

Once they were inside the door, she slung the packs off her shoulders and set them up against one wall of the entryway. Thus unburdened, she came over to him and plucked the bag from the liquor store and the six-pack out of his hands.

"Go ahead and sit down in the living room," she instructed him. "I'll put these in the fridge and get us some glasses. Unless you're a 'drink it out of the bottle' kind of guy."

He generally was, but if Laurel wanted to be all civilized, he wouldn't argue. "Whatever's easier for you."

"I'll get some glasses."

Suppressing a smile, he headed for the living room while she went off to the kitchen. The couch proved to be just as soft and inviting as it looked, and he sank down onto it with a sigh of relief, even as he hoped his pants wouldn't leave any smudges on the pristine cream-colored linen.

A moment later, Laurel returned to the living room, holding a glass full of Anchor Steam in each hand. She gave one of the glasses to Jason and then sat down next to him. Not super close, of course, but a happy little flush still went through him at the realization that she'd chosen to sit with him on the couch rather than choosing one of the side chairs.

He really needed to get a hold of himself. This was the real world, not junior high.

"To getting down off the mountain," she said, lifting her glass.

That was something he could definitely drink to. The Mt. Rose wilderness was beautiful, but right then, Jason thought he'd be perfectly happy to never see it again. Not that Laurel would give up quite so easily. He'd get a day off, maybe two, but she'd want to go charging right back up there, since the lead they'd gotten from Mel at the Hard Rock Casino was the only truly actionable piece of information they had to work with.

He clinked his glass against hers, and they both drank. The welcome, mellow flavor of the beer filled his mouth, and he swallowed, glad to feel the cool liquid sliding down his throat and into his stomach. Right then, he couldn't think of anything else he wanted more.

Well, except the girl sitting next to him.

"Better?" she asked, and he nodded.

"Much. I'm still sorry about all this, though."

She waved a hand—the one that wasn't

holding her beer. "Stuff happens. There wasn't really any guarantee that we'd find our guy up there anyway. And, like I said on the drive back here, we have a couple of things we can do while we're waiting for your ankle to heal up."

Had anyone ever looked as earnest as Laurel Wilcox as she sat there on the sofa, guileless amber-hued eyes fixed on his face, wavy locks of dark hair starting to slide out of their messy bun? Right then, Jason just wanted to pluck the glass from her hand, set down his own beer, and pull her to him in a passionate embrace. He could honestly say he'd never met anyone like her; his Ludlow cousins…those who were distant enough relations to be considered suitable as possible romantic partners, anyway…had tended to send him sidelong looks and indulge in the sort of forced flirting that made him want to cringe. The girls at Stanford had been a bit better, but a lot of them had seemed driven and focused on themselves. At the time, he'd thought their detachment a good thing, since it helped to keep him from getting too involved with anyone.

Now, though, he could only think it wasn't until Laurel entered his life that he realized someone could be so warm and open and friendly, so ready to take on any adventure that crossed her path.

She's not that *open,* he reminded himself. *It's not like she's told you she's a witch.*

But he knew he was being disingenuous. No member of a witch clan revealed that side of themselves to a civilian until they'd decided they wanted that person to be a permanent part of their lives. He and Laurel definitely hadn't gotten to that stage in their relationship.

"Do you think MaryJo Gaffney will be willing to talk to a total stranger about her experience?" he asked, and a little frown puckered between Laurel's pretty arched brows before she seemed to relax, the corners of her mouth lifting.

"Oh, probably," she said, sounding uncon-cerned. "I mean, she talked to Cole Michelson about it, so it's not as if she's trying to cover up the whole incident. Besides, when I tell her that I'm looking for this healer because a family member needs help, I'm sure she'll want to assist any way she can."

Jason made a noncommittal sound. For a Wilcox, Laurel seemed to have a pretty sunny outlook when it came to human nature.

But since he couldn't say anything like that out loud, he had to settle for a small lift of his shoulders as he replied, "I guess we'll find out, one way or another. How're you going to get in touch with her, though?"

Laurel's smile only widened. "Oh, that's not a

problem. My cousin can get me anything I need. I'll send him a text."

She set her glass of beer down on a coaster and went to the entry so she could dig her iPhone out of one of the compartments in her pack. Device in hand, she came back to the couch, unlocked the phone, and entered a quick message before putting it down on the coffee table.

"Your cousin a private investigator or something?" Jason asked.

"No," she said, amber eyes dancing. "He's just really good with computers. I mean, MaryJo is an artist, so maybe she has a website with contact info, and that'll make the whole thing super-easy, but even if she doesn't, Jeremy should be able to get me a phone number quickly enough."

Jeremy. Jason filed the name away for future use, just in case it might come in handy at some point. Laurel had only drunk half her beer, but maybe that was enough to make her slip up like that. Several times before, he'd noted the way she caught herself before saying the names of any of her Wilcox relatives, but she hadn't stopped herself this time.

"That's handy," was all he said, and she nodded.

"Very. I don't know anyone else who can do what he does with computers—and I was a computer science major."

Interesting. Laurel Wilcox was probably the last person he would have pegged as having a degree in such a technical field, but appearances were often deceiving. Jason also wondered if Jeremy's talent was working with computers. He'd never heard of such a magical gift before, although that didn't mean much. New talents did pop up from time to time, while others were rare enough that they might not appear for several generations.

However, if the Wilcoxes did actually have some kind of uber-hacker in their midst, that meant Jason would have to be extra careful. He certainly couldn't allow Laurel to take any pictures of him with her phone. Yes, he'd disguised his eye and hair color, but his features were unchanged. Any kind of facial recognition program would be able to pick up immediately that he was the same Jason Ludlow currently on file with California's DMV.

And if this cousin Jeremy of hers was at all protective, he might want to investigate the "civilian" Laurel was hanging around with….

Because he wasn't sure what he could say without giving away some of his inner turmoil, Jason picked up his beer and took another sip. A second later, Laurel's phone *binged*, and she picked it up and took a look.

"Got it!" she said gleefully. "I knew Jeremy would come through for me. He sent me MaryJo

Gaffney's address and phone number. She's in San Francisco, just like Cole Michelson told us." A pause as she stared down at the phone, and then she went on, "It's only four o'clock. It should be fine to give her a call, shouldn't it?"

"I suppose so," Jason replied. "Just don't be too disappointed if you have to leave a message."

"Oh, I know," Laurel said at once. "Most of the time, I won't even answer my phone unless I know who's calling. All those damn robocalls. Still, it's worth a shot." She reached for her beer and took a sip, as if fortifying herself to make the call. Then she took her phone and entered a number, and waited.

There wasn't much Jason could do except sit there and wait to see what happened. Part of him wanted Laurel to get MaryJo Gaffney's voicemail and nothing more. He had no idea why, but the back of his neck positively crawled with dread. Was it only that he really didn't like the notion of reaching out to someone who lived in the dead center of Ludlow territory?

"Hi," Laurel said next, so brightly that it was clear MaryJo Gaffney had, against all odds, gone ahead and taken the call. "You don't know me, but my name is Laurel Wilcox, and I wanted to talk to you about your experience with the strange man with the healing powers at Lake Tahoe."

This request was followed by a long pause,

during which Ms. Gaffney presumably made some kind of reply. Jason sat with what he hoped was a studiously neutral expression on his face, although he allowed himself to swallow some more beer. At the rate he was going, he was going to need another one soon.

Laurel spoke again, a note of pleading entering her voice. "No, it's really important. You see, my grandmother has cancer and—"

She broke off there, obviously listening again. Jason's fingers tightened on his glass, even as he allowed himself to hope that maybe MaryJo Gaffney was telling Laurel she didn't have any more information to give beyond what she'd already told Cole Michelson.

"I'm not sure…." Laurel said, her tone dubious. Then, quickly, "No, no, I understand. It's just —" A long pause, during which her expression drooped. Was that a look of real fear in her eyes? "No, we will. I mean, my friend Jason and I. He's helping me. Okay…sure. Tomorrow at three. I can do that. Thank you."

After that, she pulled the phone away from her ear and set it on the coffee table, then sent him a tremulous smile.

"She wants to talk to me," Laurel said. "Only…."

"Only what?" Jason echoed, even as all his internal alarms seemed to go off at once.

"Only she wants to talk to us in person. We're supposed to meet her at her studio tomorrow at three."

As Jason stared at Laurel, the meaning of her reply starting to sink in, two words seemed to reverberate in his brain.

Oh, shit.

10

LAUREL COULD TELL JASON WAS LESS THAN thrilled by the idea of going to San Francisco to talk to MaryJo Gaffney. Why, she wasn't sure, except that maybe he just didn't feel like cutting his vacation short to head back to home ground. While she could understand that sentiment, she knew her own situation was far more precarious.

Had she really just agreed to walk into Ludlow territory all by herself?

Because even though she had to admit that Jason was a great companion and someone she definitely enjoyed spending time with, as a civilian, he couldn't exactly provide much in the way of backup if a bunch of Ludlows decided to swoop in and grab her.

Maybe it wouldn't be that bad, though. She had absolutely no idea how strong the Ludlow *prima* actually was, so she didn't know if the woman would be able to detect her presence at all. It was the sort of thing that varied from *prima* to *prima*. However, Laurel couldn't help thinking that if the Ludlow *prima* really was all that weak, Joaquin Escobar probably would have steam-rollered right over her rather than accepting her as an ally in his plans for world domination.

Great.

Well, it couldn't be helped now. MaryJo Gaffney had told her there were things about her encounter with the healer that she hadn't revealed to Cole Michelson, but after Laurel had fed her the lie about her sick grandmother, the artist had immediately said she would tell her everything…if she came to hear the story in person.

"It'll be fun," she told Jason, who looked nonplussed. "I've always wanted to see San Francisco. And since you're a native, you'll be able to give me the nickel tour."

At that comment, his mouth quirked slightly. "Oh, I'm pretty sure that San Francisco deserves a quarter tour at least."

What could she do in response to such a remark except shoot him a grin? "Okay, the quarter tour it is. How far is it to San Francisco from here, anyway?"

"A little over three hours," he answered imme-diately, a reply that made her heart sink a bit. Was it really that far? For some reason, she'd thought Tahoe was a lot closer to the Bay Area than that. Before she could respond, he went on, "Maybe we should crash at my place. A round trip is a lot of driving to do in one day, especially since we don't know how long your meeting with MaryJo Gaffney is going to take."

Her eyebrows went up before she could stop it, and Jason chuckled.

"No, this isn't a nefarious plot to lure you back to my lair," he said. "The place is big enough that you could do a pretty good job of avoiding me if you wanted to."

From someone else, that might have sounded like a humble-brag, but Laurel guessed that Jason was only telling her the simple truth. Besides, she'd be lying to herself if she tried to deny that she'd really love to see his place. She had no idea what a trust fund baby's house was supposed to look like, but she was dying to find out.

"Okay," she replied. "If you're sure."

"Absolutely. It'll be fun." He drank the rest of his beer and put down the glass, then rubbed the condensation moisture off his fingers onto the knees of his cargo pants. "Do you mind meeting me down at my Airbnb in South Tahoe, though? It'll save us a lot of time."

The suggestion made sense, since it was about a half-hour drive one way. They were already going to be on the road for hours; no point in adding to their trip.

"No, I don't mind," Laurel said. "What time?"

"Around nine? That would put us in the city a little after noon. We can have lunch, do a little sightseeing, and then go see MaryJo."

That sounded like a great plan, almost like an extended date. And even though she'd been avoiding South Tahoe, what was the point? If she was willing to go driving right into the heart of Ludlow territory, then she certainly shouldn't be worried about roaming around in a place that was on the far eastern edge of their sphere of influence.

"Sure," she replied, then paused, giving his ankle a worried glance. Yes, she knew he was healed—but she also knew he shouldn't be pushing himself while his body caught up with the magic she'd used to fix the break. "Are you going to be okay driving?"

Without hesitation, he said, "Sure. I don't think working a gas pedal and an occasional brake for a half hour or so is going to cause any problems." He paused for a second or two before continuing. "It's probably a good idea if I let myself rest so I'm ready to play tour guide tomorrow, though. I'll head back, and see you in the morning."

"Oh, okay," Laurel said, doing her best not to

sound too disappointed. For some reason, she'd thought he'd hang around for the rest of the afternoon, maybe even into the evening. They could've ordered in, opened one of the bottles of wine she'd bought at the liquor store.

But that, she reasoned with herself, would've been pushing things. It made much more sense for him to go back to his condo and rest up. They already had firm plans for the next day, so it wasn't as if he was trying to ghost her.

A glint in his dark eyes told her that he'd probably guessed what was going through her mind. All he said was, "Oh, and if you packed a bathing suit for this trip, bring it along."

"'Bathing suit'?" she repeated, not sure what he was suggesting.

"I've got a spa in my backyard. It might be fun to hang out there and relax at the end of the day."

"No bathing suit," Laurel replied, even as she put aside her own nervousness at the thought of walking around in front of Jason Nichols in a bikini. After all, she'd be getting to see him in a bathing suit as well. "This wasn't that kind of a trip."

"Well, then," he said, rising from his seat on the sofa, "guess it's a good thing there are still a few hours left in the afternoon. You can go shopping."

Since Laurel had already told him how much

she loved to shop, there didn't seem to be much point in demurring. "True. I noticed a couple little boutiques here in Incline Village as I was driving around. I'll go check them out."

"Perfect."

He leaned down and kissed her then, a good, no-nonsense kind of kiss, one that seemed to tell her that he enjoyed doing so very much, even as he made it clear there wouldn't be any further intimacies that day. Which was fine. They'd just gone up and down a mountain, and he'd broken his damn ankle on top of it all. Yes, it was healed now, but still.

Laurel got up from the couch once Jason ended the kiss, and walked him to the door. "Tomorrow at nine," she told him.

"See you then."

Because they'd already kissed, he only raised a hand in goodbye, then headed off down the path toward the guest parking lot. Although she watched him carefully, she couldn't see any sign of a limp. That had to be a good thing.

As soon as she shut the door, she couldn't help feeling a bit deflated. They might have spent most of the day together, but that still didn't seem to be enough for her.

It's going to be fine, she told herself. *You'll see him tomorrow.*

Tomorrow, when they'd be heading right into

Ludlow territory. Sometimes she could be a real idiot.

Well, even if the worst happened, she'd just tell the Ludlows why she was there and what she was doing. The *prima* could call Connor and confirm everything if she needed to. Yes, going into another clan's territory without permission was a huge faux pas, but it didn't have to be fatal. These days, most of the other witch families seemed to be tiptoeing around the Wilcoxes. Having a reputation for being a bunch of badasses definitely came in handy.

And in the meantime, she'd get to indulge in one of her favorite pastimes.

Time to go shopping.

As Jason had expected, he'd missed two phone calls from his mother. The annoyance that flashed through him, however, was tinged with a sort of weary relief. This time, he actually wanted to talk to the *prima*…if only to give her a carefully edited version of what had transpired over the past few days. She needed to be primed before he dared bring Laurel Wilcox to San Francisco.

He eased himself down onto the couch at his borrowed condo and tried not to wince. The dull ache had returned to his ankle, probably thanks to the drive down here. By the next day, it would most likely be fine, but for now, he needed to take it easy.

The extremely mild buzz from that one beer he'd drunk had already worn off. While grabbing another from the fridge sounded tempting, he knew that probably wasn't a good idea. He needed to be dead sober when he talked to his mother.

Enough time had elapsed that he'd gotten over the shock of Laurel announcing they had to go into San Francisco to talk to MaryJo Gaffney. At the time, however, he'd barely been able to prevent his mouth from dropping open in shock. Never in a million years would he have thought she'd do something quite so crazy.

Or maybe in her mind, it wasn't crazy. She couldn't know that his mother's gift for detecting strange witches in her territory was razor sharp, or that Carolyn Ludlow's particular witchy talent—the one she'd been born with—was psychometry, or the ability to see visions based on physical objects. Over the years…and combined with her *prima* powers…she'd gotten to the point where she could pick up information from almost anything, up to and including a ring or watch a person was wearing, without her even having to touch it. There was absolutely no way in the world Laurel could go marching into San Francisco without his mother immediately detecting a strange witch in her territory. In fact, Laurel probably wouldn't get any farther than South Tahoe before Carolyn knew something was up.

Which meant he'd have to tell the truth, or at least part of it. Actually, a partial truth was all he had to offer, since he knew Laurel hadn't given him the whole story as to why she was so keen to find the Lake Tahoe healer.

He swallowed some of the water he'd poured for himself before settling on the couch, then drew in a bracing breath.

You can do this.

"Hi, Mom," he said as soon as she picked up.

"Hello, Jason," she returned, her acid tone telling him she was none too happy about the delay in his response.

"I just got back from hiking around the Mt. Rose wilderness," he told her. "I haven't found our guy yet, though. But there's something else you need to know."

"What?" she asked, voice sharpening a bit.

"We're not the only clan trying to find the healer. I bumped into a witch from the Wilcox clan in Incline Village."

"You *what?*" Before he could respond, however, his mother went on, "Does she know who you are?"

"Of course not," Jason replied, slightly irritated she would think he'd make that kind of amateurish mistake. "I've been using a slight illusion to disguise my face, and of course my talent prevents her from guessing that I'm one of witchkind. No, she thinks I'm just a guy she met who wants to help her on her quest."

"She actually told you she's looking for this man?" Carolyn inquired, her tone indicating that she didn't believe anyone—even a Wilcox witch—could be quite that much of a simpleton.

"Yes," he said. "But obviously, she hasn't said anything about being a witch. The important thing, though, is that I've gotten her to trust me. We didn't find anything up in the mountains, but we have another lead we're pursuing. And it's going to bring us to San Francisco tomorrow. I wanted you to know so you wouldn't be surprised by the presence of a strange witch so close to home."

For a few seconds, his mother remained silent. This behavior was so uncharacteristic of her that Jason held the phone out in front of his face to make sure the call hadn't dropped. But no, they were still connected.

At last, "You're bringing a Wilcox witch to our home?"

"Because she needs to talk to someone the healer helped. The woman said she wouldn't talk about her experience over the phone." He paused for a second before adding, "We need to hear what this woman has to say. It could give us the clue we're looking for."

"And you're absolutely sure this Wilcox witch knows nothing of who you really are?"

"Positive," he replied at once. Even as he spoke, however, he couldn't help experiencing a pang. He wanted Laurel to know who he was, that he was no more a civilian than she. Unfortunately, he didn't see how he could do that without destroying everything they'd already shared. "Mom, she thinks I'm some rich guy with a big trust fund."

A small sound that might have been a dry chuckle. "Well, that part's true enough, I suppose. So, she's interested in you because of your money?"

"I doubt it," he said. That was nothing more than the truth, wasn't it? After all, the attraction between them had sparked some time before he'd confessed that he wasn't exactly hurting for cash. "I mean," he went on, "it's not like a Wilcox is going to be broke."

"Possibly," his mother responded. She didn't sound terribly convinced. "Then again, Wilcox wealth and Ludlow wealth aren't precisely on a par."

Jason could have asked how she knew such a thing, since it wasn't as though the witch clans had their relative levels of wealth ranked in *Forbes*

202 | CHRISTINE POPE

or something. Then again, he supposed it wasn't too out of line to suspect that a clan which had been steadily building its holdings in one of the most expensive cities in the world might have a bit more cash on hand than one that had settled in the forests of northern Arizona.

"I suppose," he allowed. "Anyway, we're coming to town tomorrow for this interview, and we're going to be staying at my place. Just a heads-up."

"At your house?" his mother said, sounding less thrilled than ever. "Is there something you're not telling me, Jason?"

There's a whole lot of something I'm not telling you, he thought. When he spoke, however, he made sure his tone was suitably wry. "My house has four bedrooms, Mom, in case you forgot. This is all strictly platonic. Nothing to worry about."

"Hmm." To his relief, she didn't push it any further than that, instead adding, "Well, thank you for letting me know. I suppose it goes without saying that whatever the Wilcoxes want this healer for, we need him much more than they do. Make sure that if you do get any useful information out of this civilian you're coming to San Francisco to interview, you act on it before this Wilcox witch does."

"I will," he replied. It was an automatic response, nothing more.

Only another lie.

"Good." Possibly just the smallest of hesitations, and then she said, "You sound tired. You should get some rest."

Jason wished he could know whether his mother was truly concerned about his well-being, or whether she just wanted to make sure he took care of himself so he'd be in good condition for the interview with MaryJo Gaffney the next afternoon. "I've been hiking around most of the day," he told her. "But I'm back at the condo now with my feet up. It's all good."

"Make sure you don't get anything dirty," she replied at once, in typical Carolyn Ludlow fashion. "Call me when you have some more information to pass along."

She ended the call there, leaving Jason to sit on the couch with his phone pressed against his ear for a second or two before he realized he'd been dismissed.

Very slowly, he put the phone down on the coffee table, then got up from the sofa.

He'd definitely earned another beer.

11

Laurel watched Jason closely as they walked out to his Range Rover, but she couldn't see any sign of a limp. In fact, he was looking even better than usual this morning, skin just a bit more tanned, thanks to their outing the day before, his dark eyes warm with the light of adventure.

Or maybe he was just glad to see her again.

She'd brought her overnight bag with her, the swimsuit she'd bought the day before tucked safely inside. After perusing the offerings at the local boutiques, she'd chickened out and decided against a bikini, instead buying a sleek red halter that managed to show off everything without being too revealing. Her mother would have definitely approved. Dana Wilcox had never been a fan of letting it all hang out.

They had to do a bit of jockeying with the cars, since they'd decided that it was safest to put her Renegade in the space assigned to Jason's condo. That way, she wouldn't have to worry about leaving the Jeep in guest parking overnight.

Overnight. A little shiver went through her at the thought, even as she reminded herself that she'd be staying in his guest room. Perfectly innocent.

Yeah, right.

Laurel knew she should have been thinking about her upcoming conversation with MaryJo Gaffney, about what the woman wanted to reveal that couldn't be discussed over the phone, but instead her thoughts kept going to the day she was about to spend with Jason Nichols. There really wasn't any way she could think of it as anything but an extended date, even if she knew this trip was supposed to be all about business, not pleasure.

Because there hadn't been any way to let Jake —and Jeremy by extension—know about her plans without having them come down on her like a pile of bricks, she'd only texted a brief status update the evening before, telling them that she'd done some poking around in the Mt. Rose wilderness area but hadn't found anything. Jake's message back to her had been equally brief, thanking her for letting him know…and also admonishing her to be careful.

I will, she'd sent back, even though that had been a complete lie. She was pretty sure there weren't many activities that were less careful than boldly heading into the heart of Ludlow territory, even if she wasn't going alone.

For the moment, though, she was simply happy to be riding in the passenger seat of Jason's luxurious SUV, breathing in the scent of the fine leather upholstery. Her Jeep also had leather seats, but she knew they'd never smelled like this.

"How's the ankle?" she asked, mostly because their conversation when they met that morning had involved jockeying the cars and not much else.

"It's fine," he said. "Not even a twinge when I got out of bed this morning."

Those words helped her relax a bit. The night before, she'd found herself worrying that maybe Jason would start to wonder if something about the way his injury had healed wasn't quite right, and that he would ask questions she didn't dare answer. To her relief, it seemed as if he was content to let things lie, that he'd bought her story about his having a mild sprain and nothing else.

"Good," she replied. "I was worried."

"Nothing to worry about." He sent her a brief

glance before returning his attention to the road. "I'm ready to show you all over San Francisco."

"Good thing I wore my walking shoes."

Not her hiking boots, though. Since she was going to be in the city, and because she hadn't known exactly where Jason planned to take her, Laurel had put on the nicest pair of jeans she'd brought on this trip, along with one of her peasant blouses and some nice flats. Casual, but also put together enough that she should be set for just about anything other than a five-star restaurant or a night at the opera.

But since Jason hadn't shown any indication that he had a taste for opera, she figured she was pretty safe on that front.

"What kind of food are you in the mood for?" he asked next.

"Chinese," Laurel said promptly. She'd already decided that she couldn't possibly visit San Francisco without at least one meal in Chinatown.

He grinned. "That's easy enough. I'll take you to one of my favorites."

"It must be really amazing to live in such a big city and to have so many choices when it comes to restaurants."

"It definitely has its upsides." Jason paused there, something about his smile shifting just a little bit. "On the other hand, parking can be a real pain. I actually use Uber or Lyft a lot just because it's easier than trying to park this thing everywhere I go."

Laurel reflected it was sort of a shame that such a fine vehicle had to spend a good chunk of its life in a garage, but she could see why he might choose to do it that way. "If it's going to be a problem having the car, we can go someplace else."

"No worries. I know a decent parking garage not too far from where we're headed. It'll be fine."

She nodded and let herself relax against the back of her seat. After the long drive to get to Lake Tahoe, it felt good to sit here like this and let someone else handle the navigating. Pine forests flashed by on either side of the Range Rover, and she wondered how long they'd be able to enjoy such beautiful surroundings. Her knowledge of California geography was pretty hazy.

As it turned out, it wasn't until they dropped out of the foothills just outside Placerville that the landscape began to change, turned to golden rolling hills that reminded her vaguely of the landscape outside Cottonwood, although the trees here were different, not the junipers that dotted the hillsides of northern Arizona but something Jason called California live oaks.

"It's too bad we can't take a detour into Napa and Sonoma," he added. "But I don't think we'll have time for that." A pause, as if he was weighing whether to add anything to that statement, and then he said, "Maybe next time."

That comment made her feel all warm and happy inside. Maybe she shouldn't be allowing herself to consider a future with Jason, but she couldn't help herself. She'd never felt quite so relaxed around a guy, so ready to meet any adventure as long as he was by her side. That had to mean something, didn't it?

"That would be fun," she said, about the only reply she would allow herself. Maybe even that simple statement was too much, since it implied she was open to making plans with him that were farther in the future than just this afternoon, or even the next day. But it was just too hard to acknowledge the hard truth that she probably wouldn't see him again once her quest to find the healer of Lake Tahoe was completed.

If it was ever completed. In that particular moment, Laurel thought she might be okay with that. There were worse fates than being stuck in Tahoe, after all.

But no, she knew that wasn't going to happen. If nothing else, there was the obvious time limitation of Jake and Addie's wedding, now only a few days away, on this coming Saturday. She definitely didn't have months or even weeks to play with.

An image flashed into her head of arriving at the wedding with Jason as her date, and Laurel wanted to shake her head at herself. Like there was any chance she could possibly bring a civilian to an event that was going to be packed full of Wilcox witches and warlocks. As far as she knew, there wouldn't be a single civilian in attendance at the wedding, unless you counted those few Wilcox husbands and wives who hadn't been born into the clan.

Still, it was a pretty fantasy, and one she tucked away reluctantly. He certainly would have looked good at her side, if nothing else.

"Do you want to go to lunch first, or stop by the house so we can drop off our stuff?" Jason asked next, and Laurel had to shake herself loose from her reverie.

"Um…I suppose it depends if it's out of our way."

"Well, my house is in the Marina District, so it's a bit out of the way."

"Then let's just go straight to the restaurant," she replied. "I'm already getting hungry, and I don't want to wait too long to eat."

"Straight to the restaurant it is." He smiled before adding, "I was kind of hoping you'd say that. I had to scrounge for breakfast, but I figured it wouldn't matter too much since we were probably going to have a big lunch."

Laurel had done much the same, and once again she found herself wondering if all these little compatibilities were the universe's way of signaling that this guy might just be the one for her, civilian or not. And really, was that such a bad thing? If marrying a civilian and having a family with him meant that your children might not have any magic, she probably would have discarded the prospect, no matter how much she liked a guy.

But that wasn't how it worked. Having a magical ability was clearly a dominant genetic trait, because it didn't seem to matter whether a witch or a warlock had two parents who were of witch-kind, or just one—nine times out of ten, their kids had just as much magical ability as their witch parent. And really, having a decent number of civilians added to a clan only helped to strengthen it, since their presence reduced the risk of inbreeding.

She allowed herself a quick glance at Jason's profile. Once again, she had to think that she'd never seen anyone so good-looking, not even on the movie screen or in the pages of a fashion magazine. It seemed crazy to think that someone so godlike might be interested in plain old Laurel Wilcox. And okay, she knew she was pretty enough, but someone like Jason Nichols, handsome and rich and fun to be around, could have his pick of anyone he wanted. She might have worried about possibly running into an ex-girlfriend during this little trip, but she figured the odds of that happening in a city the size of San Francisco were pretty low.

"I can't wait," she said. "We have a couple of decent Chinese restaurants in Flagstaff, believe it or not, but I doubt they're anything like what you have in San Francisco."

"Probably not," he agreed. "I thought I'd take you to Hong Kong Clay Pot. Their dim sum is out of this world. It's not super fancy, but I think you'll like it."

Those words actually reassured her. She'd had visions of Jason taking her someplace formal where she'd feel completely out of place, but it seemed he cared more about the food than the ambiance. Which was just fine for lunch. It probably wasn't a good idea to go someplace that felt super romantic, not when they had their interview with MaryJo Gaffney coming up a few hours after they ate.

The drive across the San Francisco-Oakland Bay Bridge was sort of terrifying. Laurel supposed if she'd stopped to think about it, she should have realized they'd have to cross the San Francisco Bay at some point, since the city occupied a peninsula, but still, traveling across the water for what felt like miles had her gripping her purse with clenched fingers until they were safely back on dry land.

Jason had obviously noticed her reaction. However, he refrained from commenting for a few moments, waiting until they'd cut down a street whose name she didn't catch before he said, "Not used to all that water, are you?"

"No," she replied at once. "We have a couple of lakes outside Flagstaff, but that's not the same thing. Doesn't it freak you out to be driving across all that open water?"

His shoulders lifted as they came to a stop at a red light. All around them, the streets were packed with cars, and buildings seemed to loom on every side, but he didn't appear to pay any attention to the density surrounding them. "I guess I'm used to it," he said. One corner of his mouth quirked, and he went on, "I suppose it's a good thing that I didn't tell you about how part of that bridge pancaked during an earthquake back in the 1980s."

"Seriously?" she asked, her eyes widening.

"Seriously," he repeated. "Obviously, that was way before either one of us was born, but people still talk about it. Everyone's always wondering when the next one is going to hit."

That was something Laurel had never even stopped to consider. All right, she was vaguely aware of how California was prone to earthquakes, but Arizona, by contrast, was pretty geologically stable. It wasn't the kind of thing people in her part of the world had to worry about on a regular basis.

"And you're okay with that?" she asked.

He shook his head. "I don't know if 'okay' is exactly the right word. It's just one of those things we're all used to, like people in the Midwest dealing with tornadoes or people in the South and on the East Coast having to go on hurricane watches every year."

Maybe he had a point there, although Laurel reflected that at least you had some kind of warning with hurricanes and tornadoes, whereas earthquakes seemed to come out of nowhere. Still, just like so many other things in life, it was probably more what you were used to than anything else.

Jason guided the Range Rover through the packed roads, did some complicated zigging and zagging around a couple of one-way streets, and then managed to guide them into a parking structure a few minutes later. As far as Laurel could tell, he hadn't consulted the SUV's navigation system, which meant he'd come here enough times that he didn't have to stop and think about the route.

In a way, that realization reassured her. It meant he was telling her the truth when he'd said this was one of his favorite restaurants. They'd come here because he liked it, not because he was trying to impress her.

And, as he'd mentioned earlier, the interior was pretty unassuming. White cloths covered the tables, but all the furnishings were simple and unadorned. Clearly, whoever had decorated the place had decided it was better to let the food stand on its own.

Which it did. They ordered a variety of dishes because they were both hungry—egg rolls to start, followed by a dim sum platter they shared, ending up with orange chicken and fried rice. Tea to drink, which was probably a good idea, since having a glass of wine before going to talk to MaryJo Gaffney didn't seem terribly wise.

During lunch, Jason talked a bit about San Francisco, about how he'd gone to private school there and then to Stanford down on the south side of the bay, in Palo Alto. His love for the city shone through his words, and Laurel could tell he felt the same pride in his hometown that she did in hers.

However, she also noticed he didn't say much about his family. He'd already mentioned his little sister, the avid shopper, but he'd never given her name. Likewise, while he said one or two things about his parents, it was in passing, as though he didn't want to provide too many details. Well, maybe they were private people, and he didn't feel comfortable giving up too much to someone he'd only met a few days earlier.

Laurel couldn't really blame him, not when she'd remained reticent about her own family. There were so many things she couldn't say, it seemed safer to keep any details to a minimum. He knew she was an only child, and that she had a cousin named Jeremy—it had probably been stupid for her to tell Jason even that much, but the damage was done—and she figured she should leave it there for now. They certainly weren't at a point where either one of them needed to know much more.

After lunch, he drove her over to his house in the Marina District so they could freshen up a little and drop off their luggage. Laurel wasn't quite sure what she'd been expecting—maybe some kind of ultra-modern bachelor condo or something—but the house that greeted her when she emerged from the stairs which led down to the garage was so amazing, about all she could do was stand in the foyer and gape at her surroundings.

A graceful staircase curved up to the second floor, while off to her right was the living room, its walls patterned in subtle buff stripes of glossy and matte paint, with a large coved plaster fireplace dominating the far wall. The most stupendous element about the space, however, was the view. A wall of beautifully framed windows overlooked a lush green park, with what appeared to be some kind of ancient Roman structure with a curved, gilded roof set right in the center.

"What is that?" Laurel asked, moving toward the room, overnight bag still in her hand.

"That's the Palace of Fine Arts," Jason replied as he followed her. She blinked as he took her bag from her, then set it down on the subtly patterned oriental rug beneath their feet. "It was built for an exposition in 1915. They use it for weddings and other kinds of events—fundraisers, mostly—these days."

He spoke casually, as if it was no big deal for him to have such an incredible view right out his living room window. Laurel was no expert on real estate, but even she knew that a house with a view like that had to be worth a heart-stopping amount of money.

"It's amazing," she said. "How do you ever get any work done with that kind of view right outside?"

Jason smiled in response to that comment, but something about his expression seemed almost too tight, as if he wasn't quite as amused by her words as he wanted her to think. "I don't work, remember? Trust fund kid."

Right. Still, she found it hard to believe he didn't do *anything*. And okay, he'd mentioned that he spent some time with the people who oversaw his family's finances, but that hadn't sounded like enough to keep him terribly occupied. "So, what…you just spend your days roaming around, looking for some kind of new adventure to keep you busy?"

"Pretty much." He bent and picked up her bags. "Let me show you the guest room."

Sensing that he didn't want to pursue the subject, Laurel let him play bellhop, although she was perfectly capable of carrying her own luggage. She followed him up the stairs to the second floor, which was just as beautiful as the first level, with several bedrooms opening off a central hallway and tantalizing glimpses of that lush park and the bay beyond through its windows.

One of the rooms they passed held an impressive rack of guitars, and she slanted a sidelong look up at Jason. "I thought you said you didn't do anything."

"I play a little," he admitted. Before she could respond, however, he said, "Here's the guest room."

That "guest room" was bigger than her own bedroom back in Flagstaff. Nothing flashy, just a large bed with a luxurious cream-colored comforter, and dark wood furniture placed against ivory walls. This room didn't look out over the bay, but a tree with glossy green leaves stood just outside the window, making the space feel safe, sheltered.

Laurel got the feeling that Jason didn't want her to press him about the guitars, so she only said, "This is great. I wasn't expecting quite so much."

Something in the set of his jaw seemed to ease a little, as if he was glad that she hadn't asked anything further about the guitars in the other bedroom, a collection that would have been worthy of any Hall of Fame musician. With a shrug, he said, "It came this way. You're actually the first person who'll be staying here."

She tilted her head at him. "What...you bought the house with all the furnishings included?"

"Yes. The people selling it were moving back to Paris, so they didn't want to be bothered with having to ship everything."

No wonder the place looked so designer perfect. At the same time, Laurel had to wistfully think that it must be nice to have so much money, it was easier for you to sell your house with everything in it and start over fresh in a new location. Being a Wilcox made her comfortable, but it sure didn't make her that kind of rich.

"Anyway," Jason went on, "there's a bathroom past that door, and you can hang up anything you need to in the closet. I'll meet you down in the living room."

"Okay," she replied. Most of the stuff she'd brought didn't need any special treatment, but there were a couple of tops that probably could benefit from being hung up rather than staying squished in her overnight bag.

He headed back downstairs, and Laurel hurriedly unpacked the few items that needed special attention, then went into the bathroom and gave her hair and teeth a quick brush. A refresh of her lip gloss, and she thought she'd pass muster for their upcoming meeting with MaryJo Gaffney.

But even though Laurel thought she looked presentable enough, she couldn't quite help feeling intimidated by her surroundings. It was one thing for Jason to casually comment that he was a trust fund baby, and quite another to have so much evidence of his wealth everywhere she looked. Had he wanted her to see his house just so he could prove he'd been telling her the truth about his situation, or was it more that he wanted to make sure she was thoroughly impressed?

Or maybe it's just that his house makes a convenient place to crash while we're in San Francisco, Laurel scolded herself as she put away her lip gloss. *Not everyone has an ulterior motive for everything.*

True. And he must think she was doing okay for herself—her Jeep Renegade wasn't a Range Rover, but it was only a year old, not to mention the top-of-the-line Trailhawk version. Likewise, the condo the Delmonicos had loaned her in Incline Village wasn't exactly a cheap room at a Motel 6 or something. Even so, she couldn't kid herself into believing that she and Jason were on remotely the same level.

But she did her best to push those worrisome thoughts aside as she descended the staircase. As promised, Jason was waiting in the living room, his gaze fixed on the sunny, tranquil scene outside the window. Even though it was a weekday, the park looked plenty crowded, with women pushing strollers along the sidewalks and couples picnicking on the green grass.

He turned at once as she entered the room. "Ready?" he asked.

Laurel nodded. Whether she was as ready as she wanted to be, she really didn't know. She honestly couldn't think of anything MaryJo Gaffney could tell her that would surprise her too much—unlike Jason, Laurel was a part of the witching world, and therefore knew to expect the unexpected—and yet her brain couldn't quite keep itself from picking at the reasons behind the other woman's reticence on the phone.

Well, you'll find out soon enough, she told herself. *Stop worrying about it.*

They headed down to the garage and got in Jason's SUV. He backed out, managing to insert himself into the nearly nonstop cars moving along the street outside with the ease of long practice.

"MaryJo's place is in Laurel Heights," he said as he started driving in a direction Laurel thought was possibly south and west. It was hard to be sure; she didn't have any frame of reference here, and felt pretty well turned around. "That's near U.C. San Francisco."

"Is it far?"

"Not too far. Maybe about ten minutes from here, depending on traffic."

That traffic seemed pretty thick to her, even though they were still an hour or so away from the real post-workday crunch. Even so, Laurel found herself very glad that Jason was driving and not her. Even with a nav system, she was pretty sure she would have gotten hopelessly lost in no time.

It was closer to fifteen minutes from the time they'd left Jason's house to the moment when they actually pulled up in front of the building that housed MaryJo Gaffney's condo, but he'd allowed them some extra time, so they were still a little early.

The building had obviously once been a house, probably built around the turn of the twentieth century, or maybe in the 1920s. Hadn't a lot of San Francisco burned down after a big earthquake around then? Laurel thought she remembered reading about that in history class, but she had to admit that her knowledge of the exact dates involved was a little hazy. This house must have been built after that, or maybe this part of the city had escaped the disaster mostly unscathed.

Jason glanced at the clock on the dashboard—3:29. "I suppose it's okay if we go now. I doubt she's going to get too upset about us showing up one minute early."

"Probably not." Doing her best to ignore the nervous tightening of her stomach, Laurel picked up her purse from where she'd set it in the footwell and slung it over one shoulder, then reached for the door handle and let herself out.

The breeze that caught her hair was fresh and cool, almost chilly. Funny how she hadn't noticed it as much in Chinatown, but maybe that was because it was more open here, whereas the neighborhood where they'd eaten lunch had taller buildings more closely packed together.

But the sun overhead was bright and warm, counteracting the breeze a bit. The air had a faint tang to it that she guessed must be salt from the ocean, although she didn't know for sure, since she'd never been to the beach in her life.

Then Jason came around to meet her, and together they walked up the front path, which was bordered in cheerful pansies and snapdragons. MaryJo's condo was on the ground floor, so all they had to do was head to the door immediately in front of them and knock.

A moment later, the door opened, and a woman who looked like she might be in her late thirties or early forties smiled out at them. She had marvelously curly blonde hair that was only partially restrained by a purple silk scarf wrapped around her head, and she wore a purple embroidered top over slim jeans.

"Laurel and Jason?" she asked, and they nodded. "So nice to meet you. Come on in."

She held the door open for them so they could enter. At once, Laurel was struck by a sensation of light and openness, mostly because the room where she now stood held very little furniture beyond a futon with a low table in front of it, and another table under one window that held a beautifully glazed vase filled with long stalks of red gladiolas.

What dominated the space was a huge canvas on an easel at the other side of the room. The painting on the canvas had only been roughed in, but Laurel recognized the landscape at once as the sort of countryside they'd driven through on their way to San Francisco—golden rolling hills, the low, dark shapes of California live oaks.

Even in its half-finished state, it was very beautiful. No wonder MaryJo Gaffney's little sketched portrait of the Lake Tahoe healer had been so good.

"Would you like anything?" MaryJo asked. "Some green tea? Water?"

"Water would be great," Laurel said. She was already feeling jumpy enough that having caffeine probably wasn't a very good idea.

Jason also said water would be fine, and their hostess told them she'd be back in a minute, and that they were welcome to sit down on the futon if they liked. Since it felt kind of strange to be standing in the middle of the room like that, looking completely at loose ends, Laurel went ahead and took a seat, Jason settling himself next to her a moment later.

Because the futon wasn't very large, that was probably the closest they'd been to each other since she'd helped him down from the Mt. Rose wilderness. She was acutely aware of his presence —the slightest rustle of his crisp cotton shirt as he shifted on the futon next to her, just the faintest drift of the cologne or aftershave he wore. Nothing overwhelming, just a very slight scent of something woodsy and fresh, something that made her want to press her face against his neck and breathe deeply.

Since there was no way she would do anything so crazy in a stranger's house, Laurel made herself sit quietly upright. Jason remained silent, as if he'd also thought it was better to refrain from conversation until their hostess returned.

To Laurel's relief, MaryJo came back quickly enough, a pair of mason jar glasses filled with water in her hands. She gave one to Laurel and another to Jason, then went and fetched the folding wooden chair by the easel and brought it over to the futon so she could sit down and face them.

"I won't ask how you found me," MaryJo said. "And I'm sorry about your grandmother."

Her gentle condolence sent a stab of guilt through Laurel. She really hated having to spread that lie around…but she also didn't know whether she would have gotten any of the healer's "patients" to talk to her if she hadn't provided a plausible—and sympathetic—explanation as to why she was looking for the man in the first place.

"Thank you," she said quietly. "It is really important for me to find him if I can. We followed a few leads we found up in Tahoe, but none of them ended up being all that helpful."

MaryJo folded her hands on her knees. There was some dried paint around her cuticles, as if she'd cleaned up hastily after the day's painting in preparation for having company. In fact, just the faintest scent of linseed oil lingered on the air, sharp, distinctive.

"Well, I don't know if I can help you find the man," she said frankly. "He didn't give me a name, and he certainly didn't tell me where he was from. But I do remember him telling me one thing before he disappeared."

"'Disappeared'?" Jason echoed. They already knew that part of the story—or thought they did —but it seemed clear enough to Laurel that Jason was doing his best to get as much firsthand from the artist as they could.

A wry smile touched MaryJo's lips. She wasn't exactly what Laurel would have called pretty, with her sharp nose and wide mouth, but there was something about her appearance that made you feel at ease. "Yes, 'disappeared,'" she replied. "Or vanished, if you like. Either way, he melted away into thin air as if he'd never been there at all. I thought for sure I was imagining things, but then I heard about Alison Crewe's story and realized she'd witnessed pretty much the same thing. I suppose some would say we were both hallucinating, but I know what really happened."

The reporter Cole Michelson had stated flat out that MaryJo must have hallucinated the episode, but Laurel knew better. It was entirely possible for someone to vanish the way she'd described, even thought people with that sort of talent were rare in the witching world.

"What did the man say to you?" Laurel asked.

MaryJo's mouth had still been curved in a faint smile, but now her expression turned serious. "I was stammering, trying to thank him. I remember that. And he smiled at me and said it was nothing, that he always knew to go where there was need." A pause, and she went on, "I didn't tell Cole Michelson that part because I could already see in his eyes that he didn't believe anything of what I was saying. And also…." The words trailed off as she stopped there and gave a faint shake of her head.

"Also…?" Laurel prompted.

"Also, I had a feeling the man didn't want that kind of information broadcast," MaryJo said. "Otherwise, I could just see people manufacturing incidents to see if they could get him to appear, you know, so they could film something sensational for their YouTube channel or their Instagram feed or whatever. This man—whoever he is—doesn't deserve to be used like that."

Another pang of guilt went through Laurel, but she told herself that her and Jason's situation was nothing like that. They weren't going for likes on an Instagram story—they were trying to discover which clan this man was from so they could return him to his family.

Or at least, that was what Laurel was doing. Jason had come along for the ride quite oblivious to her true intentions. She wasn't up to anything nefarious, though, and so she reassured herself that what she was doing was fine.

"That makes sense," Jason said. "But if he says he goes where there's need, then you'd think he'd be visiting all the local hospitals and curing people who're terminal."

MaryJo nodded in understanding, even as she spread her hands in a gesture of puzzlement. "I thought the same thing. I honestly don't know what his motivations are. I just know he was there at the right time for me. And I know something else."

"What's that?" Laurel asked.

"I don't know who that man was…but I do know he was magic."

12

MaryJo Gaffney offered a few more tidbits after that, including the interesting detail that the man's hands had glowed as he healed her injuries. Unfortunately, none of this new information was so illuminating that Jason thought it had been worth making them come all the way to San Francisco to talk to her in person.

Well, except that the healer somehow knew who needed his help and unerringly went to them. He supposed MaryJo's worry that people might take advantage of such a trait was warranted, considering what he knew of human nature.

Still, he couldn't be too annoyed at being forced to leave Lake Tahoe for the interview, not when it meant he had Laurel here in his hometown, where he could use the rest of the afternoon to show her around. And since he'd already given a plausible story to his mother about why he'd accompanied a Wilcox witch to San Francisco in pursuit of their quest, he figured he and Laurel had carte blanche to enjoy themselves.

She thanked MaryJo for the information she'd provided, and a few moments later, they were back inside Jason's Range Rover. Only then did the smile Laurel had been wearing fade. "Well, that was a complete bust."

"Not complete," he said. "That was interesting about how the healer knows how to find people who need his help. Do you think he's psychic on top of everything else?"

A lift of the shoulders, and Laurel replied, "I suppose it's possible. He does seem to have a grab bag of different talents, that's for sure."

"Maybe Alison Crewe was right, and he really is a guardian angel."

Jason had meant the comment as a joke, but Laurel's brows drew together as she appeared to seriously consider his words. Fingers toying with the strap of her purse, she said, "I don't think the actual truth is quite that crazy. I mean, there are plenty of documented cases of people with unusual healing abilities and ESP or whatever you want to call it. Our guy probably just won the lottery when it comes to that sort of thing."

He had to hand it to her—she was definitely

good at dancing around the subject of witchy talents without ever calling them anything like that. No, she used the same terminology that any civilian might when it came to describing a person with supernatural powers, which meant she was still on her guard, no matter how otherwise relaxed she might seem around him.

"Well, whatever he is," Jason said, making sure to keep his tone light, "we probably aren't going to figure it out right this second. In the meantime, how about some chocolate to cheer you up?"

Earlier, he'd decided that if he really was going to play tour guide, then he might as well take Laurel to some of the most touristy places San Francisco had to offer. And that meant spending some time in Ghirardelli Square. Maybe such a creature existed somewhere in the wild, but he had yet to meet a girl who didn't like chocolate.

As he'd expected, Laurel's expression brightened immediately, her amber eyes glowing with anticipation. "You just said the magic word."

"Then let's get going."

He pulled away from the curb and headed north. In less than fifteen minutes, they were parked at the structure adjacent to the square and had headed out in pursuit of chocolate. Laurel looked from side to side as they walked, obviously trying to take in all the sights and sounds of the square around them.

"I didn't realize there was so much here," she said.

"Yes, it's kind of a destination," Jason replied. "But we can focus on chocolate for now. Do you want it straight up, or in a sundae?"

At once, she grinned. "Hot fudge?"

"Of course."

"Now you're speaking my language. Lead on."

Wearing a smile of his own, Jason led her to the Ghirardelli store. As usual, there was a line, and he resigned himself to a wait of at least ten minutes or so. If he'd come here with one of his Ludlow cousins—although none of them generally deigned to visit a spot so overrun with tourists —they might have tried to use the clan's local influence to jump to the head of the line.

But he knew he didn't dare try something that with Laurel watching. Maybe she wouldn't have found anything too odd about that sort of behavior, since she obviously could tell his family had a lot of money. On the other hand, she might have started asking questions, and he didn't want to risk arousing any suspicions.

So, they waited, and chatted about what else to see and where they might go for dinner. He suggested Restaurant Gary Danko, saying it was one of his favorites, and Laurel seemed amenable to that idea…with one caveat.

"Is it fancy?" she inquired.

"A little," he replied. In fact, it was a Michelin-starred establishment, one that met even his mother's exacting standards. However, he'd rather not have to provide that much detail about their destination, just because he didn't want to scare Laurel off.

To his relief, she didn't seem too worried. "Good thing I brought the dress I wore to dinner the other night. I hope you don't mind seeing me in it twice."

Since she'd looked pretty spectacular in that dress, Jason didn't have a problem with it. Not one bit.

"No, I don't mind," he said, and since he smiled as he spoke, she seemed to grasp immediately what was going through his head.

"I'm glad it meets your approval."

She looked so adorable right then, just the faintest lift at the corner of her full mouth, those amazing eyes of hers twinkling behind the sunglasses she wore, that he wished he could lean down and kiss her luscious lips. However, since they were sort of squeezed in line between two families with kids, Jason figured it was probably better to be circumspect.

Later, though….

A few minutes after that, they reached the head of the line and were guided to a table for two, where Laurel perused the menu the hostess had handed her. "I'm not sure I'm even going to want dinner after this," she remarked.

"Oh, you'll walk it off in no time," he told her. "The hills in this city are really good for working up an appetite."

"It is hillier than I'd expected." She paused there, her expression growing more serious as she appeared to ponder her surroundings. "Actually, I guess I never thought much about San Francisco. I suppose I never really expected to visit here."

"Why not?" Jason asked. Of course, he knew the real reason why Laurel Wilcox had never thought to find herself in his hometown, but he wanted to see what sort of lie she'd concoct to explain why a civilian wouldn't have any reason to visit the Bay Area.

Alarm flared in her eyes, and she reached for the glass of water the hostess had left for her and took a quick sip. "Oh," she said quickly, "I suppose I was just so wrapped up in what I was doing in my own little corner of Arizona that I really hadn't planned to do much traveling. That's all."

Somehow, he managed to keep himself from smiling. As lies went, the one she'd offered wasn't all that convincing. Still, he didn't have any intention of probing too deeply, since he didn't want her to think he had any ulterior motive behind his questioning. "I guess I can see how that happens," he said. "I suppose I'm just the opposite—I don't like to stay put."

"Really?" Laurel asked, brows lifting. "If I had a house like yours, I don't think I'd ever want to leave."

That disingenuous comment made Jason want to chuckle. Just as she had a moment earlier, he reached for his water to keep his mouth from quirking. After swallowing a mouthful, he said, "It's nice, sure, but I get itchy feet."

Of course, his desire to get out and about probably had much more to do with his wish to avoid his mother as much as possible than because he enjoyed traveling all that much. All the same, he tended to roam around Ludlow territory a good bit—spending a weekend in Santa Barbara here, wandering in wine country for a week or ten days. He supposed he should count himself lucky that he had so many destination spots right in his clan's backyard. It would have been a lot more difficult to keep himself amused if the Ludlows lived in Nebraska, for instance.

"I'll bet you've been everywhere," Laurel said next, a note of envy entering her voice. "Like Paris, or London. Hong Kong. Hawaii."

He had no more ability to visit those places than Laurel herself did, but Jason knew he had to do his best to pretend that he had. Clearly, she thought his wealth must have allowed him to travel the globe.

"Not Hong Kong," he said, figuring it was the place he knew the least about. "But Hawaii and Europe. And Mexico and Canada and Australia."

All right, maybe that was laying it on a little too thick. But since he'd already uttered the lie, he knew he had to do his best to make it seem plausible.

"Wow," Laurel replied. "Which place was your favorite?"

"Um…Italy, probably," Jason said, basing his response on pictures he'd seen of Tuscany. It did look amazingly beautiful.

"Italy," she repeated, now looking wistful.

Right then, he wished more than anything that they really were simply a couple of civilians. If that had been the case, he would have asked her if she wanted to come with him to Italy. Just the vision in his head of having Laurel at his side as they walked the streets of Florence and Rome, or to have her riding next to him in a convertible as they drove along a country road in Tuscany, was enough to make him ache for all the things he'd never be able to do, simply because he'd been born a warlock.

Most people would probably think he was crazy for viewing his inborn magical talents as a liability rather than a gift. Then again, most people had absolutely no idea how restrictive being born into a witch clan could be.

"But," he went on, "there's a whole lot to see right here. What would you like to do after this?"

"Go to Fisherman's Wharf," Laurel said promptly, then added with a smile, "mostly because it's the only place in San Francisco I've really heard of, besides Chinatown."

Fisherman's Wharf made Ghirardelli Square look like the Metropolitan Museum of Art in terms of high culture, but Jason was more than willing to do whatever she liked. Mostly, he was just enjoying the novelty of having a witch from another family sitting here with him in the heart of his clan's territory. He couldn't quite shake the feeling that his mother or some other Ludlow was going to pounce on them out of nowhere and demand what the hell Laurel thought she was doing, sitting there so nonchalantly.

But no Ludlows materialized, and so the two of them were able to order their ice cream sundaes in peace, and to eat them as well, once the food showed up. It had been years since he'd had a hot fudge sundae, and Jason had to admit it tasted better than he remembered...although that could have been the company and nothing more.

Afterward, they walked around the square a bit and looked at some of the shops, although

Laurel demurred when he suggested going into the Wattle Creek Winery tasting room.

"I'm still full from that sundae," she said. "And I assume we're going to have wine with dinner, so I'm fine with waiting until then."

He didn't bother to argue, since she was right. And after they were done at the square, they left his Range Rover in the parking structure and walked the few blocks to Fisherman's Wharf. Once there, she stood on the pier for a long moment, staring out at the water as if she'd never seen such a thing before.

"It's so crazy to think that you could sail out on that and get to Hawaii, or all the way to Japan."

Jason managed to smother a smile, reminding himself that she'd lived a landlocked existence her whole life, and probably was a bit hazy on San Francisco's geography.

"Actually, that's just San Francisco Bay," he said. "To really see the Pacific, we'd need to drive over to the west side of the peninsula, go to Ocean Beach or something."

Immediately, she looked so crestfallen that he once again had to prevent himself from smiling at her reaction. "Oh," she said. "I guess I really am turned around."

"It's okay," he replied. "San Francisco can be

kind of confusing until you get the lay of the land."

"And how long does that take?" Laurel asked. Her tone wasn't snarky at all; it sounded as though she really wanted to know.

He spread his hands wide in a self-deprecating gesture. "Since I'm a native, it's hard for me to say. Knowing these streets is just part of who I am."

Those words seemed to darken her expression. Was she also thinking of how impossible their current situation actually was? Obviously, she thought he was a civilian and nothing more, but those sorts of relationships weren't always easy to manage, either, especially with two people so geographically disconnected from one another.

Of course, those difficulties could be multiplied by infinity when the parties involved were from two clans that, if not exactly at war with one another, still weren't enjoying what anyone could call an amicable relationship.

"Well, I'll try to pay attention during the time I'm here," she said, and appeared ready to leave it at that.

Afterward, they wandered in and out of the shops. She bought a Fisherman's Wharf T-shirt, along with a couple of postcards. Jason wanted to ask her what she planned to do with those items —wearing the T-shirt would only advertise to her fellow Wilcoxes that she'd gone out of Delmonico territory, and it wasn't as though witches and warlocks tended to have friends in far-off places to whom they could send a postcard—but he refrained. He absolutely could not let a single comment slip that might raise her suspicions.

While she was shopping, he pulled out his phone and made reservations for seven o'clock at Gary Danko. Normally, it would have been impossible to get a table at the restaurant at such late notice, but the Ludlow name had considerable pull in San Francisco.

By that point it was getting close to six; at that time of year, the sun wouldn't set for several more hours, but Jason thought it was still probably a good idea to head back to his house so they could get changed for dinner. Laurel seemed agreeable to that plan; they walked to the parking structure where he'd left his Range Rover, got it out of hock, and then drove the mile or so to his place.

"We should probably leave around twenty 'til, just to give ourselves enough time to get to the restaurant," he told her as they came in through the kitchen, and she gave him a brief nod.

"Not a problem. I just need to change and fix my hair and face."

She looked glowing and lovely to him after an afternoon spent out of doors, but he had to agree privately that the wild salt wind coming in off the bay had wreaked havoc on her long, wavy hair.

"You can meet me in the living room when you're ready," he told her, and they both headed upstairs, she to the guest room, and he to the master suite at the end of the hall.

As he closed the door behind him, Jason couldn't help asking himself just what the hell he thought he was doing. If he had any common sense at all, he would've taken her to one of the numerous fun but casual restaurants he knew around the city. Instead, he was treating her to dinner at one of the city's fanciest establishments, the kind of place people generally reserved for birthdays and anniversaries...or maybe marriage proposals.

Obviously, that wasn't going to happen. No, they'd have a good meal, come back to the house, and....

His brain skittered to a stop there. He might have harbored a few private hopes as to how their evening might end, but he knew better than to give those dreamy imaginings a foothold in his mind.

For now, he was content to wait and see what happened next.

Laurel set down her hairbrush and eyed her reflection critically. She'd gotten enough sun and wind that she definitely didn't need to retouch her blush, so she'd settled for darkening her eyeshadow, adding liner, and applying actual lipstick instead of the gloss she usually wore. If time had permitted, she would've washed her hair all over again, since the salt spray made it feel sort of sticky, but that would have taken far too long. About all she could do was brush it vigorously and hope the waves she'd set in it that morning would hold through the evening.

And although she thought she looked decent, she had to wonder if "decent" was good enough for the restaurant where Jason was taking her. He hadn't given her a lot of details, but it sounded pretty ritzy.

Then again, they'd already shared a fancy meal in Incline Village, so it wasn't as though she was a stranger to the concept of fine dining with Jason Nichols. All the same, nervous flutters danced in her stomach as she descended the stairs. Something about this evening felt different from the last time they'd gone to dinner, although she couldn't say exactly what.

Maybe it was simply the realization that she really liked this guy…that she didn't want the time they were spending together to end.

There had to be a way to make it work…but how?

Worry about that later, she admonished

herself. *For now, you're just going out to dinner. Relax and enjoy it.*

Of course, her nerves started skittering all over again when she caught sight of Jason, who was standing near the unlit fireplace and watching the westering sun turn the roof of the Palace of Fine Arts to pure gold. For just a second, the light seemed to touch his hair with gold as well, making him appear almost blond. She blinked, and the illusion was gone.

But he still looked unbelievably hot in a dark gray suit with a white dress shirt underneath. No tie, though; clearly, the restaurant was fancy but didn't insist on neckwear.

"You look great," he said as soon as she entered the room, and she waved a dismissive hand at her dress.

"You've seen me in this before."

Jason's brows lifted. "So what? You looked great in it the day before yesterday, and you still look great in it tonight."

"You look nice, too," she responded. "I like the suit."

A flash of a grin, and he said, "Well, now that we've both agreed we clean up nice, I suppose we'd better get going. There's usually a line for the valet at Danko's."

Laurel nodded, and they went back out to the garage. By then, she was used to climbing into the

Range Rover and getting herself settled, so she went ahead and fastened her seatbelt while Jason backed out onto the street.

When she'd told him earlier that afternoon that she was having a hard time getting her bearings in San Francisco, she hadn't been joking. He pointed the SUV in a direction that she thought was the opposite of where they'd come in earlier that day, but she couldn't be sure. Not that it mattered—he was the one driving, not she, and she could just sit back and enjoy the ride.

If possible, the streets were even more crowded than they'd been earlier in the day. Jason drove in silence, all his attention focused on getting them where they were going. Clearly, even veteran San Franciscans didn't always enjoy themselves while negotiating the city's busy thoroughfares.

Eventually, though, they pulled up to the valet station at the restaurant, and Jason handed over the key fob and took the claim check from the man who greeted them there. Laurel wasn't sure if she would be so nonchalant about letting a complete stranger drive such an expensive vehicle, but she supposed that people living in big cities were used to that sort of thing.

The restaurant was sleek and modern, but in a warm way, with lots of bright-toned wood and interesting art on the walls. As soon as Jason paused in front of the pretty red-haired woman at the hostess desk, she smiled and picked up a couple of menus, and said, "Welcome to Restaurant Gary Danko, Mr.—"

"Thanks so much for getting us in at such short notice," Jason broke in.

The woman blinked, but then she appeared to recover herself and said, "Right this way."

An odd little exchange, but Laurel put it out of her mind as she followed Jason past the hostess station and into the restaurant. They were given a quiet table by the window and in a corner, a place where they could look out at the lights of the city and still feel private. Of course, even at the most private table in the restaurant, Laurel wouldn't feel comfortable talking about their healer…but it seemed Jason didn't harbor those same reservations. As soon as the hostess left, he said, "What do you want to do tomorrow? Head back to Tahoe and see if our guy has performed any more miracles?"

Laurel sent a quick, furtive glance around them, but everyone at the tables in the immediate vicinity seemed absorbed in their own conversations. "I suppose so," she replied. "I don't think there's much more we can accomplish in San Francisco."

"Probably not," Jason said, sounding almost cheerful. It seemed as though he was just fine with the little bit of sightseeing they'd done that day and was ready to get back to work. "I mean, unless MaryJo Gaffney has a flash of insight and calls us over to impart some fascinating new morsel of information."

"I doubt that's going to happen."

Their waiter appeared then, announced the specials, and asked if they had any questions about the restaurant's offerings. Laurel couldn't quite help giving a guilty start, since she hadn't even looked down at the menu the hostess had given her.

Was that a wink Jason had just sent in her direction? He said, "Do you think you're going to want red meat tonight...fish...fowl?"

"Red meat," she replied at once, since that seemed the safest thing to say. Even if they got slightly different entrées, it would be easier to choose a wine if they were in the same basic category.

He looked up at the waiter. "We'll have a bottle of the 2002 Opus One Cabernet. We'll order when you come back with that."

The man nodded. He looked as though he was in his early forties, with clean, angular features that seemed to hint he might be part Asian. "Of course. I'll get the wine now."

He left, and Jason said, "Want any

suggestions? The bison is amazing, and so is the filet."

Laurel had had elk, but not bison, so that sounded like something fun to try. "Oh, I'll have the bison, then."

"Perfect. I'll get the filet."

That matter settled, they chatted a little about the drive back to Tahoe as they waited for the waiter to return. He did so promptly, uncorked the wine and had Jason take the ritual first taste, and then took their orders and departed again.

"That's what I like," Jason commented once they were alone. "A waiter who's all business. The ones who hover drive me nuts."

"Especially when you're trying to discuss something you don't want overheard," Laurel replied, and he nodded.

"Exactly. I mean, I suppose this isn't exactly privileged knowledge, since MaryJo's story was in the paper and Alison Crewe publishes her blog for everyone to see, but still...."

"You still don't want someone listening to every detail."

"Right." Jason picked up his glass and paused. Belatedly, Laurel realized he wanted to toast, so she raised her glass as well and clinked it against his. She'd never heard of the wine he'd ordered for them—no big surprise—but it was delicious, dark and smooth. Once they'd both had their first swallow, he continued. "I suppose we should head back out to the Mt. Rose wilderness area…but I promise to be more careful this time."

His expression was almost rueful. Since Laurel figured he'd given himself enough crap over the careless injury, she only nodded and said, "I think it's still our best lead. Now we know to take the other fork."

"And pray that our guy hasn't already moved on to another location."

About all she could do was give a helpless lift of her shoulders. Since neither one of them had any idea what the healer's plans were—if he had any, other than hanging around in an area that probably had more than its fair share of hiking mishaps—it seemed the best thing to do was to follow the one real lead they had.

The food arrived soon after that, and they both dug into their meals. Laurel found she was hungrier than she'd thought she would be—her hot fudge sundae had been amazing, with the decadent addition of a little pitcher of fudge on the side to make it extra gooey—but it hadn't stayed with her for too long. Too much sugar and not enough substance, probably.

They made plans for hiking, leaving out any mention of the healer. If anyone had been listening to them, they would have sounded like a normal couple making plans for a getaway in Lake Tahoe.

Too bad they weren't a normal couple. Laurel still hadn't quite figured out exactly what they were, but she told herself she should relax and allow herself to enjoy this time in Jason's company…however long it lasted.

The meal stretched out longer than she'd thought it would…moving on to dessert and two more glasses of wine as they lingered at the table, caught up in their conversation. Eventually, though, Jason paid the bill and they headed back out to the valet stand.

Feeling definitely hazy, Laurel got into the Range Rover and leaned against the seat back as they drove the mile or so to his house near the Palace of Fine Arts. Once they were inside, Jason paused in the kitchen, asking, "Do you want some water?"

"Yes, please," Laurel replied, thinking it was probably a good idea to hydrate after all that wine.

He got out a couple of glasses, filled them from the dispenser in the door of the big stainless-steel refrigerator, and handed one to her. She sipped from it gratefully, then paused, her attention caught by the shimmering blue-green circle of the spa in the backyard. A nod toward it, and she said, "Are we going to try that out?"

Jason followed her gaze, then lifted an eyebrow. "Now?"

"Why not? It'll be warm, won't it?"

"Very."

"Well, then."

He grinned. "I like you, Laurel Wilcox. You keep me on my toes."

"I like you, too," she replied. Deep within, she knew what she felt for him was more than merely "like," but she wasn't tipsy enough to be uttering those sorts of truths…thank God.

"I'll find a robe for you," he said next, his tone almost too casual. Had he been thinking the same thing, that this was turning into something neither one of them had expected? "The spa will be warm, but it'll be cold coming and going."

Right. She supposed she should've thought of that. The night breeze here was cool, brisk in a completely different way from Flagstaff's mountain winds. Probably because of the moisture from the ocean, but still, walking from the house out to the spa—even in a one-piece—probably would be a little nippier than she would like.

"Sounds great," she said.

They drank some more water, then went upstairs to their separate rooms to get changed. As Laurel climbed out of her dress and into the bathing suit she'd bought in Incline Village, she wondered if she was being crazy for suggesting a midnight dip. Okay, it was probably just a little past nine, but still.

Well, she couldn't exactly back out now. She rummaged through her luggage and found a clip so she could pull her hair up and out of the way. A rustle outside the door made her think Jason had stopped by to leave the promised robe for her. When she peeked out into the hall, she didn't see him, but sure enough, a thick white terrycloth robe was hanging from the doorknob…and dragging a bit on the polished wood floor.

She slipped into the robe gratefully, then headed back down to the kitchen, her flip-flops making little slapping noises on the steps. Jason waited for her there, wearing a robe similar to the one he'd loaned her, only navy blue instead of white.

Like her, he was also wearing flip-flops. Even the bit of muscular chest and bit of his strong legs that the robe revealed was enough to make her catch her breath. If he could have this effect on her when he was mostly covered up, what the heck was she supposed to do once he took off the robe and got in the spa with her?

Don't stare, whatever you do, she told herself. *You got this.*

He didn't seem to have noticed her discomfiture. Or maybe he was just pretending not to notice. "Ready?"

She nodded.

"We should bring some water with us," he said. "You can get dehydrated in a spa."

That was a little factoid she hadn't known, but then, she hadn't spent a lot of time in hot tubs or spas. Quite a few of the Wilcoxes had them, but her own immediate family had never gone to the expense of having one installed. "Okay," she responded as she scooped up her glass from the counter.

Jason retrieved his glass as well, then opened the back door. At once, a rush of cool, damp air greeted them, making Laurel both glad of the robe Jason had loaned her and worried that this whole thing had been a ridiculous idea.

But since they were committed to it now, she didn't say anything, only followed him across the yard, which was really more like a large patio, with beautiful herringbone brick covering the ground and trees in planters lining the walls. When they reached the spa, she wouldn't allow herself to feel self-conscious, but only dropped the robe as soon as Jason turned on the jets, then climbed into the water.

He got in a moment later after also letting his robe fall to the immaculate bricks. Laurel did her best not to stare, but it was difficult with someone so eminently stare-able. His body was lean and sculpted enough to be on the cover of *Men's Fitness* magazine or something like that, his chest smooth, although he had just the right amount of masculine hair on his legs and arms. Nicely tanned, too, or at least, she thought he was. The illumination from the landscape lighting provided enough light so you could find your way easily enough, but it didn't do a very good job of showing true colors.

"This is great," Laurel said, figuring that sitting there in dead silence probably wasn't a good idea. And she wasn't lying; the hot water felt delicious, a wonderful contrast to the cool night air. "Was the spa here when you bought the house, or did you have it put in?"

"It was here," Jason replied. He reached for his water and took a sip, then added, "I wanted a house where I wouldn't have to do anything to it, and so this one was perfect."

Right—he'd bought it with all the furnishings included. Laurel thought that would take some of the fun out of buying a place, since getting to decorate a home just the way she wanted was something she looked forward to one day, but she supposed there was something to be said for not having to worry about a bunch of nit-picky details.

"The previous owners did a really nice job," she said. "This backyard is gorgeous. It sort of reminds me of a villa in Italy—or at least, what I imagine a villa in Italy would look like."

"It's close enough," Jason responded. He set his glass down, and his gaze locked with hers.

A not-unpleasant thrill ran down her spine. She had a feeling that the warmth currently pooling in her belly didn't have much to do with the hot water surrounding her.

She didn't know which one of them moved first. All she did know was that in the next moment, his arms had gone around her, pulling her close, his mouth locking on hers. She pressed herself against him, all too aware of the thin fabric of her swimsuit the only thing separating her breasts from the hard muscles of his chest.

They remained that way for a long, breathless moment. Then Jason pulled away just a little, dark eyes intent on her face. Voice husky, he said, "Do you want to go inside?"

Laurel knew exactly what he was asking. The rational part of her was saying no, it was too soon, and besides, there was no way she could really have a future with Jason Nichols, so why go any further than they already had?

But her heart and her body ignored the rational promptings of her brain, and she replied, "Yes."

No other words, just the two of them climbing out of the spa, pausing to grab their robes and throw them on to wick away some of the moisture from their brief dip in the water. They left shimmering footprints on the bricks as they hurried to the back door, telltales of their haste to get inside.

And then it was up the stairs and down the hallway, passing the guest room, continuing to the master suite at the end of the hall. Laurel didn't get much more than a brief glimpse of warm-hued walls and simple, dark-toned furniture before Jason was yanking back the covers so they could fall on the bed.

His fingers found the clasp that held the halter of her swimsuit closed, and he undid it so the straps fell down on her shoulders. A moment later, he was pulling down the suit so her breasts were exposed. At once, his hands moved over her, caressing, and she gasped. Every single nerve ending in her body felt as if it had come vibrantly, joyously alive, a sensation she knew she'd never experienced before.

Not like this.

That was only the beginning, though. Soon after, he grabbed her suit and pulled it all the way off, tossing the damp garment onto the floor. Then his hand slid up her thigh, strong, deft fingers slipping into her, making her moan out loud this time.

Well, two could play at that game. She

grasped the waistband of his swim trunks and pulled them down as well, then threw them onto the carpet next to her bathing suit. The only light in the bedroom was the illumination from the sconces in the upstairs hall, but that was enough for her to see how big he was, how hard and ready for her. Without hesitation, she reached out and touched him, took him in her hand and began to stroke him up and down.

Now it was his turn to moan, to let out a gasping breath at her touch. Laurel bent and took him in her mouth, tasting the faint tang of chlorinated water, need pulsing in her even as she pleasured him.

He seemed to sense that need, because a moment later, he shifted, pushing her down against the pillows so he could taste her as well. She let out a startled gasp, then let herself relax into the sensations pulsing through her, the growing certainty that he was about to make her come harder than she ever had before.

Which she did, with a moan that was almost a scream. He shifted again, and she could feel his hardness against the inside of her thigh, tantalizingly close.

"Should I get a condom?" he asked, and she shook her head. The McAllister witches had taught their Wilcox counterparts the charm of Brigid, the one that would ward off unwanted pregnancy. Maybe she should be worried about disease more than pregnancy, but somehow Laurel knew that wouldn't be an issue with Jason.

Even if it were, she could have Eleanor fix her up. That was the one limitation of a healer's talent; none of them were able to heal themselves.

All those thoughts flashed through Laurel's mind in a microsecond. After that, she couldn't think of anything except the exquisite sensation of Jason sliding into her, of the way their bodies seemed to fit perfectly together. She wrapped her legs around him, drawing him in deeper as they fell into a perfect rhythm, their breaths combining so they sounded like a single being rather than two people with their own hearts and minds... their own secrets.

Another orgasm rocked its way through her, and she cried out again. A few seconds later, Jason shuddered his way to a climax as well, his arms tight around her as they clung to one another.

They remained that way for some time, neither one of them wanting to let go. Eventually, however, she kissed him on the cheek and made her unsteady way to the *en suite* bathroom to get cleaned up. Afterward, she murmured the words of the charm.

"Blessed Brigid, now is not the time. Bestow your blessings elsewhere."

Would that time ever come for her and Jason?

Laurel wasn't a seer, and so she couldn't say for sure. As she returned to the bed and slipped under the covers, felt him press his warm body against hers, she only knew one thing.

She loved him…and had absolutely no idea what to do about it.

13

Jason opened his eyes and blinked up at the ceiling. For a second, he was only aware of an immense sensation of well-being. Then reality slammed down, and a bolt of panic flashed through him.

His power of illusion didn't work while he was sleeping.

At once, he summoned the disguise he'd worn for the past week—dark hair and eyes, skin deeper-toned than his own. He looked over at Laurel, but she seemed to be fast asleep still, eyes shut, a smear of mascara on her cheek showing how they'd both passed out after their lovemaking sessions and hadn't bothered to do anything to truly get ready for bed. Her hair straggled out of the clip she'd used to put it up for their dip in the spa, and he was pretty sure she was the most beautiful woman he'd ever seen.

Thank God he'd woken up first. If she'd looked over and seen his true appearance, had realized he wasn't the person he was pretending to be....

But she hadn't. The disguise was the most important thing, because although he'd also had to hide his warlock nature from her during their first meeting, now that they'd been together for days, it was no longer necessary to conceal that part of himself. That was always how it worked for witches and warlocks—once they got past that initial meeting, they no longer experienced the signal which told them a newcomer was one of their own kind.

Once the panic had subsided, however, he still wanted to smack himself upside the head. What the hell had he been thinking?

Well, he hadn't been thinking. Not clearly, anyway. Too much wine with dinner, and then the sight of her as she let the robe drop and he was able to see clearly the perfection of her body—the swell of her breasts in that sleek swimsuit, those legs that seemed to go on forever.

No wonder he'd lost control. Problem was, now he had to figure out what in the world to do about it.

Was Laurel expecting more from their relationship than she'd let on? As far as he could tell, she appeared to want to keep things at least semi-casual. There wasn't much chance of a future between a witch and a civilian who lived so far from her home territory, and so maybe she was just doing her best to amuse herself while looking for her elusive healer.

Last night, though…that hadn't felt like casual sex. Not at all.

And he didn't want it to be casual. He wanted…well, he wanted to tell her the truth. He wanted to tell her that he'd fallen in love with her and wanted her to stay here with him in Ludlow territory.

It was only until those words reverberated in his brain that he realized what he'd done to himself.

How could he be in love with Laurel Wilcox? He barely knew her.

That didn't matter, though. He knew enough. He knew she was the only woman who'd set his heart on fire like this, who made the hours they'd spent together slip by like pearls strung on a cord of pure silk, lustrous and perfect and each one a jewel.

Damn it.

She stirred then, and Jason forced away the frown he'd felt etching his brow. "Morning," he said with a smile.

Her eyes widened for a second, as if she hadn't quite recalled where she was until he spoke. Enough light slipped past the shutters to reveal how truly beautiful those eyes were, amber in hue overall, but flecked with deeper shades of brown and lighter tones of gold. They were absolutely spellbinding, like a vein of pure crystalline citrine.

"Morning," she said, and her mouth curved in response to his. "I must have really passed out. What time is it?"

Such prosaic words after a night of passion. But Jason thought he understood—she was trying to act as normal as possible so things wouldn't be too awkward between them.

He glanced at the clock on the nightstand. "Eight forty-five. Not too late."

"Good." She sat up then, but he noted the way she kept the covers clutched against her breasts, as if she feared showing her naked body to him might lead to more sex.

Was she regretting what they'd done? He gazed down into her face for a moment, but he didn't see any guilt or worry there. No, it was more that they'd had a plan for this day, and if they allowed themselves to get sidetracked, they'd lose valuable time.

In a way, he had to admire her single-mindedness. Besides, his body was telling him it was sated…for now. Better to get on with their day.

"I figured we could go out for breakfast on our way out of town," he said, watching the way her body seemed to relax as he made the suggestion. "I know a great place not too far from here."

"That sounds perfect," she replied. "I'll just get in the shower, then."

Before Jason could reply, she'd slipped out from under the covers. He caught the briefest glimpse of her lithe, nude body before she scooped up her borrowed robe from where it lay on the floor and slid it on. She bent again, this time to grab her discarded swimsuit, and slipped out of the room.

That seemed to be the signal for him to get up as well. He went into the bathroom and closed the door, and briefly contemplated abandoning his illusory appearance while showering. However, that didn't seem like a very good idea—what if Laurel came back for some reason?—and so he maintained the dark hair and eyes as he showered, and afterward while he brushed his teeth, shaved, and got dressed.

When he emerged from the bedroom, he could hear the sound of Laurel's blow dryer emanating from the guest bathroom.

A thought crept into his mind, one he wanted to ignore and knew he probably shouldn't.

He really should sneak a peek at her driver's license and get her home address.

Just in case.

The blow dryer kept going. Jason hurried into the guest room, located her purse, and pulled out her wallet. Yes, that was the address—1522 North San Francisco Street, Apartment A. He wanted to smile at the irony but decided he didn't have the time. Instead, he returned the wallet to her purse and hurried out of the room.

To his relief, the blow dryer was still humming away in the guest bath. Trying not to feel too guilty about the way he'd just intruded on Laurel's privacy, Jason continued down to the kitchen and popped an Italian roast pod in the Keurig. Yes, they were going out to breakfast, but he needed caffeine sooner than that.

A glance at his phone had told Jason he hadn't missed any calls from his mother. No doubt her spies had already told her that Jason was showing a Wilcox witch around San Francisco—as they'd left the restaurant, he'd thought he glimpsed his cousin Ben sitting at the bar—and so she was content to sit back and see what happened next. Honestly, Jason wasn't even sure whether Carolyn would be angry with him for sleeping with Laurel. She might very well view the shift in their relationship as a sign that he might try to convince the Wilcox healer to stay in Ludlow territory.

At any rate, he allowed himself to relax slightly as he poured coffee into his favorite red-glazed mug and leaned against the counter. He might as well allow himself to enjoy some of the afterglow, since he couldn't tell whether Laurel was interested in further intimacies or not.

She appeared a few moments later, sniffing appreciatively at the warm scent of coffee on the air. Her hair lay in rich waves on her shoulders, and she wore a cheerful orange top that only intensified the warm hues in her extraordinary eyes.

"Want some coffee?" Jason asked, doing his best not to stare. You'd think after spending several days around Laurel Wilcox, he'd be used to her appearance, but every time he looked at her, he only wanted to drink her in that much more.

"Yes, please," she replied. "Normally, I'd wait until breakfast, but after all that wine last night…."

The words trailed off there, and a faint flush tinged her high cheekbones. Maybe she was reliving the activities of the night before, and thinking that maybe things would have turned out differently if they'd had just a little less wine.

"No worries," he said. "Italian roast okay?"

"Sounds great."

He hurried to put another pod in the Keurig, and the awkward moment passed. Still, he was glad when the coffee was ready, and he was able to hand her a mug and ask, "Do you want any milk or sugar? I don't have creamer."

"No, I take it black," she replied with a smile.

A girl after his own heart. Of course, he'd already known that about her.

"Are you packed?" he asked next. "I figured we'd go straight from the restaurant to Tahoe if you're ready to go."

"I'm mostly packed," Laurel said. "I have some toiletry stuff I need to put away, but that'll only take me a couple of minutes."

"Great." Jason wasn't exactly sure why he wanted to put San Francisco behind them as soon as possible, although he had a feeling the longer they stayed, the greater the chance that his mother would get tired of hanging back and waiting to see what happened next, and would directly intervene. A quick breakfast followed by immediately getting on the road to Tahoe seemed the safest way to head her off at the pass.

The coffeemaker beeped, so he went ahead and poured a mug for Laurel. She seemed glad to take it from him, although she wisely didn't try to drink any right away, but stood there and blew on it a few times. Her attitude seemed diffident, although Jason couldn't really blame her for that. He also wasn't sure what to do about this awkwardness that had sprung up between them. Although he didn't regret what had happened the night before, he also didn't want the physical intimacy they'd shared to change the easy dynamic they'd developed over the past few days.

She finally sipped some coffee, then blurted out, "When we get to Tahoe, maybe you should come stay at my condo. It would make the logistics of looking for the healer a lot easier."

For a second, Jason could only stare at her. Of all the things he'd thought she might say to him on this morning after their worlds had changed, he definitely hadn't expected her to invite him to her condo for an indefinite amount of time. Clearly, she wasn't trying to avoid a repeat of the previous night.

Well, unless her condo had two bedrooms and he'd utterly misinterpreted her comment.

Because he didn't respond right away, she added quickly, "I mean, if you want to. I just thought it would save you having to drive back and forth between Incline Village and South Tahoe all the time."

Might as well make things utterly clear between them. He met her gaze and said, his tone level, "Is that the only reason?"

The flush in her cheeks was all too obvious in the bright morning sunlight streaming through the kitchen windows. "Well, no," she said, meeting his eyes without a blink. "I don't want last night to be a one-time thing. But if you don't want to—"

He had to stop her right there. Without thinking, he stepped forward and gave her a kiss, tasting coffee on her tongue and knowing she must have tasted it on his as well. "I want to. I definitely want to." Even as he spoke, though, he couldn't quite hold back some inner misgivings. Staying in Incline Village with her meant he'd have to be even more on his guard, since that was Delmonico territory and he absolutely couldn't allow any of them to discover there was a Ludlow in their midst.

Still, a bit of extra caution seemed like a minor price to pay when balanced against being around Laurel Wilcox day and night…with being able to share her bed.

She smiled back at him, relief clear in her expression. "Great. We'll still have to stop at your condo in South Tahoe to pick up my car, but otherwise, we can make my place in Incline Village our base of operations."

"Sounds like a plan."

They finished their coffee after that, and then Laurel went upstairs to finish packing. Jason followed her, since he had a few odds and ends he needed to put together, too.

As he zipped up his overnight bag, though, he

had to hope he hadn't just made a huge miscalculation.

Jason took her to breakfast at a funky little spot not far from his house. They had to eat at a tiny table crammed into a corner, but Laurel's quiche Lorraine was so sublime, she really couldn't complain about the lack of atmosphere. They chatted about the restaurant and other places in town that were his favorites, all the awkwardness of earlier that morning gone. And she was relieved by that, because she definitely didn't want to feel as though she had to go on tiptoes around him.

Maybe it had been crazy to ask him to stay at her condo, but the idea had leapt into her mind as she stood there facing him in his kitchen, and she'd decided to go with it. If nothing else, at least she would have learned quickly enough if he intended their relationship to be nothing more than that one shared night of passion, and whether he'd decided he'd had his fun and wanted to move on.

She should have known Jason wasn't like that. He'd accepted her invitation immediately, with no sign that he wanted to second-guess his decision. And now they were heading north on 580, going back to continue their quest.

It felt so natural to be sitting here in the passenger seat of his Range Rover, watching the golden landscape flash by outside the windows, listening to the warm tones of his voice as he talked about prosaic topics, such as whether they should stop at a grocery store in South Tahoe to stock up on some groceries so they wouldn't have to keep going out to eat all the time.

She agreed that sounded like a good idea. "I'm not much of a cook," she confessed. "But I can throw together a few things. And there's a barbecue on the patio at my condo."

"Well, then, that's definitely enough to keep us going for a while," Jason said. "We'll get some steaks and cut-up chicken to put on the grill, that kind of stuff."

"And then we won't have to worry about watching what we say every time we eat," Laurel replied, and even in profile, his smile was dazzling.

"Yeah, that was starting to cramp my style a bit."

She smiled in response, although inwardly, she couldn't help wincing just a little. Even when they were alone together, she'd still have to be careful and make sure she didn't let slip a single detail of her real reason for searching out the healer.

But that inner worry smoothed itself away as they drove, and then they stopped at a grocery store in South Tahoe and spent way too much money on steak and chicken and potatoes, makings for salad and pasta, and anything else that sounded good. Jason insisted on paying for the whole thing, and after making a few feeble protests, Laurel went ahead and let him whip out his credit card at the checkout line. He obviously wasn't hurting for money, so what was the point in arguing about him footing the bill?

From the grocery store, they went to his vacation condo, where he packed a few more things, and where she collected her Jeep so she could drive it back to Incline Village. It would have been much more fun to be with Jason for this final portion of the trip, but of course, she needed to bring her car back to the place where she was actually staying. Honestly, she was just glad that she hadn't gotten a parking ticket for leaving it at Jason's condo for so long. He'd assured her it would be fine, but she knew if the condo complex had wanted to get pissy about it, they could've made a stink about a vehicle that wasn't registered to that particular unit being left in its designated parking space.

They made it back to her condo in Incline Village without incident, however, and they unloaded the groceries and took their bags into the suite's master bedroom.

"I'm only using the top two drawers in the dresser," Laurel said hastily, figuring she might as

274 | CHRISTINE POPE

well get past the awkwardness of them sharing a room by focusing on practicalities. "So take whatever else you need. And there's plenty of space in the closet, too."

"Thanks," Jason replied. He went ahead and put his jeans and T-shirts in one drawer, socks and underwear in another. She noticed at once that he'd also brought along a pair of dress trousers and a couple of button-up shirts, as though he wanted to make sure he was prepared just in case they decided to go out to dinner at some point.

Which would be fine. The main point about getting groceries was so they wouldn't be forced to go out to eat all the time. There wasn't any problem with going occasionally, just to break things up.

Laurel realized then that she was thinking of Jason's stay as if it would be of indeterminate duration. True, there didn't seem to be any end point to their mission, so to speak, at the moment, but she had to believe that sooner or later, they'd find the man they were looking for. Sooner, she hoped, since Addie and Jake's wedding was coming up awfully fast, and she knew she couldn't stay here in Tahoe forever, enticing as that prospect might seem.

And once the healer was found, she and Jason would have to go their separate ways. A pang went through her at the thought, and she realized she wouldn't have a problem if they never located the healer, if she and Jason continued to hang out together and explore the wilderness around Lake Tahoe as summer faded into fall.

It's not going to work out that way, she told herself. *If it really starts to look as though we can't find the guy, then we're both going to have to give up and go home. It's not as though the Delmonicos are going to let me camp here indefinitely, even if I didn't have a reason to leave much sooner than that.*

True enough. They'd purposely left things open-ended, since obviously, no one knew exactly how long the search was going to take, but Laurel knew she couldn't impinge on their hospitality by taking up permanent residence in the place.

Well, she wouldn't think about that right now. After all, she'd only been here for four days so far; it felt as though a lot of time had passed, but she doubted the Delmonicos would be kicking her out quite so soon. She'd be long gone before anyone in that clan started to get antsy. And at least she and Jason would be together this entire week.

It was probably wrong to be thinking of the situation in those terms, but she knew her search for the healer had taken a back seat to making sure she spent as much time with Jason Nichols as possible. They'd keep looking, of course, and yet she was just fine with that search extending for an indeterminate number of days. After all, she could always run back to Flagstaff for Jake and Addie's wedding and then return to Tahoe as soon as the big event was over….

They headed back into the kitchen and started to put together the ingredients they needed to make some sandwiches. Only partway into this process, Jason gave a disgusted shake of his head. "I knew we'd forgotten something. We didn't get any mustard or mayo."

Great. Laurel had had a niggling feeling in the back of her mind that she'd left something out, but condiments were the kind of item you had to buy so rarely, they often snuck up on you when it was time to actually purchase some. "There's a little grocery store down on Tahoe Boulevard," she said. "I can run over and see what they have."

"No, I'll do it," Jason replied. "It's probably better if I move my car around from time to time anyway."

"You're sure?" Laurel asked dubiously. "I mean, I know where the store is, and you don't."

"The nav will find it." He bent and kissed her on the cheek, and pushed a stray strand of hair away from her face. "I'll be back in a few."

No point in arguing over something so trivial. "Okay," she said. "I'll work on getting these tomatoes cut up."

"Perfect."

Another kiss, this one on the mouth, and then he was headed out the front door. A happy little glow remained from his kisses, although Laurel could tell he was only being casually affectionate and not trying to actually start anything.

Well, plenty of time for that later.

Her phone buzzed, and the afterglow from his kiss vanished as she pulled the iPhone out of her purse and looked down at the screen. A message from Jeremy, in the singularly cranky way only her cousin could manage in a simple text.

I hope you have a good reason for the radio silence. What's going on up there?

She frowned, even as she sent a silent thank-you to the universe that Jason had stepped out before she received the message. At least this way, she wouldn't have to explain who she was texting with.

I haven't said anything because nothing's happened, she replied. *I wasn't aware I had to give a status report when there wasn't any status to give.*

Another pack of lies. But no way in the world would she try to explain Jason Nichols to her cousin. She could only imagine the intensity of Jeremy's eye rolling if she tried to tell him she'd hooked up with a civilian during her stay in Tahoe.

You still need to check in, Jeremy wrote back. *Anything could be going on up there. You could've fallen down a hill. You could've gotten in a car accident. Being hundreds of miles away is no excuse for being thoughtless.*

Damn, he sounded like her father. Laurel almost wrote back that he needed to ditch the scolding, but she knew doing so would only irritate her cousin that much more. *Sorry,* she said. *I guess I just didn't see the need to bug you with irrelevant details.*

Well, bug me. I hate not knowing that's going on.

Fine, she sent back. *I'm probably going to go check out another part of the Mt. Rose wilderness after lunch, so if I find anything, I'll let you know.*

Let me know even if you don't find anything, he replied. *It can be dangerous hiking by yourself. When you don't check in, we get worried.*

Great, now he was laying on the guilt. Laurel couldn't even get angry with him for that, although she had to wonder if he was doing the guilt trip thing precisely because he knew it was one of the more effective ways of getting her to keep in touch more often.

No worries, she answered. *I'll send you a ping when I get back to the condo.*

You'd better.

I will.

No response, which seemed to indicate Jeremy thought he'd gotten his point across and didn't see the reason for any further conversation. Which was just as well, because a few minutes later, Jason returned with a reusable grocery bag stocked with mustard and mayonnaise and ketchup, and also fun stuff like aioli and fry sauce.

"It's a very well-stocked store for a small place," he said, setting his purchases down on the counter.

"I guess they have a lot of gourmets in Incline Village," Laurel responded as she sliced the tomatoes she'd set out before Jeremy messaged her. From the sideways glance Jason gave those tomatoes, she got the impression that he'd expected her to be further along with the task, but to her relief, he didn't ask any awkward questions.

Soon enough, they had lunch ready, and because it was a beautiful day, with a bright sun rippling on the waters of the lake and not enough breeze to create any chills, they took their food out onto the patio so they could sit in the sunshine.

No alcohol with lunch, which was probably a good thing. They'd had plenty the night before, and Laurel hadn't suggested any, even though she still had the leftover beers from the six-pack she'd bought a few days earlier sitting in the fridge. At the grocery store in South Tahoe, they'd purchased a couple more bottles of wine, but that didn't seem like the kind of thing you drank with deli-style sandwiches.

"I think I could get used to this," Jason remarked, gazing up at the tall pines that ringed the complex. "It's so quiet here."

"It is," Laurel agreed, even as she thought that she, too, could get used to hanging out with Jason and letting the world go by. She added with a grin, "City life getting to you?"

For a moment, he didn't reply, only sat there, sandwich in hand, as his mouth drooped and his brows drew together. "I'm not sure if that's the best way to phrase it," he said. "There's a lot to love about San Francisco. But I have to admit that peace and quiet are sort of in short supply. Even the parks are usually filled with people. It's hard to just…get away, you know?"

She nodded. "I like that about Flagstaff. It's pretty easy to go off to places to be alone. Sure, the really popular trails always have people on them, but overall, it's a tranquil kind of place." A pause, and then she added, "Well, except around the college. The traffic can get pretty crazy there."

"I can imagine."

For a moment, they both fell silent as they munched on their sandwiches, interspersing bites with swallows of water. Then Laurel asked, "Do you want to head out to Mt. Rose this afternoon?"

"I guess we'd better," Jason replied, although he didn't look overly thrilled at the prospect.

She supposed she couldn't blame him. After all, the last time they'd gone up there, he'd gotten hurt pretty badly...not that he would ever know how bad that injury actually had been.

"We'll take the west fork this time," she said. "I'm not sure how far we'll be able to get, since we're starting so late, but I'd feel weird about coming back here today and not trying to look."

"It's fine." Jason took another bite of his sandwich and added, "I suppose I need to get back on the horse, so to speak. And who knows? Maybe we'll get lucky."

Laurel summoned a smile, although she honestly wasn't too thrilled by that prospect. Yes, they needed to find the healer...but not today.

The sort of luck she was hoping for was an entirely different kind.

14

RUNNING OUT FOR THE MISSING CONDIMENTS had given Jason a chance to send a quick text to his mother.

Back in Tahoe. Searching. Will keep you posted.

After that, he put his phone in airplane mode. He guessed Carolyn would try to text him back immediately, and he didn't dare get interrupted while he was with Laurel. Better to let his mother think he was already out in the mountains somewhere, looking for their elusive healer.

It felt good to know that more than a hundred miles separated them, and that Carolyn really couldn't come after him here. His mother was a take-charge sort of person, but even she knew better than to intrude on another clan's territory without a specific invitation. And after the way the Ludlows had joined forces with Joaquin Escobar several years earlier, there wasn't much chance of any of them getting an invitation from the Delmonicos...or from any of the other witch clans, for that matter.

It also felt good to sit on the patio with Laurel and try to act as if he had nothing more pressing on his mind than locating the mysterious healer who'd made Lake Tahoe his haunt, for whatever reason. The bright sunlight found golden high-lights in her dark hair, and although she was wearing sunglasses to protect her eyes from the glare, he could still see the occasional amber glint from behind the dark lenses. Once again, he thought of how she was the most beautiful woman he'd ever met—the most fun, the easiest to talk to.

The most off-limits.

Well, he'd already crossed those limits, and the world hadn't ended. He had to hope there was some way to make this thing work, even if he couldn't quite see his way clear to that particular conclusion yet.

In the meantime, though, he would have to survive another trek into the Mt. Rose wilderness area.

They finished their lunch, cleaned up, and then changed into their hiking clothes. Once again, Laurel drove. Jason was fine with that; he'd spent enough time behind the wheel the past few days, and she was right—her little 4x4 was much better suited to the rough terrain, even if his Range Rover also had four-wheel drive.

Today, the parking area at the trailhead was less crowded, and he had to take that as a good sign. Somehow, he had a feeling the healer wouldn't want to be in an area that was overrun with hikers.

Laurel consulted the .pdf of the trail she'd stored on her phone, then said, "It looks like this part of the trail is what takes you up to the summit of Mt. Rose."

"We're not going all the way there, are we?" Jason asked, feeling vaguely alarmed. He'd brought along his little tank of oxygen, just in case, but he didn't see the need to get crazy.

A quick grin, and she said, "Nope. There's no point in going all the way to the summit. But if we follow the trail, we'll get to a place where it branches off and sort of winds around the base of the mountain. It looks like there are a lot of spots in the area that people use for camping, so maybe that's where we'll be able to find our guy."

She sounded hopeful, but Jason wasn't quite so sanguine. An area that was popular with campers seemed like exactly the sort of place the healer would want to avoid. But since he didn't have any better ideas—and because he didn't care about the success of that day's quest nearly as much as he did simply having the chance to spend the day with Laurel—he nodded. "Sure. It sounds like a good place to start."

One last glance at her phone's screen, and then Laurel stowed it in a pocket of her cargo pants, buttoning it closed so there wasn't the slightest chance of the iPhone sliding out while she was traversing rough terrain. Jason had to marvel at the way she seemed equally at home on the trail or in a sexy dress at a fine restaurant. He hadn't met many women like that before.

Actually, he'd never met anyone like Laurel Wilcox, which was probably the main reason why he wanted to do whatever he could to keep her in his life.

They began to make their way along the trail, which rose more steeply than the one they'd traversed a few days earlier. The sharpness of the incline, along with the thin air, made Jason wonder yet again why people did this sort of thing for fun. True, the scenery was beautiful—alpine meadows, stretches of dark pine forest, with majestic mountain peaks ahead and the shimmering blue of Lake Tahoe behind them—but he still thought there had to be easier ways to look at scenery.

He didn't complain, however. No, he made himself follow Laurel as she led him up the trail, even while he did his best not to pant or show in any way that he was exerting himself. She didn't seem affected at all by the climb, but then, she'd grown up in a place whose altitude was similar to their current surroundings. Being accustomed to those sorts of conditions was her own kind of superpower.

Eventually, though, it seemed as if even she needed to take break, because she paused at a relatively flat spot and pulled a bottle of water out of her pack. "Time for a breather," she said.

"Good idea," Jason responded, glad that he didn't sound too out of breath. He also got out one of the bottles of water he'd brought with him and took a long, welcome swig. "Not a lot of people up here," he added, which was only the truth. They hadn't seen a single soul so far.

"No, there aren't," Laurel said. She now looked vaguely troubled. "I'm kind of surprised by that, to tell the truth. You'd think the rockfall on the other fork of the trail would have pushed everyone over to this part of the wilderness area."

"Maybe they're worried there could be rockfalls here, too, and are hiking in other areas," Jason suggested.

"Maybe." Her expression didn't clear, however. "I checked the USFS website this morning, though, and didn't see any warnings posted. There was one about the problem on the north fork...

which means I'm even more of an idiot for not looking before we went out hiking the other day."

"It's not your fault," he told her. "Or, if anyone's at fault, then I am, too. It's not as though I couldn't have looked at the website before we went. I just never thought of it."

"Do you hike a lot?"

"What do you think?"

Laurel sent him a flash of a grin, the only answer he needed. "Exactly. But I hike all the time, and unless it's a trail I know really, really well, I try my best to check the website for the area to make sure there aren't any warnings or restrictions. It was really stupid of me not to look that first time, especially since I was dealing with a location I'd never hiked before."

He didn't like how she called herself "stupid." At the same time, he got the feeling if he tried to defend her too much, she'd only dig in her heels. "It happens," he said, and figured he might as well leave it at that. "Any ideas on what we're going to do if we don't find anything out here today?"

"Try again tomorrow," Laurel replied. Her smile had slipped a little, but she didn't look too concerned. "I mean, there's a lot of ground to cover here. Which means we should probably keep going."

Jason wasn't overly thrilled by the prospect, but he reminded himself it was the reason why they'd come out here in the first place. So he nodded and swallowed some more water, and then stowed the bottle in his backpack once more.

The going was steep enough that there wasn't much energy left over for conversation. In a way, that was good. When he was hiking in silence, he didn't have to worry about slipping up and saying something which might hint to Laurel that he wasn't quite the civilian he was pretending to be. Once again, he berated himself for not having the guts to tell her the truth about himself. But he was enjoying being with her so much that he didn't dare do anything that might make their time together any shorter than it already promised to be.

After a while, however, the ground leveled out somewhat as they entered a large meadow, not unlike the one they'd encountered during their first aborted hike. This time, though, the campsites were obvious, with their campfire rings and areas of flattened grass.

In fact, at one of the sites closest to the pine forest that ringed the meadow, someone had erected a small yellow tent. Laurel sent him an eager look.

"Do you think…?" she began.

The same thought had entered Jason's mind, even as he'd told himself that the chances of encountering their healer on basically the first try like this were pretty slim.

Even that faint hope was dashed soon enough, because as he and Laurel were gazing at the tent, an older man with gray hair pulled back into a ponytail emerged from the tent, a big black dog at his side.

"Well, that's not our guy," Jason said, trying not to sound too disappointed.

"No," Laurel replied. Her mouth had drooped a bit at his words, but then she lifted her chin. "But maybe he's seen him. We should go and ask."

This didn't seem like the world's greatest idea to Jason. As far as he was concerned, anyone camping out in the woods alone like this probably didn't want to be accosted by a couple of strangers. If their presence initiated some kind of a confrontation, he wasn't sure what they would do. Yes, they were a witch and a warlock, but neither of them had the kind of powers that would be of much use if the stranger turned out to be hostile.

Any warnings he might have uttered would have been of no use, since Laurel had already started walking purposefully toward the campsite. A narrow trail branched off from the one they'd taken here, and Jason followed her doggedly, wondering whether he would be any help at all if the camper made some kind of aggressive movement toward them.

But as Laurel raised a hand in greeting, the man lifted his in reply. From this distance, Jason couldn't make out too much of his expression, but he appeared startled more than anything else by their appearance at the campground.

Up close, the camper didn't look like the sort of person who made a habit out of attacking unwary hikers. His blue eyes were bright against his deeply tanned skin, and he appeared ready to wait while they approached.

"Hi," Laurel said brightly. "We're so sorry to bust in on your campsite like this, but we were hoping you could help us."

"Are you lost?" the man asked. "All you have to do is follow the trail you were on, and it'll take you straight down the mountain. You'll be back at the parking area at the trailhead in about forty minutes or so."

She shook her head, even as she offered him a smile. After all, it hadn't been that crazy an assumption. People probably got lost up here all the time, even when armed with maps and GPS.

"No, we're not lost," she said. "I'm Laurel, and this is my friend Jason. We're looking for someone who's been camping around here. We were hoping you might have seen him."

"Who're you looking for?" the man responded.

A logical enough question. Unfortunately, neither of them had a name to give him.

Without answering directly, Jason said, "He's in his late thirties, with brown hair and brown eyes. Tallish, sort of athletic build."

"Oh, you mean Nathan?"

Jason and Laurel exchanged a glance. Her eyes were wide, shining with excitement behind her sunglasses.

"Yes," Jason replied, hoping the man hadn't noticed the brief pause before he'd responded. "He said we should meet him up here, but we haven't seen him, and our phones don't have any reception."

"Nope, they won't," the camper said, sounding pretty happy at that prospect. Then again, anyone who was camping out here in the middle of nowhere was probably doing so because they wanted to get away from it all, and that included avoiding interruptions from cell phone calls. "You should really carry walkie-talkies out here."

Laurel nodded. "I know. But we figured since we knew where we were going...."

Her words trailed off there, and the man only shook his head. Jason had a feeling the guy thought they were a couple of rubes, which was fine by him. He really didn't care what the man's opinion of them was, as long as he was willing to give up some more valuable information.

"Well, you missed Nathan," the man said. "He was camping up here until a day or so ago. But he packed up and moved on."

"Did he say where he was going?" Jason asked. That question had probably sounded a little too desperate, but too late now.

The man shrugged. "Not really. You know how he is. Tends to talk in riddles, or maybe he does that just because he doesn't see the point in letting the world know all his business. He said something about heading to the next place that needed him, but he didn't give me any real details."

The next place…or the next person who needed him? MaryJo had made it sound as though this healer—Nathan, if that really was his name—somehow knew exactly when and where someone would be hurt and would require help, so if he'd seen in advance where the next accident would occur, then it made sense that he would have hurried off to be there when needed.

Once again, Jason had to wonder exactly how many powers the man possessed. He knew he'd never heard of anyone being both a seer and a healer at the same time. Those were both powerful gifts, and obviously made a potent combination.

"Oh, that's just like Nathan," Laurel said, sounding so chirpy that Jason knew she was overcompensating to hide her disappointment. "But he really didn't give any details at all?"

"Not really," the man replied. "Except he said he didn't think he'd have to go far." A shrug, and he bent to place a fond pat on the head of the big dog who'd sat patiently next to him during this entire exchange. Maybe the animal was as much a guard dog as he was a companion, but he clearly didn't view either Jason or Laurel as much of a threat. "Sorry I can't tell you more than that."

"It's all right," Jason said. "We're kind of used to Nathan living in his own world. And he has a few other favorite camping spots in the area, so we'll check there next."

"Tomorrow, maybe," the man offered as he glanced up at the sky. The sun was dropping toward the west, although dusk wouldn't arrive for a few more hours. "You only have enough time to get down the mountain and to the parking area before it gets too dark to be wandering around up here."

Laurel looked as though she wanted to protest…but then defeat flickered in her expression, as if she knew they shouldn't be taking those sorts of chances. "Yes, tomorrow," she repeated. She glanced over at Jason, and he nodded. Frankly, he was more than happy to regroup and try again the next day. Afternoons lingered for quite a while at that time of year, but there wasn't much point in pressing their luck.

"Thanks for your help," he said. "And if Nathan does come by for some reason, let him know we were looking for him."

"Sure will," the man responded. "But now it's time to take Ringo for his afternoon constitutional. You have a good one."

He nodded at both of them and then headed off across the meadow, the dog trotting alongside him without any need for a leash. Well, there probably wasn't much point in bringing a dog up to a place like this if you couldn't let it run free.

In silence, Jason and Laurel headed back to the main trail. They walked for a few more minutes without saying anything, and then she finally spoke.

"Well, at least we have a name."

Only a first name, and a pretty common one at that, Jason thought, but he didn't bother to point out those depressing truths. She probably knew them just as well as he did.

"Yes," he allowed. "And it also sounds as if Nathan plans to stick around Lake Tahoe, even if he's taken off for someplace other than the Mt. Rose wilderness area."

"I hope so," Laurel said. "I mean, I know there are miles and miles of trails around here, and plenty of places he could be holed up, but at least it's not as if we have to start searching the entire state for him."

"True."

They walked in silence for a bit more. Although Laurel's chin was still up, he could tell she wasn't too thrilled by this latest setback.

Hoping to cheer her up, Jason said, "Well, it'll feel nice to get back and have a grilled steak dinner at least. That bottle of cab we bought should be perfect."

She glanced up at him, her eyes an amber flicker behind the Ray-Bans. "Trying to cheer me up?"

"Yes," he said honestly. "Besides, she who eats a steak dinner lives to fight another day, right?"

"That's totally not that saying."

"It's close enough."

An unwilling grin pulled at her lips, and she came closer and slid her hand into his. It was the first time since they'd started on this hike that she'd initiated any kind of physical contact, and a funny little flush of warmth went through him. Yes, they'd gotten to a part of the trail that wasn't quite so steep, and therefore they didn't need both their hands to keep their balance, but it still felt good to have her fingers twined with his, warm and slender and strong.

No, it felt better than good. It felt *right*.

The sun was already slipping behind the

western hills as Laurel backed out of their spot at the trailhead and pointed her little Jeep toward Incline Village. Jason had forgotten that dusk could come earlier in mountainous country like this, and found himself glad of the stranger's warning that they needed to get back to their vehicle and try again the next day. He definitely didn't like the idea of tromping around in the wilderness with no sun to guide them.

Dusk had just begun to settle on the lake when they parked at the condo complex and headed toward the unit Laurel was renting. After washing up, the two of them went into the kitchen and started getting out the various bits and pieces of their dinner—a pair of lush-looking T-bone steaks, one of those ready-seasoned packets of baby potatoes that only needed to be put in the microwave, a bagged Caesar salad.

"I'll go ahead and set the table while you're putting those on the grill," she said.

"Sounds good."

She smiled at him as he let himself out onto the patio, then set the plate holding the steaks down on the table there so he could fire up the grill. It was a newish propane model, and appeared to have been cleaned off in preparation for Laurel's stay at the condo, so all Jason had to do was wait a minute for it to heat up before he slapped the steaks down on the grill.

The air temperature here was noticeably warmer than it had been up on the mountainside, and yet the breeze coming off the lake was cool enough that he thought they'd probably eat inside, even though the patio looked inviting, with its wrought iron furniture and carefully tended flowers blooming in pots.

Laurel opened the screen door and poked her head outside. "How's it going?"

"Fine," he replied. "I was thinking it might be a little cool for an *al fresco* dinner, though. What do you think?"

She stepped out on the patio and stood there for a moment or two, obviously trying to gauge the comfort level of the early evening air. Jason wondered if she would declare it just fine—after all, she was used to much colder temperatures than he was—but after that brief pause, she said, "I think you're right. I never saw the point in shivering through dinner just to prove you were using your patio. I'll set the table in here. When do you think the steaks will be ready?"

He glanced over at the grill, where their dinner was just beginning to sizzle. "Probably another fifteen minutes or so. Those steaks are pretty thick."

"Got it."

A brilliant flash of a smile, and she headed back inside. While Jason maybe would have liked for her to stay and talk with him while the meat was grilling, he had to admit to himself that there was something oddly comforting about the thought of her just inside, as well as the mental image of her busying herself with setting the table and getting the other odds and ends ready for their dinner. It felt almost…domestic.

If asked, Jason would have said that he really didn't care about tying himself to someone, of having the sort of cozy suburban life that most witches and warlocks eventually settled into. Right then, however, he thought he might be able to picture such an existence with Laurel…and he also thought he would be very happy with that kind of life.

A pang went through him. He could conjure whatever fantasies he wanted, but he doubted any of them would survive her finding out who he really was. No, about all he could do was try his best to enjoy the time he was spending with her now…even while he had to admit that they weren't accomplishing a hell of a lot.

Well, besides getting to know one another better.

He forced his attention back to the grill, where the steaks needed to be flipped. Honestly, he hadn't done much outdoor cooking in his life, although his cousin Leo had tried to show him the basics a few summers ago, declaring that every man needed to know how to lay down a neat cross-hatch of char on a steak.

Leo would probably shake his head at Jason's efforts, but that was okay. He sort of doubted Laurel cared whether a steak was picture perfect as long as it tasted good. That was another thing he liked about her—she was refreshingly down to earth.

A light came to life under the eaves, and he glanced toward the sliding glass window to see her giving him a smile and a thumbs-up as she passed by, plates in hand. It actually was getting dark enough that he needed the extra illumination, and he waved back, smiling as well.

How like Laurel to do something so casually thoughtful. No need to ask—she just noticed that there probably wasn't enough light for him to work by, and had taken care of it.

He really didn't deserve someone like her.

But since he didn't feel like getting into self-recriminations right then, he did his best to push the thought aside as he tended to the steaks. Soon enough, they were ready, and he used the tongs to lift them from the grill and put them on their plate, then headed back inside and closed the sliding door behind him.

The dining area was just past the small but well-appointed kitchen. The square table there had two place settings across from each other, and a trio of candles in bronze holders flickered on the tabletop, flames moving gently in the draft from an open window.

"I hope you don't think it's too much," Laurel said. She was standing by the table, bottle of cabernet in hand. "But they already had the candles on the table, and I found a lighter in the kitchen when I was getting the utensils out—"

"It looks great," he cut in, but gently. He definitely didn't want her to give herself grief over trying to make their dinner a romantic one. "I always was a sucker for candles."

Her amber eyes lit up. "Me, too. My friends always tease me about running up the national debt whenever Bath & Body Works has a sale on their three-wick candles, but I do love them."

"Good to know." Jason put down the plate with their steaks, noting that a bowl of salad and another of potatoes already waited on the tabletop. "Do you want me to open that?"

"Yes, please." She handed him the bottle of wine and a waiter-style corkscrew. "I'm not very good with these things. I like the jumping-jack kind."

Well, those were easier to work with, although the wine snobs in the Ludlow family probably would have sneered at such an admission. "I think I can manage."

Because the bottle they'd bought wasn't old

enough that its cork had had time to get compromised, the cork came out easily enough. Jason poured a bit into each of the glasses Laurel had set out, and then they both sat down.

He lifted his glass. "To finding Nathan."

"To finding Nathan," she echoed, although some of the cheer seemed to leave her expression. "Wherever the hell he is."

Jason couldn't help but grin at her comment. "He isn't making this easy, that's for sure. But I'm sure we'll track him down."

In actuality, he wasn't sure at all, but he didn't see the point in telling Laurel that. If he made it sound as if the situation was hopeless, then she might give up and go back to Flagstaff. Selfishly, he wanted to keep her hopes alive for as long as possible.

"I admire your optimism," she replied, but a corner of her mouth had lifted, and a glint showed in her amber eyes, telling Jason that she wasn't quite as cynical as she pretended to be.

"It doesn't take any more energy to be optimistic than the opposite," he told her. "So, that's what I choose to be."

"Words to live by."

They both drank some wine. It was better than he'd expected, and he gave an approving nod. Laurel seemed similarly impressed, although she didn't say anything, only picked up her steak knife and cut into the T-bone in front of her.

"Is it okay?" he asked. "I tried to go for medium rare, since you didn't say how you wanted your steak cooked."

"It's perfect," she said. "Medium-rare steak is my favorite."

Relieved, he took a bite of his own steak. Yes, that was a medium-rare T-bone even his cousin Leo should approve of, despite the char marks maybe not being as perfect as they could be.

The conversation afterward was prosaic enough, about their favorite places to get steak in their respective hometowns, but Jason was glad of that. He was glad of every moment with Laurel Wilcox when he could forget what he was hiding from her and simply interact with her as a human being.

Toward the end of the meal, she did bring up the elusive Nathan, but only to say that in the morning, they could look over some maps of the area and see if they had any flashes of intuition as to where he might have headed.

"Of course, I suppose if he's really meant to cross paths with us, then it doesn't matter what we plan," she said as she took the final sip of wine from her glass and then set it down. "He'll just naturally appear."

"That seems like kind of a fatalistic way of

looking at the situation," Jason replied, and she shot him a rueful smile.

"Maybe it's my way of trying to avoid disappointment. I mean, if something is meant to be, it'll happen no matter what either of us does."

Was this meant to happen? he wondered. *Was it inevitable that I would meet Laurel Wilcox, since she's clearly the woman I'm supposed to be with?*

He wanted to think so. If fate had guided them to be together, then that had to mean they would somehow find their way to a happy ending, even if he couldn't quite figure out how that implausible outcome might occur.

"I guess we'll find out sooner or later," he said lightly, figuring it was probably better to leave the matter there for the moment.

Laurel seemed inclined to agree, because she nodded, then pushed her plate away and set her napkin down next to it, seeming to signal that she was done with her meal. Jason had already demolished pretty much every speck of meat on his own T-bone, so he ate the remaining potato on his plate and rose from his seat, even as he reached for Laurel's dish.

"You don't have to do that," she said.

"No biggie," he responded. "I'm pretty sure I can manage putting a couple of plates in a dishwasher."

She chuckled, then got up as well. "Okay, you get the plates and glasses, and I'll get the serving stuff."

"Deal."

They cleared the table, and he stowed the dirty plates and glasses and utensils in the dishwasher. When he was done, he turned to see her watching him, expression serious.

"What is it?" he asked.

"Nothing," she answered. "It's just…."

The words trailed off, and she made an odd, almost futile gesture with one hand, as though she knew what she wanted to say but wasn't sure she should say it.

"Just what?" Jason prompted.

"Just that I think I'm liking this too much," she said after a pause. "Like…it feels too natural, if you know what I mean."

He did, actually, because he'd been thinking much the same thing while he was out on the patio, grilling their steaks. Because he wasn't sure how much he wanted to reveal, however, he only nodded, then stepped toward her and took her by the hands. Her fingers were warm and smooth, and tightened on his.

That definitely felt like a signal.

No hesitation. Jason pulled her toward him and kissed her, reveling in the fullness of her lips and the tang of wine on her tongue. She pressed against him, and he wrapped his arms around her, wanting to savor the moment, since he had no idea how many more moments like this they would be able to share.

Neither of them said anything. They didn't have to. In the next moment, she was leading him out of the kitchen and through the living room, and down the short hallway that led to the ground-floor master bedroom. They went inside, still in silence. Jason got a brief impression of cool tones of pale gray and dark lilac—he hadn't really looked around when he'd been in here earlier to unpack—but then all his attention was drawn to Laurel, who'd already slipped off her T-shirt and begun to undo the cargo pants she wore.

That seemed like a clear enough signal. He took off his clothes as well, and a minute later, they fell onto the bed, limbs entwined around one another as they touched and tasted and caressed.

It seemed even better than the first time they'd been together, maybe because there was already some familiarity, some knowledge of what the other person preferred. She reached a climax almost as quickly as before, body warm and lush beneath him.

Had he ever felt this close to a woman?

He doubted it. As she snuggled into his arms afterward, he held her almost fiercely, willing the moment of perfect togetherness to last as long as possible.

Problem was, he knew it couldn't last forever.

And he didn't know what he was supposed to do about that.

15

THEY SHARED A SHOWER THE NEXT MORNING. Laurel had made the suggestion, a little surprised at her own boldness. But it was something she'd always wanted to do, and Jason hadn't demurred. No, he'd been ready to climb into the large, glass-enclosed space and let the warm water sluice over both of them, washing away the scent of the previous night's lovemaking...but not the sensation of closeness it had created.

Something did feel different this morning, although she couldn't exactly put her finger on what it was, or why. Maybe it was only that they'd shared a second night together, and so were feeling as if they were settling down into a routine.

No, that wasn't it. Last night had definitely been anything but routine.

A warmth filled her as she remembered the way he'd held her, had caressed her, had made her come over and over until she pretty much passed out from exhaustion. A good night's sleep had taken care of her weariness, though, and now she felt fired up and ready to go. This might not be the day they located the mysterious Nathan, but it would be another day spent with Jason, and that was good enough for her.

They went out for breakfast, since they'd made the mistake of not buying much at the store that would work for a morning meal, unless they both wanted toast. Since a few slices of bread didn't seem quite enough to keep them going on an all-day hike, they'd agreed that it would be better to grab something on their way back to the mountain.

The place was busy, which meant they didn't have much of a chance to discuss their mission. In a way, though, Laurel was just fine with that. She wanted to focus on the food, and revel in Jason's presence. No, it wasn't as though they could really talk about what had happened between them the night before, either, but again, that was all right. Sometimes it was better not to analyze things too deeply. For the moment, she thought it was just fine to look across the table and meet those dark eyes of his—not dark, dark like some of the Wilcox men, but a warm, chocolate-y brown—and to commit every detail of his face to memory.

Because as much as she didn't want to think about the future, she knew that sooner rather than later, his face would probably be nothing more than a memory.

Well, no reason to torture herself right now, though. They knew where they were going—a trail near Galena Creek—and, while Laurel had no reason to believe they'd have any more luck there than they had in the Mt. Rose wilderness, at least it was something they could focus on.

"…need anything else?" Jason asked, and she blinked at him.

"Sorry," she said. "I guess I was zoning out there. What were you saying?"

Instead of being annoyed with her, the way some of the civilian guys she'd dated might have been, he only looked amused, a twinkle glinting in his eyes. "What's the matter? Didn't get enough sleep last night?"

"Not really," she admitted, and even though she did her best to sound severe, she knew she'd spoiled the impression by letting a corner of her mouth quirk into something that wasn't quite a smile. "And I think we all know whose fault that is."

"Oh, I'd say there were a couple of guilty parties involved."

Since she couldn't argue that point without being a total liar, she conceded the argument with a lift of her shoulders, then reached for her mug so she could take a final swallow of coffee. They'd fallen asleep in each other's arms, but when she'd awakened a few hours later, she hadn't rolled over and quietly gone back to sleep, had instead reached out to him so they could make love again. In the past, she'd never thought of herself as being quite so insatiable. Now, though, she couldn't seem to get enough of Jason Nichols.

"Anyway," he went on, "I was just asking if there was anything else we needed to grab while we're here in town before we head out."

She considered his comment, then shook her head. "No, I think we're good. We've got plenty of water, and I packed some Kind bars in case we get the munchies. Although I doubt that's going to happen soon after this kind of breakfast."

Because they'd both known they were going to be tromping around on some rough trails for the next few hours, they'd ordered big breakfasts—a Denver omelet with hash browns and fruit on the side for Jason, huevos rancheros with tortillas and beans for her. At the moment, the food making her feel a little sluggish, and she hoped she'd be past the heavy digesting by the time they actually hit the trail.

"Yeah, I don't see any munchies in my near

future," Jason agreed. "I think I ate my weight in hash browns. But if you're ready—"

She nodded, and he got out his wallet and dropped three twenty-dollar bills on the table. Their breakfast had been only a little more than half that, and so he was leaving their waitress a heck of a tip.

But then, as he'd pointed out when he bought the groceries the day before, he could afford it.

They got up from their table and headed out to the car, and within a few minutes, Incline Village was behind them and they were ascending into the pine forests that encircled Lake Tahoe. Not for the first time, Laurel wished she really was here on vacation so she could spend the day doing touristy stuff with Jason—going on a glass-bottom boat cruise, or exploring Emerald Bay State Park…visiting one of the casinos in Stateline at night for dinner and a show.

But she wasn't on vacation. She was supposed to be locating Nathan, the healer—if that really was his name—not playing footsie with a hot civilian she'd picked up in town.

Describing Jason that way did him a disservice, though. He was so much more than just a civilian; he was someone she could spend a whole day with and never get bored, someone who seemed to fit all her quirks and odd angles. In the past, she'd wondered how a witch or a warlock could even find something appealing enough in a nonmagical person to want to spend the rest of their lives with them, but now she was starting to understand. It wasn't someone's magical gifts that made them attractive. No, it was the way their mind and heart and soul meshed with yours. And she was meshing with Jason in a way she'd really never thought possible.

He'd been sitting quietly in the passenger seat, watching the ponderosa pine forests pass by outside the car windows, but he spoke now. "Does your grandmother know?"

Laurel blinked. "Does my grandmother know what?"

"Know that you're looking for a supposedly magical healer to help her."

Damn. Not for the first time, she silently cursed that particular lie, even though she knew she'd needed to give him some sort of explanation as to why she was looking for the mysterious man. "No," she replied, glad that her voice sounded even, that she hadn't hesitated for too long before responding. "I didn't want to get her hopes up in case this all came to nothing."

Jason reached over and touched her hand, gave her fingers a reassuring squeeze. Right then, Laurel hated herself for keeping the truth from him. Here he was being all sweet and understanding, and there was no reason for him to be that way, not when she kept telling him lie after lie.

"You're going to have a great surprise for her after we find Nathan," he said.

"If he can even help," Laurel responded. "I'm a little worried after some of the stuff MaryJo said."

"She might not have understood what he was trying to tell her," Jason said reasonably. "She was stressed out and in pain, and that guy we met yesterday up in the Mt. Rose wilderness made it sound as if Nathan doesn't always try too hard to be clear."

Damn it, there he went, being all nice again. A sour taste rose in the back of her throat...the taste of guilt.

Or maybe it was just too many refried beans.

"I hope so," Laurel replied, trying to keep her tone light. "It would really be awful to finally track him down, only to find out he can't do anything to help."

And there, she realized, was just another part of the problem. She would have to give this Nathan the lie about her grandmother, but then do her best to find a way to speak to him privately without Jason around so she could tell him the truth. If he really was a warlock, he'd be able to sense right away that she was another of his kind...but he'd also be able to tell that Jason was a

316 | CHRISTINE POPE

civilian, and so would—she hoped—understand that he couldn't say anything too revealing in front of him, and would also want an opportunity for private conversation.

So much could go wrong. For just a second, Laurel wished she hadn't insisted so hard that she be the one to go on this mission, and to do it alone. If Jake were around, he'd probably have some good advice to help her find a way out of her current conundrum.

But if she'd traveled here with Jake, then she probably would never have met Jason. It was a pretty good bet that he wouldn't have approached her if she'd been accompanied by a big, good-looking guy. After all, there was no way he could have known that the good-looking guy in question happened to be her cousin.

"It sounds as though Nathan can do a lot," Jason said. Nothing in his tone or expression appeared to have changed very much, so it didn't seem as if he'd noticed anything more than the ordinary worry her previous comment had revealed. "There's no point in borrowing trouble."

That was a favorite expression of her mother's, and one Laurel tried to live by. Problem was, her current situation could dish up a whole heap of trouble if she didn't handle things right.

A sign coming up ahead pointed toward the turn-off for the hiking trail they'd planned to explore. It wasn't particularly scenic compared to a lot of the other trails that wound around Lake Tahoe, but it did have the benefit of being off the beaten path—no pun intended—and one that didn't attract as many hikers as some of the showier routes.

And even if it didn't offer any spectacular vistas, it still cut through a forest that was beautiful in its own right. Having grown up in Flagstaff's ponderosa woods, Laurel found something deeply soothing about the tall trees, about the mournful sigh of the wind as it moved over their slender needles.

Once again, she'd downloaded a .pdf of the trail to her phone. She got the iPhone out of her purse after she parked the car, then slid the phone into a pocket and snapped it shut. Looking up, she saw Jason unfastening his seatbelt and realized there was no reason to ask him if he was ready.

They got out of the car and walked over to the trailhead. Unlike the Mt. Rose wilderness trail, which had offered several different forks in the road, this one was pretty straightforward. It wound through the forest and ended up in an alpine meadow, another place where camping was permitted. If they couldn't find their healer somewhere along this trail, they wouldn't have to second-guess themselves over the route they'd taken. Of course, they'd also be back to square one and have to start all over again with a different trail, but at least they wouldn't have as much guesswork to deal with.

Jason looked at the rough chart of the trail on the sign next to the trailhead and ran a hand through his hair. He'd woken up with some serious bedhead and hadn't done much with it, but Laurel thought the tousled look only made him that much sexier.

"Seems pretty basic," he commented.

"It is," she agreed. "So here's hoping our healer is also feeling basic today."

He grinned. "Seems like a funny thing to hope for, but I get it."

They began to make their way up the trail. The going was rough in spots, but nothing that either of them couldn't handle. In fact, because the path wasn't as rocky as the trails they'd explored in the Mt. Rose wilderness, many more wildflowers bloomed here—deep blue gentians, and bright red Indian paintbrush, along with black-eyed Susans and others Laurel couldn't even identify.

"Do any of these flowers have medicinal uses?" Jason asked out of the blue, and she blinked at him.

"I don't know. Why?"

"Because I was just thinking that if they did, maybe the healer would be out here gathering them. Maybe this is exactly the kind of place he'd be headed."

If they were talking about a holistic healer, someone who created potions and tinctures to cure his patients, then that would have been a good theory. However, it sounded as though this Nathan cured people by laying on hands, the same way witchy healers had treated their patients for generations.

Unfortunately, Laurel couldn't offer that particular rebuttal without giving away information she needed to conceal. Trying to sound enthusiastic, she replied, "That's a good idea. It would be really great to know we were on the right track."

Jason sent her an encouraging smile…but then his expression sobered. "Although no one who was treated by our guy seems to have been given any kind of medicine. He just touched them and healed them that way."

"True," Laurel said, a little relieved he'd come to that same conclusion himself, even if that particular conclusion might be leaving out some fairly large puzzle pieces. "But then, he was treating physical injuries—bone breaks and bruises and sprains. He might still need to make medicine for stuff like cancer and other diseases."

"Makes sense." Jason paused and pulled a bottle of water out of his backpack, and so she figured she might as well do the same. Despite stopping for breakfast, they'd made decent time, and it had only been a little past nine-thirty when they parked at the trailhead. They certainly had enough time to take a break and have some water. He glanced away from her and up along the trail, which wound through the forest for another fifty yards or so before jogging to the left and disappearing into the trees. "How far is it to the end of the trail?"

"A little over four miles."

Which was no big deal to her, although she could tell he was less than thrilled by her reply. An outdoorsy kind of guy, he was not.

It was probably the only dissonance between them. But even though Laurel enjoyed hiking and spent a good chunk of her downtime outdoors, she'd never put being outdoorsy at the top of her list when it came to desirable traits in a romantic partner. While she would have liked a hiking buddy, she thought it much more important that she be with someone who made her feel like herself, like she didn't have anything to prove.

She definitely felt that way around Jason... even with having to conceal a large portion of who she really was.

He didn't comment, only took another swallow of water before replacing the bottle in his pack. Then he shifted the pack to settle more comfortably on his shoulders and said, "Ready?"

Laurel nodded and resumed their uphill trek. It wasn't too bad an incline, just enough for her to feel it a bit in her calf muscles. They followed the jog in the trail that took them toward the west briefly before it resumed its more northerly direction, all the while climbing gently, heading toward the meadow that was their destination.

And if the healer wasn't there, well, they'd take a break and eat their Kind bars, drink some more water, and head back to Incline Village. It would probably be early enough in the day that they could go exploring along the shoreline of the lake, or maybe take a drive in Jason's plush Range Rover, head over to Paradise Bay and wander there for a bit. Afterward, they might have another dinner at the condo, or even go out if they didn't feel like making burgers or whatever. There was that tapas restaurant she'd passed several times while driving around. It looked interesting, and would definitely be a change of pace from the sort of stuff she'd been eating lately. And if Jason wasn't interested in that, they could maybe just order pizza and watch movies and snuggle on the couch.

Or maybe—

She actually heard the *crack* of her ankle before she saw the rock-strewn hole in the trails. Pain flared a moment later, and she let out a gasp, just before she stumbled and fell. Instinct kicked in, and she put out her hands to break the fall. Pebbles stung her palms. She sucked in a hiss as she rolled and came to rest in something resembling a sitting position.

Jason was there at once, kneeling next to her, face tight with worry. "Laurel? Are you okay?"

Somehow, she managed to blink. Actually, blinking was a good thing, since it flicked away some of the tears of pain that had gathered in her eyes. "I'm fine," she said, another lie. Her ankle was already a red-hot ball of agony, and she knew she must have broken it, probably in several places. She forced herself to add, "I mean, I think my ankle is trashed. But the rest of me is okay, except for some scrapes on my hands."

"Do you want me to take a look?" he asked. "I don't know much about first aid, but—"

The mere thought of clumsy, unpracticed hands fumbling with her ankle made Laurel clench her teeth. "No," she said. Her voice sounded strange to her, high and tight with the effort to keep herself from moaning in pain. "I think it's probably better to leave it as it is. At least right now my hiking boot is sort of holding things in place."

"It's broken?" Jason went pale under his tan, and he gave a quick, worried glance around them. What he was looking for, Laurel didn't know.

They hadn't seen a single soul on their hike today. Without waiting for her to reply, he reached in his pocket and pulled out his phone, then swore. "No signal."

Of course there wasn't. They were out in the middle of nowhere, a long way from line of sight of any cell towers in the area. She let out a breath and said, "You'll have to hike back down to the car and drive to the ranger station. I saw a sign for one as we were driving in. I think it's probably about five miles from here." Even as she spoke, she fumbled with the snap on her pants pocket. Once it was undone, she reached inside and got out the fob for her Jeep and extended it toward him.

"I can't just leave you here—" Jason began, not making a single motion toward the key fob, and Laurel shook her head.

"Well, I can't walk, so we don't have a lot of options. It's okay—I'm sure I'll be fine." She was actually proud of herself for sounding so calm. Yes, her voice was just about as clenched as the rest of her body, but she wasn't crying, even though her ankle hurt worse than anything she'd ever experienced. The only thing that even came close was the first stabbing pains of her appendix starting to fail on her when she was fourteen, but Eleanor had come along and used her gift to keep the annoying organ from causing any more trouble. If only the Wilcox clan healer was here now!

But she wasn't, and one of the quirks of a healer's power was that she couldn't use it on herself. Otherwise, Laurel would have wrapped her hands around her ankle, mended the broken bones, and then told Jason she'd only wrenched the damn thing.

"There could be bears," he said, still kneeling next to her. His brows were drawn tightly together, etching a line in the otherwise smooth, tanned skin. "Or mountain lions. Or—"

"True," she responded. "But we've been making enough noise that I'm pretty sure any wild animals in the vicinity have found better things to do elsewhere. Going for help is our only real option here."

He hesitated, handsome face still etched with worry. Then his mouth compressed, and he got up, brushing at the dirt-smudged knees of his cargo pants. "If you're sure—"

"I'm sure," she cut in. Actually, she didn't know if she was…the thought of being left here alone with a broken ankle scared her more than she wanted to admit…but she also knew they couldn't wait in the hope that someone might eventually come along the trail. Already she was starting to feel a little lightheaded from the pain, her forehead beading with cold sweat.

Shock setting in, which meant they really couldn't waste any more time.

Jason gave a single nod, took the key fob from her, and then said, "I'll be as fast as I can," before he placed a reassuring kiss on her cheek.

Even as he turned to start walking down the path, however, dead leaves crackled in the wild forest that surrounded them. From a ways further down the trail and off to one side, the young trees parted, and a tall man with shaggily cut brown hair emerged. He wore a Hard Rock Casino T-shirt and camo pants and hiking boots, and had a sturdy walking stick in one sun-browned hand.

Laurel blinked at the apparition. Was it possible?

No, she couldn't possibly be that lucky. She wasn't her cousin Lucas, after all.

"Hi, there," the man said, his voice friendly and warm, like sunlight coming through the leaves. "It looks like you could use some help."

16

JASON WAS PRETTY SURE THE LOOK OF stupefaction on Laurel's features was mirrored on his own face. "N-Nathan?" he blurted.

The stranger grinned. He had several days' worth of stubble going on, so the contrast made his teeth flash that much whiter. "You've been talking to Hank, haven't you?"

"Is Hank the guy camping with the dog up in the Mt. Rose wilderness?"

"The same," Nathan replied. His grin disappeared as he glanced down at Laurel. Voice gentle, he said, "Is it okay if I take a look?"

"If you're going to fix me up the same way you fixed up MaryJo Gaffney, absolutely," Laurel said. Her voice was still strained, but she somehow managed to make her mouth curve in a ghost of a smile.

"You've been doing your research, I see," Nathan said. He knelt down next to her, and deftly undid the laces of her hiking boot, then pulled off the thick sock she wore underneath.

Jason couldn't help wincing in sympathy at the sight of Laurel's ankle. It had already swollen a good bit, and the flesh was turning angry red and purple. There was also a frightening knob on the inner side, probably where the bone had snapped.

Despite the stories he'd heard from MaryJo and Alison Crewe, Jason really didn't see how such an injury could be healed outside a hospital's emergency room.

"Well, that's a nasty one," Nathan commented, although his tone was still mellow and he didn't look particularly perturbed by Laurel's injury. "It's going to hurt a bit when I touch your ankle, but I promise the pain won't last long."

"It's fine," she said. "Whatever you need to do."

After delivering that statement, however, her teeth clamped down on her lower lip, as if she wasn't sure she'd be able to hold back a groan and was trying to be proactive about preventing any sounds of pain from slipping out.

Nathan didn't respond, only shut his eyes for a moment. Was he somehow reaching out with his strange talent, mentally probing the injured ankle and doing his best to discover exactly where the break—or breaks—were located?

Maybe. Jason still didn't know much about how a healer's gift worked. For all he knew, the process differed from person to person.

Then Nathan reached out and wrapped his hands around Laurel's ankle, his tanned fingers a few shades darker than her skin, even though she also had a light summer tan. Watching this, Jason couldn't quite prevent a strange flicker of jealousy from moving through him, even though he knew there was absolutely nothing sexual about the way Nathan was touching her.

Or maybe it was partly frustration at not being able to help the woman he loved, at the way he had to stand off to the side and watch as someone else worked.

The moment didn't last very long, however, because just a few seconds later, Nathan lifted his hands from Laurel's ankle and sent her a sunny smile.

"How does that feel?"

Expression wondering, she ran her hand over her skin. The bruises and swelling were gone, along with the scary little knot to one side of the joint. It was as if the injury had never happened— in appearance, anyway.

"It's fine," she said. Then she shook her head.

"No, I mean it's great. It's perfect. The break is healed. How did you do it?"

For a few seconds, Nathan only regarded her in silence, his head tilted to one side as he appeared to contemplate her question. "I think you know that just as well as I do, Laurel Wilcox."

Her amber eyes flared wide with surprise. "How—?"

"Because we're the same, aren't we?" he broke in, but gently. Without waiting for her to reply, he extended a hand. She took it and let him pull her to her feet. "Both healers, both people born with a particular talent."

"I—I don't know what you're talking about," she stammered. Just the briefest guilty glance in Jason's direction before she went on, "I mean, I'm not—"

"Oh, yes, you are," Nathan said. A pause, and then the man glanced over at Jason, his gaze steady.

Oh, shit, Jason thought.

Because what he'd seen in the other man's eyes was knowledge—knowledge of who and what Jason was, even though there was no way in the world he should have been able to detect such a thing. How many different talents did the guy have, anyway?

Jason's gut clenched, and spiky tremors of panic flooded through his limbs. He knew he needed to say something, needed to cut in and steer the conversation in a different direction before he was hopelessly exposed. Problem was, he had no idea what those magic words were supposed to be.

"Just as your friend here is as well," Nathan continued. "Not with your exact gift, but one of your kind."

Laurel's eyes widened even further. "Jason, what is he talking about?"

"I—"

Nathan gave a nod of understanding, although the pleasant expression he wore didn't budge an inch. "Ah, I see. You were hiding this from her."

Voice strangled, Jason managed to grind out, "I wasn't hiding anything."

But the damage was done. He could tell from Laurel's stricken expression that she believed what the healer had said, was now beginning to realize that everything Jason had ever told her was a lie. Maybe he should be offended that she was willing to believe an utter stranger over the man she'd spent the last few days with, but there was some quality about Nathan that was oddly confidence-inspiring.

Besides, he'd just healed her ankle. He'd appeared when he was needed, just as he had told Hank…and told MaryJo Gaffney as well. How much more evidence did anyone need to know the healer was on the up and up?

"Is it true, Jason?" she demanded, brows drawn together into a fearsome frown. "You're a warlock?"

Desperate, Jason responded, "I can explain—"

"Yes or no," she cut in. "Are you?"

"Yes," he said simply.

"You two need to talk," Nathan said. He touched Laurel on the arm. "I'd be easy on that ankle for the next day or so, but you shouldn't have a problem getting down the trail as long as you don't push it. Take care of yourself."

He moved away from them, heading back into the forest. Laurel stared after him for a moment, then burst out, "Wait!"

Not even a turn, just the briefest shift of his glance in her direction. "You're healed, Laurel," Nathan said. "You don't have any further need of me."

"But I came here to find you!"

A smile. "Which you did. I can tell your cause is pure, but I have no wish to be catalogued by the Wilcox clan. I walked away from all the clans many years ago."

"Which one are you from, though?" she asked desperately. "Please just tell me that much!"

All she got in response was another smile, and then Nathan disappeared into the trees.

Deprived of her quarry, Laurel rounded on Jason. "You lied to me!"

"So did you," he countered, even though he knew his argument was a weak one.

"Because I thought you were a civilian!" she flared, amber eyes flashing with inner fire. Right then, she looked like some kind of avenging goddess, despite her smudged T-shirt and cargo pants. "Is that your talent? Hiding your magical nature?"

Because the gig was up, he didn't see the point in hiding any longer. "One of them," he admitted, and released the illusion he'd been holding for so long, the one that hid his dark blond hair and blue-gray eyes.

Laurel stared at him for a long moment, chest heaving with angry breaths as she took in his altered appearance. "So, which clan *are* you from?"

The one thing he *really* didn't want to tell her. "What does it matter?"

"It matters to me," she replied. She sounded a little calmer now, but the fire in her eyes told him she was still as angry as ever.

He knew he shouldn't answer. Whatever had begun to grow between them was now probably gone forever, and so there didn't seem to be much point in trying to mollify her.

Only…he was so very tired of lying.

"The Ludlows," he said, not bothering to hide the defeat in his voice.

Some of the color had returned to her cheeks, thanks to the way Nathan had healed her ankle, but now she went pale again as she stared back at Jason. When she finally spoke, her tone cut like a knife. "Oh, the criminals who hooked up with Joaquin Escobar and tried to kidnap Levi McAllister. No wonder you didn't have any problem lying to me."

"It's not like that——" Jason began, but she only shook her head.

"How can I trust a single thing that comes out of your mouth?"

Obviously, she'd intended that question as a rhetorical one, since she didn't bother to wait for an answer. No, she snatched the key fob to her Jeep Renegade from him, then turned on her heel and began to walk swiftly away from him, proving that Nathan really had done a great job of healing her ankle.

Jason almost called out to her to stop, but then he realized such an effort would be fruitless. Laurel seemed like an easygoing person, but he could tell she was the type who was mellow… right up until the moment she wasn't. Clearly, she needed some space.

Well, she would get all the space she required. He wouldn't bother to pursue her, because he knew she wouldn't believe a single thing he said… even if he told her the truth.

She's abandoning you on the side of a mountain, he thought, but he couldn't even feel angry. Not really. He deserved to get dumped like this.

It was a long walk to Incline Village, however.

For a few moments, he stood there on the trail, listening to the wind moving through the trees. Then he blew out a breath and began to walk down the trail, following the same path Laurel had taken just a moment earlier. He wouldn't hurry, though.

He knew there was no point in trying to catch up with her.

Just a few minutes earlier, she'd been holding back tears of pain. Now tears of hurt and rage streamed down her cheeks. If anyone had encountered her on the trail, she probably would have looked like a crazy woman, but Laurel was way past caring about any of that.

Jason Nichols was really Jason Ludlow.

How could she have been so blind?

And all right, apparently his talent involved hiding the fact that he was a warlock, and also allowed him to alter his appearance. That sort of illusion ability wasn't so rare; Connor possessed much the same thing. But being able to hide his magic at the same time?

Laurel didn't think she'd ever heard of such a thing.

So, maybe it wasn't so strange that he'd been able to fool her so completely. At the same time, she still wanted to kick herself for being taken in. More than once, she'd thought that no one could be as perfect as Jason Nichols…and it turned out she'd been right. Jason Ludlow had been putting on an act, being the person she wanted him to be so she'd have a reason to keep him around.

She couldn't believe she'd been idiotic enough to sleep with him.

Well, done was done. She wasn't stupid enough to think she'd be able to hide most of what had happened from Jake and Jeremy, but she'd do her damnedest to make sure they never discovered that embarrassing tidbit.

And to top it all off, she'd actually found their elusive healer…only to have Nathan wander back into the woods without revealing a single detail about who he really was. Laurel knew she had to be grateful to him for the way he'd healed her ankle, but at the same time, she was also right-eously ticked off that he hadn't even stuck around to hear her sales pitch, so to speak.

No, he'd been much more interested in outing Jason. Who deserved it, but still.

Her ire hadn't died down noticeably by the time she reached her Jeep. As she took hold of the door handle, just the faintest wave of guilt washed over here. After all, she'd ditched him on that trail, leaving him to get out of there by himself.

Jason's a big boy, she told herself as she got in the driver seat and grimly buckled the seatbelt. *He can figure it out.*

However, she took out her phone and glanced down at the screen before sticking the phone in a cupholder. Only one bar of LTE, but that was probably enough to get a text message out, or to make a phone call…or even summon an Uber. There were probably a couple in Incline Village who would be willing to drive all the way out here and earn a juicy tip.

Because there were a lot of things she'd like to call Jason Ludlow, but cheap definitely wasn't one of them.

Were all the Ludlows that rich? They'd been in the Bay Area for a long time, and considering the crazy prices of real estate there, if they'd bought a lot of land early on, they probably could have made insane amounts of money. It was the sort of thing Jeremy would be able to find out. Of course, if she asked him to investigate the Ludlows, he'd want to know why. And that would circle back to the series of embarrassingly bad decisions she'd made over the past couple of days.

What a nightmare.

She drove back to the condo, blind to the beauties of the lake and the countryside around her. Once there, she stomped into the master bedroom, packed up all of Jason's things, and then marched right back down and out the front door. Part of her wanted to head over to guest parking where his Range Rover still waited, but she didn't think that leaving his stuff next to the SUV was a very good idea. It seemed like an open invitation to theft. Too bad her witchy talent for opening locks didn't extend to getting past car doors…too many electronics involved.

Compromising, she left his overnight bag and toiletry case on the doormat at the condo. That should leave a pretty clear message that she didn't want anything else to do with him. And sure, it wasn't as if he couldn't afford to replace the items in his luggage, but she figured this was best. He could pick them up, get in his Range Rover, and drive back to San Francisco and right out of her life.

That image sent a pang through her, but she clenched her jaw and told herself she needed to put on her big-girl panties. Okay, he'd seemed perfect in every way, but everything between them had been a lie.

Which made her wonder exactly why he was so interested in getting close to her. Laurel doubted it was simple curiosity about a Wilcox witch. She supposed it was just barely possible that he'd been curious about a Wilcox wandering around apparently unfettered in Delmonico territory, but she had a feeling there was more to it than that.

Had he been trying to find the healer, too?

The more she thought about it, the more plausible that explanation felt. Why the Ludlows would be interested in Nathan, Laurel wasn't sure, but maybe that was just because she couldn't get in the headspace of a clan nasty enough to think that joining forces with Joaquin Escobar was a good idea. That guy had been pure evil.

Her phone buzzed with a new message, and she glanced down at the screen, mouth twisting in annoyance.

Jeremy. She knew his real talent was working with computers, but sometimes she found herself thinking that his secondary one must be irritating people. His bad timing was downright impeccable.

At least he'd texted and hadn't called. Her cousin might not have been the most perceptive person in the world, but even he probably would have heard her voice and immediately known something was wrong.

One word.

Anything?

Damn it. Her fingers tightened on the phone. As much as she wanted to tell Jeremy to go to hell, she knew that wasn't an option. For one thing, he wouldn't be deterred by that sort of brush-off. No, he'd just keep picking at her until she gave him the information he wanted.

Well, since he'd asked….

The healer's name is Nathan, she typed back. *He's real, but he doesn't want to have anything to do with us. He took off into the woods, and I couldn't follow him. This whole thing was a bust. I'm heading home just as soon as I pack.*

Before she'd started composing the message, Laurel hadn't even begun to formulate a clear plan, although she'd vaguely thought that she'd head out early the next day. It was sort of crazy to leave for Flagstaff now, since that meant she probably wouldn't get there until four in the morning at the earliest.

But she didn't want to stay. She wanted to get the hell out of Lake Tahoe and never look back. Maybe with time, the sting of all the mistakes she'd made while here would eventually fade.

Resolute, she went back upstairs and hurriedly started packing her clothes and toiletries, not bothering to fold things neatly or put them away in any order. All that mattered was getting this condo—and the search for the healer—in her rearview mirror as quickly as possible.

In less than five minutes, she was back out in her Renegade and heading toward Reno. One nice thing about being a witch—she didn't have to worry about returning the condo's keys to the Delmonicos. She simply left them on the kitchen counter, along with a hastily scrawled thank-you note, then locked the door using her witchy ability. A quick text to their contact in Incline Village, saying her work there was done, and she'd tied off that thread.

The whole time, though, she couldn't stop looking behind her, wondering if she'd see Jason's black Range Rover. No sign of him, though; his bags were still sitting on the doorstep when she left, which meant he hadn't even made it back to Incline Village yet. An image of him trudging along next to Highway 28, looking disconsolate, flashed through her mind, and she pushed it resolutely away. He was a warlock with tons of resources. He'd make it back just fine.

Jeremy had responded to her bombshell of a text with a flashing cascade of messages, each one increasingly agitated. It was probably killing him that she had the luxury of ignoring them all… which was exactly what she happened to be doing at the moment. Very likely he was ripping her a new one for not chasing Nathan into the forest or whatever, but he hadn't been there. When someone wanted to be lost, they generally stayed that way.

And yeah, she knew Jeremy would give her a mountain of grief the second she walked through the door at Trident Enterprises, but she found herself surprisingly unconcerned by that prospect.

He could hit her with his best shot…but it couldn't possibly be any worse than what she'd already done to herself.

His mother leaned against the antique desk that was her pride and joy, brows drawn together—but not too tightly, because that might mess up her latest Botox injections. Even the matriarch of the Ludlow clan wasn't above a little civilian intervention when it came to disrupting the aging process.

"You mean to tell me that you had the healer in your hands, and you let him go?" she demanded.

"Nice of you to think I had that much control over the situation," Jason replied calmly. On the drive back from Lake Tahoe, he'd played as many possible variations of this conversation as he could think of over and over in his mind, and at the end of the exercise had concluded that he really didn't give a shit. He'd been disappointing Carolyn Ludlow his entire life, so why should he stop now? As his mother continued to stare at him, blue eyes hot with fury, he added, "Considering that I'm not a martial arts expert and my magical powers aren't the kind that give me any kind of advantage in a fight, I don't see how I was supposed to keep the healer from walking away."

"You could have done *something!*" she snapped. "You could have explained what life in the Ludlow clan could have offered him. You could have told him that he would be a member of a very elite group."

Those words only made Jason want to laugh outright. He'd met Nathan, and she hadn't, and even that brief meeting had been enough for Jason to take a good guess at the other man's measure. It was clear the healer followed his own path, sought his own truth. The sort of material comforts that Carolyn might have offered wouldn't have tempted him at all.

But Jason knew there wasn't much use in explaining any of this to his mother. She had a transactional view of the world, one where she believed everyone could be bought…as long as she knew the price. That the healer couldn't care less about any of that didn't even enter into her mental equations.

"At the very least, you could have brought the Wilcox girl back here with you."

This time, he did chuckle. The look of outrage that passed over his mother's carefully preserved features was worth the trouble he knew such a display of defiance would earn him.

"Right," he drawled. "I could've tied her up and thrown her in the back of my Range Rover, and dragged her here. I'm sure that sort of thing would go over really well with Connor Wilcox and his wife."

At the mention of the couple who'd caused so much trouble to the Ludlow clan—Connor Wilcox and Angela McAllister-Wilcox had stripped the powers from the Ludlow witches and warlocks sent to attack tiny Jerome, and those powers had never returned—real hatred flashed in his mother's eyes. However, she didn't respond directly, probably realizing this was an argument she couldn't win.

"I never suggested *force*," she said, shooting him a dark glare. "It seems you were getting along quite well with her. At least, that's what your cousin Ben told me. He saw you leaving Gary Danko's."

Since Jason had spotted Ben at the bar and had guessed exactly why his cousin was loitering there, he couldn't even be surprised by this admission. Maybe a little angry, in a weary sort of way, but that was about it. He knew his mother too well not to believe she'd had people spying on him and Laurel the entire time they were in San Francisco.

Before he could say anything in reply, Carolyn went on, "With the way you were wining and dining this Wilcox witch, I thought you might be using subtler methods to make sure she stuck around."

He had a brief mental flash of Laurel as she'd run, laughing, from the hot tub into the house. Everything about her had seemed so wild and free, so different from everyone and everything in his life here with the Ludlow clan. Anger stabbed through him as he stared at his mother, at the infuriating smile she now wore.

No…that wasn't even fury he was feeling.

It was hate.

He hated Carolyn right then. It didn't matter that she was his mother. What mattered was that she'd spent her entire life manipulating people to get what she wanted, and no one had ever stood up to her because she was the darling of the clan, the beautiful *prima*-in-waiting who'd become their leader, the person who'd ordered her life to suit her own whims, right down to the handsome but ineffectual man she'd chosen as her consort because she wanted to ensure attractive children and at the same time know he would never interfere with anything she did.

Well, all that needed to stop, here and now.

"Laurel Wilcox is a better person than anyone I know," he said clearly. "And that includes you, Mother. I wouldn't do something like that to her. She deserves better than to be used and manipulated."

His declaration only earned him an amused lift of one of his mother's carefully groomed eyebrows. "If you want to insult me, Jason, you're going to have to do better than that. I never pretended to be Mother Teresa. I've always done what was best for this clan."

"I'm sure that Michelle and Todd and Lou might have a different opinion about that," Jason shot back, naming a few of the witches and warlocks who'd had their powers stripped by Connor and Angela Wilcox.

Carolyn's lips thinned. "They knew the risks. They were proud to fight on behalf of the Ludlow clan."

"I doubt they knew they were risking having their powers taken away forever."

A negligent lift of her shoulders. In that moment, Jason saw once again that even the members of their clan were no more than pawns to her…and she numbered him among those pawns as well.

Well, it was time for this pawn to remove himself from the chessboard.

"I'm not going to be your lackey anymore," he said, and turned toward the door.

Her laugh stopped him. "What exactly do you plan to do, Jason? Without this clan, you're nothing."

A dramatic statement. She probably even thought it was true. Sure, she could cut off his stipend, which was pretty hefty. But he hadn't exactly lied to Laurel when he'd told her his work involved managing his investments. He had a very healthy portfolio, one sufficient to keep him living in style for the rest of his life, even without the Ludlow stipend. And with the San Francisco real estate market continuing to boom, he knew he could probably get a healthy seven figures for his house without even blinking.

Thank God he was the only person on the title. The place was his to do with as he wished.

He realized that leaving wasn't the real problem…it was having a place to land.

Well, sometimes you just had to throw caution to the wind, and hope to hell that the wind would blow you in the right direction.

Tone casual, he said, "I guess we'll just have to see about that. Goodbye, Mother."

Without waiting for a response, he headed out the door. Behind him, Carolyn said, "Jason—"

He ignored her, hastening his steps as he hurried down the staircase. When he reached the bottom, he pulled his iPhone out of his pocket and put it in airplane mode. After all, the only person he would have wanted to hear from probably had no intention of calling him.

About all he could do was hope she wouldn't tell him to go to hell when he turned up on her doorstep.

Jake and Jeremy both faced her, arms crossed, in the "conference room" at the converted Craftsman house that served as Trident Enterprise's headquarters. Laurel supposed she should have known that Jake would be here for this interview, even though she thought that someone who was getting married the day after tomorrow would have better things to do with his time.

Unlike Jeremy, who wore a scowl that seemed destined to permanently etch a line between his brows, Jake's face bore a studiedly pleasant expression, as if he'd told himself that he needed to get through this discussion without losing his cool, and therefore faking a look of mild interest seemed the best way to handle the situation.

She hadn't even told them about Jason Ludlow yet. During the drive back to Flagstaff—all eleven hours of it—she'd come up with and discarded roughly a dozen stories she hoped would sound plausible. However, even though neither of her cousins was a mind reader, they both knew her well enough to be able to tell when she was lying.

Honestly, she hoped she would be able to leave that part of the story out of it entirely. It wasn't as though Jason had stolen Nathan from under her nose or something, so she reassured herself that he wasn't really integral to the story.

Well, except the part where he'd stolen his way into her heart, but Jake and Jeremy didn't need to know that. Anger at Jason's lies still burned inside her, although it had died down to a simmer rather than a full boil.

Much as she didn't want to admit it to herself, she missed him. How someone she'd only spent five days with could have left such a big hole in her life when he was gone, she had no idea. She'd pulled into Flagstaff at a little past four in the morning and had crawled into bed without even stopping to wash her face or brush her teeth, and had found herself hoping that if she stayed in there long enough, she could sleep her way through the worst of the soul ache she'd been suffering ever since she left Lake Tahoe.

Most likely, she would have slept the entire day away, except that the buzzing of her cell phone had finally penetrated her consciousness a little before eleven. Jake, calling to see if she was all right, and asking her to come over to Trident HQ that afternoon so they could talk about what had happened in Tahoe.

He'd phrased it like a request, but Laurel had known she didn't have much chance of wriggling her way out of the interview. She'd told Jake she could meet him and Jeremy at two, which was why she sat here now, staring at her cousins and hoping she could successfully lie her way through this without either of them suspecting anything about her extracurricular activities.

Never mind that she'd done enough lying over the past week to last her for the rest of her life.

"Did you explain to this guy that we're only trying to help?" Jake asked. His jaw was taut, and despite the mixture of guilt and worry and anger twisting her insides, Laurel couldn't help feeling sorry that he'd been put in this position at all. He should be off working through all the last-minute wedding stuff with Addie, rather than wasting his time here.

"I didn't get that far," she replied. "He made it pretty clear that he didn't want anything to do with any of us. I have no idea how he knew why I was looking for him. Maybe he's a mind reader on top of everything else."

"A guy who's a healer *and* a telepath?" Jeremy

interjected, looking skeptical. "I've never heard of that."

"Just because you've never heard of it doesn't mean it can't exist," she shot back, and Jake leaned forward in his seat, expression quelling as he gave them both a sharp look.

"There's no point in squabbling," he said. "We all knew this was kind of a long shot from the beginning. But you were able to confirm his healing powers."

"Yes," Laurel replied, after shooting Jeremy a serious side-eye. She loved her cousin, but sometimes he really plucked her last nerve. And she figured she might as well relate how she'd injured her ankle, and how Nathan had come along and fixed it. Again, leaving Jason out of the story wouldn't be too difficult. "I lost my footing and hurt my ankle pretty badly. Actually, I'm pretty sure it was broken. But all he had to do was hold it for a few seconds, and it was good as new."

"No recuperative period?" Jake asked. Their own healer Eleanor did a marvelous job, but you could still feel it for a few days after she'd fixed a broken bone.

Laurel shook her head. "Not really. I mean, it felt a little sore, but I was able to get back down the trail without any problem."

"So, this Nathan is really powerful."

She gave a helpless little shrug. The strength of

the healer's gifts seemed obvious enough to her… just as it also appeared glaringly obvious that he wanted to use them on his own terms, where he thought they would do the most good. Actually, she could relate to his desire not to be controlled by the commands of his clan's *prima*. Not that Connor or Angela would ever ask her to do anything she didn't want to do, but still, she knew there were some members of the Wilcox family who weren't too thrilled with her decision not to apprentice with Eleanor beyond learning the basics, who thought you had to use the talent you were given no matter how much you would prefer to avoid doing so.

"I don't know what happened to him to make him walk away from his clan, but it must have been something big," Laurel said. "Problem is, I didn't get the chance to ask him any questions, so I can't tell you anything more than that."

"What did he look like?" Jeremy asked.

Luckily, the sketch MaryJo had made of Nathan had been tucked away in an inner pocket of Laurel's purse this entire time, so she had that much to show for her efforts. She produced it now and handed it to her cousin, who stared down at the paper, eyes narrowing.

"Where'd you get this?" Jeremy asked.

Obviously, he knew she couldn't have created the sketch, since her drawing skills stopped abruptly at stick figures. "From one of the people Nathan healed."

"Is this accurate?"

"Pretty accurate," she said. "In person, his mouth looked friendlier. His hair was a sort of medium brown, and so were his eyes. He definitely wasn't dark enough to be a Wilcox…or a de la Paz or a Castillo."

Jeremy studied the portrait for a moment longer, then remarked, "He sort of looks like he could be a McAllister."

Again, all Laurel could do was shrug. "I'm pretty sure if the McAllister clan had a healer who'd disappeared on them, we would've heard about it. I think our guy is from an entirely different part of the country."

"Why?" Jake asked, dark eyes gleaming as he seized on her comment. "Did he have some kind of an accent?"

"No," she said. "I just got the feeling that he'd put some distance between himself and wherever he started out. Isn't that what you would've done if you were trying to get away from your clan?"

"Probably," he admitted.

"Well, this is something," Jeremy put in. He smoothed the slightly crumpled paper of the sketch, adding, "I'm going to scan this and run it through my facial-recognition program. If this guy ever had a driver's license or any kind of photo I.D., I should be able to pick up something."

Laurel supposed that sort of trace was the logical next step, although she found herself hoping Jeremy's algorithms wouldn't find anything. Nathan wanted to be left alone, and they should respect his wishes.

"And if you find him?" she asked, crossing her arms.

Jeremy glanced over at Jake, who gave a very slight shake of his head. "Nothing," he said. "I know when to back off. But I hate unsolved mysteries. This would be to satisfy my own curiosity, nothing more."

"Promise?"

He let out an exasperated huff of a breath. "Yeah, I promise."

She supposed she would have to be satisfied with that. Jeremy could be annoying sometimes, but when he told you he would do something, he stuck to his word. "Sorry I don't have any more information to give you, but, like I said, I probably spent five minutes at the most around the guy."

"It's all right," Jake said, and now he sounded soothing, as if he knew they needed to stop pushing her. He pulled his phone out of his pocket to check the time, then said, "I need to go.

I'm meeting Addie at the restaurant to do a final rundown with the caterer."

Thank God. With Jake leaving, that meant Laurel could flee before Jeremy asked any more questions. So far, she'd managed to leave out anything that might have raised his suspicions, or made him think there was more to the story than she'd let on, but she knew the longer she was around him, the bigger the chance that he might be able to cajole something out of her that she'd prefer not to reveal.

"Okay," she responded, doing her best not to sound too relieved. "I'm going back to my apartment and putting my feet up. That drive was brutal."

"Yeah, you should probably rest." Jake looked over at Jeremy. "You can hold down the fort here, right?"

That question earned him a raised eyebrow. "Don't I always?"

Yeah, you're a real martyr, Laurel thought, although she wisely kept her mouth shut. True, Jake had been pretty busy lately with the wedding preparations, and she knew that she probably found more excuses to find herself occupied outside Trident Enterprises than was strictly necessary, but it still wasn't as though Jeremy had to do everything himself.

Jake got up and went out, and Laurel rose as

well. Before she reached the door, however, Jeremy said, "Is there something you want to tell me, Laurel?"

She stared at him, unease creeping its way down her spine. "I don't think so," she replied, doing her best to sound casual and unruffled.

His dark eyes narrowed slightly. "Why'd you go to San Francisco?"

Oh, shit. No point in asking Jeremy how he knew she'd made that side trip to the Bay Area; he obviously had been tracking her cell phone. Laurel knew she should probably count herself lucky that he hadn't been accessing the phone's microphone and camera as well, although maybe even Jeremy had decided that was too large a breach of her privacy. Obviously, she should have put her phone in airplane mode the whole time she was in Northern California. That seemed to be the only way she could have prevented her cousin's snooping.

She swallowed a breath and said, "I went to San Francisco to interview MaryJo Gaffney, the woman who made that sketch."

Jeremy stared at her as if he thought she'd lost her mind. "And you thought it was okay to take such a huge risk? To go right into the heart of Ludlow territory?"

Her heart began to pound against her ribcage,

but Laurel made herself respond coolly, "Nothing happened."

"That's not the point," he snapped. His dark eyes were blazing with anger—and with worry. Had he been genuinely concerned that she might fall into the Ludlows' clutches? "It *could* have happened. And you—and this clan—would have been in a world of hurt."

I'm already in a world of hurt, she reflected. *Just not the kind you're thinking of.*

That inner realization sounded melodramatic even to her, and she did her best to push the thought away.

"Calculated risk," she said lightly. "I figured in a city that size, the chances of encountering a Ludlow weren't all that big."

"It's not like you would've had to bump into one of them," Jeremy returned. "What if their *prima* had detected a strange witch entering her territory?"

"Well, obviously she didn't," Laurel told him, even as she realized that the Ludlow *prima* must have known she was there the whole time and had held back, waiting to see how things would pan out with her and Jason. The thought that the woman had known of her presence and did nothing about it made a weird little shiver creep its way down her spine. "Or we wouldn't be having this conversation."

For a second or two, Jeremy was silent, most likely trying to think of a way to counter that argument. Of course, he really couldn't, because here she was back in Flagstaff, safe and sound. "Still," he said, which she knew was his way of getting in some kind of response, even if he didn't have anything to say to counter her argument.

"It was stupid, I know," she said. And she sincerely hoped he would never discover exactly *how* stupid she'd been. That was a secret she'd take with her to the grave. "And I guess it proves I'm not really cut out for fieldwork. Anyway, I need to go home and take a nap. I feel like I'm crashing already, and I don't want to look like death warmed over at the wedding. It would ruin Addie and Jake's pictures."

Jeremy shrugged. Someone else might have told her she looked fine—her reflection as she'd put on her makeup prior to this meeting had told her she appeared a little tired, but nothing too terrible—but this was Jeremy. "Sure. Guess I'll see you Saturday, then."

Technically, they should have been working all week, but Jake wasn't coming in, not with the wedding the day after tomorrow, and he'd let her and Jeremy know he didn't expect them to show up, either. Jeremy probably would come and work anyway, just because he didn't seem to grasp the notion of a day off too well. Luckily, he was Sloane's problem.

"See you Saturday," Laurel responded, and picked up her purse and slung it over her shoulder. She gave him a quick wave, then hurried out of the conference room and to the front door.

Her exit felt way too much like an escape.

Jason paused on the sidewalk and pretended to be looking in the window of the art gallery that occupied one half of the ground floor of the building where Laurel's apartment was located. There were some really fine landscapes displayed there, the sort of thing he would have considered collecting if he were still interested in decorating his home. However, the place already felt like something from the past, even though he hadn't yet put it on the market. During the drive to Flagstaff, he'd reached out to a civilian agent who specialized in high-end properties such as his, and she'd assured him she could probably sell it without even publicly listing the home.

"In fact, I have a client who's looking for something just like your house," she'd said, eagerness at the prospect of a big, fat commission seeping past her crisply professional tone. "I can give her a call—"

"Better wait," he'd cut in. "I haven't made up my mind yet. I just wanted to gauge interest."

"Oh, there'll be interest," she replied, and he'd told her he'd get back to her in the next day or so.

Funny how his fate could be decided in such a short amount of time.

He'd booked a room in a historic hotel just down the street from Laurel's loft apartment. No, he wasn't proud of himself for lifting her address from her driver's license while she was blow-drying her hair, but at least he'd kept that information to himself, since at the time he didn't even know what he'd planned to do with it.

Now he was here, though, he found himself hesitating. Pure cowardice, of course; as long as he stood out here on the sidewalk, his future with Laurel was completely in limbo. But as soon as he went upstairs and knocked on her door, her reaction would set the course the rest of his life took.

Just do it, he told himself. *Did you really drive eight hundred miles to stand here like an idiot?*

Well, when he put it that way....

He opened the discreet door that stood between the two ground-floor businesses—the other one was a coffee shop—and found himself facing a set of stairs. There wasn't anything to indicate that the second floor was composed of apartments, but he supposed that was better, considering how the place was right in the heart of Flagstaff's downtown.

Nothing to do but go up.

His footsteps sounded way too loud on the concrete stairs, echoing off the ceiling far above him. Would Laurel hear them?

Was she even home?

Well, if she wasn't, he'd go back to his hotel room and try again later. At the moment, he had nothing but time on his hands. Maybe if he was forced to go to the hotel to regroup, he'd be able to figure out the perfect thing to say to her. He'd run one speech after another through his brain, and none of them had sounded right. None of them could possibly convey how much she'd come to mean to him.

He stopped in front of the apartment door to his left. It had a cheerful doormat patterned with flowers and dragonflies in front of it, the bright colors so singularly Laurel that he thought he would have guessed she lived here even if he hadn't known her actual address.

You can do this, he told himself. *You walked away from your clan. What do you have to lose?*

Everything, if Laurel told him to go to hell.

But he was here now, and he would do this thing.

He raised his hand and knocked on the door.

~

Laurel startled at the sound of a knock at her apartment door, then reached for the remote and paused the episode of *Say Yes to the Dress* she was watching. Why she'd decided to torture herself by watching strangers try on wedding dresses, she wasn't sure, except that possibly the show did do a good job of reinforcing her belief that most people had terrible taste.

That better not be Jeremy coming over here to give me more grief, she thought, even as she pushed herself up from the sofa. Then again, showing up in person wasn't really her cousin's style. He was much more likely to bombard her with nagging text messages, although her phone had been ominously silent ever since she left Trident HQ.

When she opened the door, worried gray-blue eyes stared down at her. Since she'd only seen Jason's true appearance for a very brief few moments, it took her a second or two to realize who was standing there on her doorstep.

Then shock pulsed through her, and she demanded, "What the hell are you doing here?"

"I need to talk to you," Jason Ludlow said.

Her brain was spinning. How could he be here in Flagstaff? All right, he'd probably driven— or maybe used some of his apparently vast amounts of money to charter a flight—but the logistics involved weren't the real issue.

He absolutely could not be here in Wilcox territory. Panic flared for a second, and then she reassured herself that his gift would have prevented any of her relatives from realizing that a strange warlock was roaming around downtown.

Still, it probably wasn't a good idea to leave him standing there on the landing.

"Get in here," she ordered him, voice taut with anger.

A flicker passed across his face, one that probably meant he'd heard the fury in her tone. But he didn't argue, only stepped inside so she could shut the door behind him.

Annoyingly, she found herself somewhat relieved that she'd put on makeup for her meeting at Trident HQ, and hadn't changed into something sloppy like yoga pants or a tank when she got home. She frowned. What the hell difference did it make what she looked like?

"You need to turn around and go back where you came from," she said, and his jaw set.

"I can't."

Laurel crossed her arms. "What do you mean, you can't?"

Jason shoved his hands in his trouser pockets. He was dressed almost formally, in summer-weight wool trousers and a button-up shirt, and would have looked wildly out of place roaming around downtown Flagstaff. Even in the midst of her anger, his good looks struck her like an almost physical blow, although Laurel told herself she had way more important things to be focusing on at that particular moment.

"I mean that I basically told my mother to go to hell, that I was done with her crap. I walked out." A pause, and he added, "My mother is Carolyn Ludlow, the *prima* of our clan."

Oddly, Laurel didn't find herself quite as surprised by this revelation as she probably should have been. Rank and file members of a clan, even one as wealthy as the Ludlows, generally didn't have Jason's kind of money to throw around.

"Are you expecting a medal or something?" she asked.

He didn't even blink. "No. I just figured I'd told you enough lies already, so I wanted to tell you the truth about that. She wanted me to bring Nathan back to be with our clan because we don't have a healer…but when I told her I suspected you had healing abilities, too, she said you would be an acceptable alternative."

"Nice to know I was the runner-up," Laurel remarked. Maintaining a sarcastic tone helped her to keep her emotions at bay, because being around Jason again was a lot harder than she'd thought it would be. Yes, she was still angry with him…but she also wanted nothing more than to close up the distance between them so he could put his arms around her.

Well, that wasn't going to happen.

"You weren't the runner-up," he said, and now there was an edge to his voice, as if he was also having a hard time keeping everything under control. "I told her there was no way I would do something like that to you."

"And so…what?" Laurel asked. "I mean, what was your game plan? You got close to me, but why?"

A long, long pause then. His hands were still shoved into his pockets, but now it looked as if the fabric was cutting into his skin, as if he was straining against the thin wool material because that was the only thing preventing him from reaching out to her. "At first, it was just to find out what you were doing in Delmonico territory. When I realized you were looking for the healer, too, it made sense to work with you. After that, though…."

The words faded away, and Laurel tilted her head up at him. "After that, what?"

"I fell in love with you," he said simply. "I never meant for you to get hurt."

His words were like a shock to her system. Right then, she found herself having a hard time breathing. Somehow, though, she managed to pull in some air. Jason Ludlow loved her. She'd hoped for that when she'd thought he was Jason Nichols, but what was she supposed to do with such a declaration when it was coming from one of her clan's enemies?

A tremor went through her voice as she said, "But you thought it was fine to keep lying to me."

At last, his paralysis seemed to break, because he pulled his hands out of his pockets and took a step toward her, then another. Before she could move away, he'd reached out and grasped her hands in his. She remembered the strength of those fingers, even though now they were cold, as though his worry had moved all the way down to his fingertips.

"I was going to tell you the truth," he said, his tone urgent. "I just couldn't figure out a way to break it to you. I knew you would hate me for lying...would hate me for who I was."

And then Nathan had come along and exposed Jason's lie. For all she knew, he could be lying now, trying to cover his ass, but she didn't think so. Sincerity shone out of his blue-gray eyes, the same shifting color as the cool Pacific waters that surrounded his hometown.

The words slipped past her lips before she could stop them. "I don't hate you."

It was hope she saw now in his features, terrible and fragile. "You don't?"

Laurel shook her head. "I probably should. But you're here now, which has to mean something." It was no small thing to stand up to the *prima* of your clan...especially if she also happened to be your mother. "Um...what *does* it mean, exactly?"

Jason's fingers tightened on hers. "That's up to you, Laurel. I came here because I want to be with you. I want to leave the Ludlows behind. I can't fix what I did—or what my clan has done—but I can try to make it up to you...if you'll let me."

Would she? Once again, she found herself hesitating. Not because she didn't know the truth of her own heart, but because she wasn't sure how she could explain any of this to her family. Would they accept her being with a Ludlow?

Well, they're going to have to, she thought as she came to a sudden conclusion. *It's not like the Wilcoxes are saints, after all. We might have cleaned up our act lately, but we of all people should know that we don't like having our clan defined by the actions of a single person, even if he happened to be our* primus.

"Oh, I'll let you," she said, and didn't get any further than that, because Jason had pulled her to him and pressed his lips against hers.

How in the world could she have ever thought she could live without being kissed by Jason Ludlow? All her exhaustion was gone, banished by his touch, by the taste of his sensual mouth. Once again, she was alive in a way she knew she couldn't be with anyone else.

When the kiss ended, however, she couldn't keep herself from saying, "You're really going to give up that fabulous house and everything else? Just for me?"

"You're worth it," he said, one hand brushing a stray strand of hair away from her face. "Also," he added as a smile quirked at the corners of his mouth, "it's not like I'm showing up here penniless or something. The house is mine to sell, and I have a very good portfolio."

"So, you really are a trust fund baby?"

"More or less."

The only way to answer that comment was with another kiss. Yes, this was exactly where she was meant to be—in Jason's arms, and the hell with anyone who tried to give her grief about it. When she pulled away, she found she had a smile of her own lifting her lips.

"This is perfect timing, actually," she said. "I want you to come to a wedding with me on Saturday."

"'A wedding'?" he echoed, looking vaguely alarmed.

Of course, she'd let Jake and Addie know about Jason. It wasn't as though she would dump a complete bombshell on them in the middle of their special day. Still, Laurel was now very, very glad that she hadn't tried to find a date for the wedding, not when the universe had dropped the perfect man right into her lap.

Taking pity on him, she said, "My cousin Jake and his fiancée Addie are getting married the day after tomorrow. If you really are serious about being a part of the Wilcox clan, I can't think of a better way for you to meet everyone."

Some men might have looked dismayed at the prospect of having to meet the clan all at once. Jason, however, only nodded. "Sure. It sounds like fun."

"Really?" she asked, and he grinned.

"Okay, not really," he said. "But I'll do it for you. I'll do whatever you need me to do, if that's what it takes to prove I'm serious."

"Oh, I won't make you jump through too many hoops," Laurel said. "Because you know what?"

"What?"

"I love you, too, Jason Ludlow," she told him. "All I ask is that you tell me the truth from now on."

"Always," he said, his expression now deadly serious. "You can trust me."

And she did. The lies he'd told before had been in the service of his clan, but he'd left the

Ludlows behind. Now he would be a Wilcox, if not in name, then in heart and mind.

Who could ask for anything more than that?

The Witches of Wheeler Park series will continue with Autumn's story in *Wishful Thinking*, releasing in September 2021.

ALSO BY CHRISTINE POPE

HEDGEWITCH FOR HIRE

(Mystery/Paranormal romance)

Grave Mistake

Social Medium

Household Demons (July 2021)

Perpetual Potion (October 2021)

THE WITCHES OF WHEELER PARK

(Paranormal romance)

Storm Born

Thunder Road

Winds of Change

Mind Games

A Wheeler Park Christmas

Blood Ties

Healing Hands

Wishful Thinking (September 2021)

Smoke and Mirrors (January 2022)

PROJECT DEMON HUNTERS*

(Paranormal Romance)

Unquiet Souls

Unbound Spirits

Unholy Ground

Unseen Voices

Unmarked Graves

Unbroken Vows

THE DEVIL YOU KNOW*

(Paranormal Romance)

Sympathy for the Devil

Charmed, I'm Sure

A Wing and a Prayer

THE WITCHES OF CANYON ROAD*

(Paranormal Romance)

Hidden Gifts

Darker Paths

Mysterious Ways

A Canyon Road Christmas

Demon Born

An Ill Wind

Higher Ground

Haunted Hearts

THE WITCHES OF CLEOPATRA HILL*

(Paranormal Romance)

Darkangel

Darknight

Darkmoon

Sympathetic Magic

Protector

Spellbound

A Cleopatra Hill Christmas

Impractical Magic

Strange Magic

The Arrangement

Defender

Bad Blood

Deep Magic

Darktide

Rising Dawn

THE SEDONA FILES*

(Paranormal Romance)

Bad Vibrations

Desert Hearts

Angel Fire

Star Crossed

Falling Angels

Enemy Mine

TALES OF THE LATTER KINGDOMS*

(Fantasy Romance)

All Fall Down

Dragon Rose

Binding Spell

Ashes of Roses

One Thousand Nights

Threads of Gold

The Wolf of Harrow Hall

Moon Dance

The Song of the Thrush

THE GAIAN CONSORTIUM SERIES*

(Science Fiction Romance)

Beast (free prequel novella)

Blood Will Tell

Breath of Life

The Gaia Gambit

The Mandala Maneuver

The Titan Trap

The Zhore Deception

The Refugee Ruse

STANDALONE TITLES

Hearts on Fire

Taking Dictation

Golden Heart

Night Music: A Modern Reimagining of The Phantom
of the Opera

Ghost Dance: A Sequel to Gaston Leroux's The
Phantom of the Opera

Flight Before Christmas

* Indicates a completed series

ABOUT THE AUTHOR

USA Today bestselling author Christine Pope has been writing stories ever since she commandeered her family's Smith-Corona typewriter back in grade school. Her work includes paranormal romance, fantasy romance, and science fiction/space opera romance. She makes her home in New Mexico.

Christine Pope on the Web:
www.christinepope.com

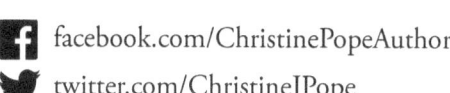

facebook.com/ChristinePopeAuthor
twitter.com/ChristineJPope
pinterest.com/ChristineJPope

www.ingramcontent.com/pod-product-compliance
Lightning Source LLC
Chambersburg PA
CBHW021131260626
47169CB00005B/1555